JDangerous
Journey

Dangerous Journey

By

Joseph W. Myer

iUniverse, Inc.
Bloomington

DANGEROUS JOURNEY

iUniverse books may be ordered through booksellers or by contacting:

iUniverse
1663 Liberty Drive
Bloomington, IN 47403
www.iuniverse.com
1-800-Authors (1-800-288-4677)

ISBN: 978-1-4759-0146-7 (sc)
ISBN: 978-1-4759-0148-1 (hc)
ISBN: 978-1-4759-0147-4 (ebk)

Printed in the United States of America

iUniverse rev. date: 08/21/2012

To my brother, Richard . . .
who finally saw the light

CHAPTER 1

He stared hard and long at what he had written on the yellow paper of the legal pad. Finally, he read the words out loud to himself: *I don't know what I'm going to do. I don't want to live, but I don't want to die either. As painful as my life has become I cannot envision or contemplate the alternative. And the fear of the unknown, of death, keeps my finger paused on the trigger. The truth is I don't want to blow my brains out . . . not yet anyway. J.R. Cronyn, (a.k.a. J.R.) July 1, 2002.*

J.R. sat at the desk, his pale face close to the whirring fan and thought of the time when he felt sorry for all those poor people who lived in this vile little place called Hell's Kitchen. Now he was one of those people.

He was well into his fifties and he had lost his publicist job at Girls Town almost two years earlier. It didn't take him long to learn that there were no jobs for a man his age, only an occasional part-time job that he usually lost to one of the hundreds of younger, out-of-work, New York actors.

Most of his savings gone, and with little money in his checking account, he was forced to move out of his stylish bachelor pad into the small, four-story walk-up. Two windows in the small, dark living room looked out onto the backyards of more dreary apartment buildings where lines of faded white sheets flapped in the stale air sounding like a hundred flightless birds.

After drinking several glasses of cheap wine, he tried to sleep, but sleep, however, eluded him. He chain smoked, and, in spite of the fact that the night was heavy with humidity, he paced back and forth like a caged animal.

It was dark except for rays of flickering moonlight that played across the old wooden floor. His head ached and the shirt on his back was drenched. He got up and ambled to the kitchen and squinted at the clock. It was close to eleven. He splashed some water on his gray face, reached for a dry shirt that hung over the tub and put it on. After he combed his rumpled hair, he patted his face with after shave lotion, opened the door, looked around, then stepped into the hall closing the door behind him. No one greeted him on the front stoop as he headed for Eighth Avenue in search of something to relieve the tension of unrelenting and joyless days. He needed a woman.

In a few short blocks, stretching from 42nd Street up to 45th along 8th Avenue, friendly bars, great restaurants, and a number of Broadway theatres can be found, including, of course, lovely ladies of the evening.

J.R. found the avenue crowded with late night carousers, including the after-theatre crowd, looking for fun and frolic. The noise was deafening but it didn't bother him; in fact, he took pleasure in it. It made him feel alive, invigorated. He crossed 8th Avenue. As he neared 42nd Street, a shapely lady of about thirty caught his eye, and his fancy. She saw him staring at her and she smiled. He approached her.

He greeted her with a soft hello and she purred something sweet to him, but when he made the proposition, the unexpected happened: she whipped out her cop's badge and shoved it in his face. In seconds, adrenalin took over his body, and, before she could say, 'You're under arrest for solicitation,' he made his escape.

He didn't know what happened next except that, before he knew it, he was dashing across the street dodging screeching cars, and running as fast as he old legs would take him.

Glancing over his shoulder, he saw the undercover cop on a phone, raising her left arm and waving it about. He knew immediately that she was calling backup police.

And, as he ran up 8th Avenue, dodging groups of tourists who quickly side-stepped to let him pass, he spied two immense muscle-bound cops with crew cuts and surly faces crossing the avenue from the opposite side, pushing their way through the crowd and shouting at J.R. Turning west at the corner of 43rd Street, J.R. ran as fast as he could toward 9th Avenue. Looking back, he saw the cops on the opposite side of the street running and waving their arms, yelling at him to "Stop. Stop."

At the same time, J.R. saw what he thought were police cars; they turned sharply down 43rd Street, their brakes screeching, their lights flashing and their sirens blaring. The sound was deafening. *Good Lord,* he thought. *Are they coming after me too?*

He picked up his pace, and, looking ahead, he saw a large truck backing out of a warehouse about halfway up the street. It was so large that it blocked the entire street making it impossible for another car or truck—or even a human—to pass.

He thought to himself that if it didn't clear the sidewalk, he'd be trapped. Approaching the warehouse, he heard squealing tires burning rubber into the pavement. The nose of the truck cleared the walk, and just seconds after passing it, he heard a tremendous impact as a car hit the truck causing an almost immediate explosion so loud and powerful that it nearly knocked J.R. off his feet.

At first he thought the truck had been loaded with explosives, but he was wrong; it was carrying Fourth of July fireworks. When J.R. turned he couldn't believe his eyes. The explosion blew the top of the truck off, and an astonishing array of fireworks shot high into the air creating a stunning array of colors and shapes that lit up the night sky turning it into day. The almost deafening POP, POP, POP was an appropriate accompaniment to the incredible pyrotechnic display.

J.R. looked for the cops but he didn't see them. He imagined they had fallen victims to an unplanned, unprecedented Fourth of July fireworks display that rained down on them causing suffering and severe, possibly fatal, burns. He knew he should make a run for it, but he couldn't move. He was held spellbound thinking about the time he was four-years old.

The year was 1944. He had gone to Coney Island with his mom and dad on the Fourth of July to watch the fireworks. Just before they were set off, his father lifted him up onto his shoulders. J.R. felt like he was on top of the world, high above everyone. It was a happy time, not only for J.R. but for his parents as well. His father had a new job and making money and mother was pregnant with his sister. Sadly, the joy didn't last. His dad lost his job a few months later and his mother suffered a miscarriage. Her depression developed into a nervous breakdown, and she never fully recovered. She was lost to J.R. forever.

At 9th Avenue, J.R. knew he'd have to decide whether he was going to try to make it three blocks to his apartment, or half a block to an abandoned apartment house where he could hide out for a while until the heat was off.

When he saw the police car coming fast down 9th Avenue, he made a quick decision. Running across the avenue he heard thunder in the distance. When he reached a broken fence that ran the length of the deserted building on the north side, he ducked down, trying to make himself look as small as he could. Scurrying down the garbage-laden alley, he heard the sound of thunder and echoed blasts of sirens as the police approached.

J.R., out of breath and frightened, realized he had but a few seconds to find a hiding place. Near the back of the building he found a basement window open. As he climbed in, he lost his footing, causing him to fall about six feet to the cement floor below. A sharp pain shot through his left leg, but he stifled a groan, fearing the police might hear him. Not hearing the siren, he assumed they were now on their feet looking for him. They were probably moments away.

As a strong odor of bleach and cleaning fluid filled his nostrils, he thought he heard voices. *They're coming.* Raising himself up on his right leg, he groped his way until he felt a wall. Side-stepping to the right a few feet he felt a door. He tried pushing it with his right hand, but it wouldn't budge. Then, in front of him, he saw a flash of light. *They're here.* He felt his heart pounding in his chest.

J.R. threw all of his weight on the door; it creaked and then fell forward, taking him with it. When he landed on the cold cement he saw a light creeping slowly across the floor. He knew that if he didn't move now he would be caught. Taking a deep breath, he rolled over on his left side until he thought he was clear of the doorway and out of sight.

He stopped and listened. *Did they see me?* He couldn't be sure.

He waited a few agonizing moment, daring not to breath. When the light flicked off, he waited. Silence.

That's strange. I was sure they saw me, but I guess they didn't.

Relieved, he took a deep breath and thought: *What to do now? I can stay still for a while and take a chance of making it home in an hour or so. Or I could . . .* A cold chill interrupted his train of thought; it swept through his body. He shivered. He needed to move away from the open window.

If he were lucky, he thought, maybe he would find a blanket discarded by a homeless person. But when he tried to move, pain gripped him again. He knew his ankle wasn't broken but he also knew it wouldn't be easy moving about. Damning the pain, J.R. pulled himself up, and, feeling his way, limped forward a foot or two at a time, stopping now and then peering into the darkness and listening. For a moment he thought he heard something like a kind of shuffling sound. Then nothing. Again he took another step. Silence. Nothing.

Then, when he tried to take another step, his foot hit something. Whatever it was it felt soft. Maybe it was the blanket he was hoping for. Before he could reach down, the room flooded with light. At first he thought it must be the police, but he couldn't tell because he was blinded. Ever when he shielded his eyes, all he could make out were vague shapes, shadows of creatures that moved slowly, menacingly toward him.

If they weren't the cops, who the hell were they? While his cloudy, muffled mind tried to grope with reason he tried to take a step back. When he did so, he was hit by something so hard that he was knocked off his feet. As he crashed to the floor, excruciating pain wracked his body.

To J.R. it felt like some huge muscular monster had picked him up in one hand and had slammed him against a brick wall. He knew his head must be split open because he could taste his own blood.

Male voices started shouting: "Kill him. Kill him. Kill him." A chorus of female voices accompanied the death call with laughter and gleeful shrieks of approval. When he tried to pull himself up in a feeble effort to escape the onslaught, he was grabbed and thrown to the floor. The monsters continued to kick, pound and pummel his body.

A moment later he caught a glimpse of shimmering silver being raised over his head. The hand holding the knife stabbed him repeatedly in his chest and abdomen. Sharp, stinging pain ravished his body, and he could hear his own screams coming to him as if through an echo chamber. Then, as he lay trembling from the onslaught, he slipped into a state of torpid darkness.

J.R.'s return to life was anything but blissful. The monsters, probably thinking he was dead had discarded his bloody body in the alley like a putrid pile of discarded garbage. He was conscious only of the fact that he was cold and that an insistent drizzle drenched his face. He shivered.

"Dear God," he cried out, "I don't want to die like this. Not in this dark, stinking hell hole." With that, he lost consciousness.

CHAPTER 2

Manhattan General Hospital
Two Weeks Later

When J.R. awoke from his coma he was greeted by young Dr. Morgan who wanted to know who Elizabeth and Bobby were.

He stared at the doctor but was unable to speak.

The doctor pressed forward. "As you were coming out of your coma you spoke their names repeatedly. Are they members of your family?"

Family? J.R. heard the word in his head. At first he was a little confused then he realized what it meant. "Family," he said, the word seeming to burst from his mouth. "They're my family. My *children!*"

"We've got to notify them, Mr. Cronyn."

"Yes, yes, we must find them," he cried. "I want them near me. They're my family. They're all I've got left. Oh, dear God. You must help me, doctor."

"I'll do all I can, Mr. Cronyn."

"Please," he said, putting a hand on the doctor's arm. "Call me J.R."

"All right, J.R.," he said. "Just tell me where they are."

Turning his head away, J.R. said in a weak voice: "I feel ashamed, doctor, but I don't know where they are. I haven't seen them in thirty years."

"Get some rest, J.R.," the doctor said. "I'll check back with your later."

When Dr. Morgan returned that evening, he and J.R. got into a conversation about the big fire works explosion on Forty-third Street. J.R.

explained why he was running from the police and that when he neared Ninth Avenue he turned and saw two police cars driving at high speed toward the truck. When he started to run he heard a crash and a terrible explosion and when he turned he saw a spectacular Fourth of July fire work display. "At that moment I knew I was in big trouble."

Smiling broadly, Dr. Morgan told J.R. that the police were not after him. That they were chasing a fugitive in a stolen car who had killed his girlfriend. When he got to Forty-Third Street he turned right and headed straight for the big truck that by then was blocking the street. That crash you heard was his car hitting the truck. He hit it with such force that he was killed instantly."

J.R. gasped, staring at the doctor. "Oh, my God."

There was a long silence. The young doctor observed J.R. for a moment then asked: "What made you go the abandoned apartment house?"

"I was running from the police."

"Do you think that's all it was? Or is it possible you were running from something else? From yourself perhaps?"

Oh, doctor, good doctor, you are digging for something now, aren't you? Digging at my soul. Digging for answers that I, myself . . . Oh, my God. A sudden flash of light, a moment of awareness struck him with such an intensity of feeling. The answer came to him in an instant. "If I had known in the moment of the crash on Forty-Third Street that I was not the one the police were chasing, I would've gone home to my filthy little flat in Hell's Kitchen and forgotten everything that had happened that evening.

"I would've forgotten to be afraid, forgotten to care. I would've gone on with my miserable little life and been caught up in all the meaningless things that muddies a man's soul and makes him numb. Oh, God, doctor, am I glad I fled to that abandoned apartment? Am I glad I sort refuge in that dark and stinking building? You bet I am.

"I'm even glad that I was beaten to the point of unconsciousness and possible-death. Even though I tasted the dust of death, I didn't die. I lived. I'm here now to tell my story. Doctor, I'm alive because I was meant to survive, to live, to thrive . . ." J.R. felt that he could cry tears of joy, but, instead, he looked up at the doctor and smiled a renewed declaration: "It's a new beginning, doctor."

"And that means?"

"It means finding my children and becoming a family again. That's all I want. My God, doctor, I could've died in that stinking building without ever having seen them again. You've got to help me!"

Days later, after the headaches had passed and his head had cleared, J.R. began to read and to think about the future and what it might hold for him. With the notebooks the pretty day nurse had given him, he started a journal. The first entry read: *As soon as possible I want to start on a new path, a journey of enlightenment, a journey of love, not only for my children, whom I miss more than I can say, but for a woman, one special woman I can love and who will love me. I know she's out there. And I will find her as I will find my children. This is the beginning of a new and wonderful life!*

While J.R. pondered his future, young Dr. Morgan entered the room. "Good news, J.R." His manner was cheerful. "You'll be going home soon."

"Not soon enough," he said. "I've been giving it a lot of thought. Actually, all these magazines around here have helped me, inspired me. I have a lot to say about a lot of things, and I'm convinced that magazine writing is what I want to do."

"Ever been published?"

"No."

"Well, then, you'd better get the hell out of here, J.R., because you're not getting any younger." J.R. didn't respond. "What's the matter?"

"I may not have a place to live," he began. He explained that he had a small apartment on Ninth Avenue, but that he hadn't been there in weeks, and, well, he hadn't paid any rent and he was sure the old landlady had gotten rid of his stuff, and . . ."

"This might be your lucky day, J.R." the doctor interrupted. "Ever been to Brooklyn?"

"Are you kidding? I grew up in Brooklyn."

"Do you know Bay Ridge?"

"Sure I know it; that's where you get on the Verrazano Bridge to cross over to Staten Island."

Morgan told J.R. that he had a friend who owned a three-story apartment house on Eighty-Eighth Street and that he had one vacant apartment for rent. "It's actually the garden apartment on the first floor."

"A garden apartment?"

"It's not huge but it's very cozy, and there's a big maple tree in the back yard."

"A *maple tree?* I'm sold. How much is it?"

"Can you afford one-twenty-five?"

"Is that a week?"

"No. That's a month."

J.R. stared in disbelief at the doctor. "There's a small catch." Morgan smiled. "I thought so."

"The building doesn't have a janitor so you'd have to, well, you know, clean up once in a while, sweep the halls, shovel snow in winter. That sort of thing. What do you say?"

"I say it sounds like paradise. When can I move in?"

"There's just one more thing, J.R.," Morgan said, sitting on the edge of the bed. "I'm sorry we couldn't find your children, but I'm sure you will. And I hope you succeed in whatever you desire to do. But I don't want you to isolate yourself in that little apartment. Get to know the other tenants; they're all older than you, but they might inspire you or teach you something you don't know. Don't shut them out, J.R. While you're looking for your family, let yourself be a part of their family. I think you need that right now. In the long run, I'm sure you'll be glad you did,"

"Did you ever see the light, doctor? A light so brilliant and so beautifully mysterious that you never forgot it? I saw it when I was ten years old. I saw it again when I was about twenty; it saved my life. I thought it was my guardian angel. Whether it was or not I never saw it again. I strayed from the path and stopped believing in angels and in God. I became smug and arrogant. Oh, was I arrogant. I thought I knew everything, but, of course I didn't. I didn't know anything. But now I'm so grateful to you, doctor. I believe in my heart I'm about to embark on a journey that will have a profound affect on the rest of my life. I don't know where it will take me, but I believe you're right. I need to be part of something strong and solid and spiritually inspired. I need to be part of a family—*my* family. That's a big part of my journey."

CHAPTER 3

The three-story apartment building on Eighty-Eighth Street, with its brick façade, dated back to 1911.

The moment J.R. walked into the cozy one-bedroom apartment, he immediately felt an aura about the place. He looked through the kitchen into the living room and to the bedroom beyond where someone had left the large double hung window open allowing a gentle breeze to play with pale blue curtains. He laid a large bag of staples on the kitchen counter, then carried his luggage to the bedroom and put them on the comfortable-looking double bed.

He took a deep breath. He felt alive and new and energized. It was time, he thought, to look for his children.

Opening the smaller of two suitcases, he rummaged through it for his old phone book, and when he found it, quickly flipped the pages looking for old friends that he and Edith had known when they lived in Los Angeles.

The first name that popped up was Stan Jones, his old poker buddy. He and his wife, Judy, had been their best friends for years. *If anyone knows where Edith is, they'll know.*

He entered the number on his cell phone and waited for a connection. Soon he heard a woman's voice. He said *hello* and asked to speak to Stan Jones.

"Stan who?" was the reply.

He said the name again, louder. The woman said she couldn't hear him. "It must be the connection," she said. "You're breaking up a little.'

After he took several steps into the living room, he asked: "Can you hear me now?"

She said she could, so he said the name again: "Is he there?"

A moment. Then she replied that she did not know a Stan Jones."

After he repeated the cell number, she confirmed it, and said that she was sorry.

He thanked her and cancelled the call. When he set his cell phone down on the end table, next to the couch, he noticed a large city phone book on the bottom shelf. *Of course,* he thought. *I'll go to the library and look Bobby up in a California phone book. Why didn't I think of that before?*

J.R. went to the bathroom, threw some cold water on his face. When he reached for a towel he heard a knock on the door. He patted his face quickly and made a dash for the door. "Coming," he called out. When he opened it, he was confronted by a short, healthy-looking gentleman in his mid-seventies. He had broad shoulders and a barrel chest and he spoke in a voice that was pure tenor. "Are you J.R. Cronyn?" he asked.

"Yes, I am," J.R. answered. "Who are you?"

"I'm Carl from the top floor," he said, offering his hand.

J.R. smiled and shook the old man's hand. "I'd like to stay and chat but I'm off to the library. Very important research . . ."

"Are you writer?"

"Uh, yes," J.R. responded. "I'm doing research for an article I'm writing."

"Well, Mr. Cronyn," Carl began, "I'm sorry to have to tell you this, but your research will have to wait. You see, the library is closed today. And today being Friday, it will not open until Monday."

"You wouldn't be fibbing now, would you Carl?"

The old man looked miffed. "I never fib, Mr. Cronyn."

"Call me J.R."

"May I come in, J.R.?"

He opened the door wide with a grand gesture. "Welcome to my humble abode, sir."

They sat in the living room. And, while J.R. sipped a diet Coke, Carl went on about his life and loves and everything in between. When he mentioned that he had a Masters degree in the humanities, J.R. quipped: "Ah, literature, language, and philosophy. No one could have a *higher* calling."

"You got that right." Carl smiled. My first job after school was with the *High* End Taxi Company driving a cab."

"Tell me it was a spiritual experience for you."

"Oh yes. I met the love of my life in that cab," he sighed. "The experience could not have been more . . . spiritual."

J.R. laughed.

"I'll bet you have a Masters degree."

J.R. shook his head. He explained that when he was in his forties he worked for a prominent non-profit agency as a publicist and they helped finance his education. For three and a half years he attended night school at New York University where he took classes in creative writing and journalism. His favorite free-time activity was acting in student films. He made several of them and was told that he was a natural.

"You've got the good looks of a leading man," Carl offered. "You remind me of . . . what's-his-name?" He thought a moment, then: "I know. Newman."

"Paul?"

"That's it. Paul Newman. You've got those blue eyes, but I think you're taller."

"I'm not interested in an acting career. Writing is my game."

"Non-fiction?"

"Yes."

"I was a journalist for a while. I used to write a *special interest* column for the old *Brooklyn Eagle*." He hesitated, shaking his head. "God, that seems like a zillion years ago. Where does the time go?"

J.R. was thoughtful. "That's a question I've been asking myself."

"What are you going to write about next?"

"I've been thinking a lot about that lately and I've come up with a title: SEX, in bold type, of course—to grab the reader's attention—with a sub-title that reads, *and sex addiction.*

A strange little smile crossed Carl's face. "I can hardly wait," he said. "I may be old, but I can still turn a lady's head."

"I'm sure you can, Carl."

"Well," he said, shaking off a memory or two, "how about a thumb-nail sketch of the other tenants?"

"Shoot," J.R. said.

Holding up one thumb he began with his third floor neighbors, George and Gertrude Kendall. He described him as a semi-invalid with a gruff manner. Dear Gertrude, it seems, was sweet and painfully thin. "They're very old, and, by all appearances, completely devoted to one another. I think they'll die in each other's arms."

"The lady beneath me, pardon the pun, is Mrs. Molly Miller. She's very secretive; doesn't talk very much, but she's at least civil. Personally, I think she was once a madam of a low class brothel. She's got to be in her sixties, and she wears too much makeup. And she dyes her hair bright red."

"You like her, don't you?"

"I'm *mad* about her," Carl blurted out. "The problem is I think she killed her husband." Regaining his composure, and with a slight clearing of his throat, Carl continued to tell his story about the strange little man down the hall from Mrs. Miller. His name's Tony Argoni, a man in his late forties.

"He's a loner," he said. "A classic case." Carl lowered his voice and said in a confidential tone: "Personally, I think he has ties to the mob; but, believe me, I wouldn't spread a word around. All we really know about him is that he smokes and reads a lot. Once a month he leaves stacks of newspapers, all neatly tied with string, outside his door." Then, leaning forward, he whispered that Tony had brought a lady home one evening and that she hasn't been seen since.

"When was that?" J.R. asked.

Carl couldn't remember exactly, but it was more than a month ago. J.R. opined that perhaps the woman had left. When Carl stated, rather emphatically, that she had not, J.R. answered: "What? You keep watch on the neighbors twenty-four hours a day?"

"Of course not," he snapped back. "It's just that I heard them talking."

"You just *happened* to hear them talking?

"No." He looked a little flustered. "As I passed by his door I heard voices: a man's voice and a woman's voice."

"Well, what did you hear?"

"Not much, except it sounded like they were arguing about something. I don't know."

"Well, Mr. Olson," J.R. said, getting up from the couch, "you certainly are an interesting old guy, and I've enjoyed our little chat. But I must get back to work."

"But J.R.," Carl said, following his host to the door, "I haven't told you about Johnson, your neighbor . . ."

"I know all about him," J.R. said, opening he door. "Have a good day!"

Carl stood as tall as he could, staring up at him. "Have you family, J.R.?" he asked.

J.R. thought a moment. "Yes," he said. "I'm divorced, but I have two children."

Carl smiled and turned away. "I'm alone now, you see. An orphan." He turned and looked up at J.R. His eyes were bright and his smile seemed to bring color to his cheeks. "But I consider myself a lucky man to be living here in this old house that'll turn one hundred soon. I hope you'll be happy here."

"Thank you, Carl."

With that, he turned and walked briskly down the hall.

What a strange but funny little man he is, he thought, closing the door. Turning his attention back to finding Bobby, he realized that there must be a hundred or more California phone books covering every city in the state. And he had no idea where Bobby was living. So . . . *back to my old phone book,* he thought. *There must be someone I can call.*

Sitting on the couch, he leafed slowly through the old book. He got to *R* and still nothing. But, when he turned the page, a small piece of paper fell to the floor. When he picked it up and unfolded it, he saw the name Jerry Swain. He recognized it at once. He and Bobby had attended school together and had been great pals.

J.R. didn't recognize the phone number but he decided to try it anyway; he knew he had nothing to lose. He picked up his cell phone and entered the number. A moment later he heard a male voice say "hello."

"Hello," J.R. said loudly. "Can you hear me? This is J.R. Cronyn for Jerry Swain." There was no answer. "Hello? Hello? Can you hear me? Hello?"

"I can hear you," a man answered. "Did you say J.R. Cronyn?"

"Yes. I'm looking to get in touch with my son, Bobby Cronyn. I haven't seen or talked to him in years, but I must find him." J.R. listened intently as the man told him that his son Bobby just happened to be the owner and CEO of a huge computer company called Bobby Computers.

"Where've you been all these years, mister?"

"Who are *you,* sir?"

"I'm Jim Swain, Jerry's brother," he answered. "I haven't seen *him* in years either. He's probably off shacking up with some dame somewhere. Hold on. I'll see if I can find a number."

This is amazing, he thought. *Bobby's the owner and CEO of a computer company?* His thoughts were interrupted by the man's voice. "Here's the Bobby Computer office number. Got a pencil?"

"I'm ready." After he wrote the number on a pad, he said: "You'll never know how happy you made an old man today, Jim Swain. G'bye, and God bless you."

I should make this call, but I'm starving. I haven't eaten since yesterday. But I must make this call. I must. What time is it in California? Three hours difference. It'd be just ten there. Perfect. I'll have some diet Coke, make the call, then eat a substantial breakfast. Here goes.

He got a Coke from the refrigerator and took several sips. Sitting at the small, round kitchen table, he set his cell phone down and just stared at it. *What am I going to say? Hello, Bobby, this is your father speaking?* He thought for a moment. *Good Lord, suppose he asks 'Father who? I don't have a father. He's dead!'*

He got up from the table and paced the floors. *I suppose I'd say the same thing if I were in his place. I don't think I'd want to have anything to do with my father if he hadn't called me for thirty years.*

He walked through the apartment to the bedroom window and stared out into the garden. The grass was a shimmering green and rows of red, purple, and yellow petunias adorned the edges of the garden adding an array of color to please the eye and a dash of perfume to soothe the senses. J.R. took a deep breath and sighed. *It has to be done,* he thought. *I have a fifty-fifty chance of succeeding. I have no other choice but to take it.*

With phone in hand, J.R. went out through the kitchen door to the garden and sat in a folding chair. He looked for a moment at the numbers on the pad and then entered each one from memory. Holding the cell close to his ear, he waited for an answer.

A woman's voice said: "Welcome to Bobby Computers. How may I help you?"

J.R. said hello and introduced himself. Silence. Then he asked if she had heard him. She said she had and was sorry but Mr. Cronyn was out of the country and would not return until Monday. "This coming Monday?" he asked.

"Yes," she replied.

"Would you mind giving him my cell phone number? I'd like him to have it."

After taking his number, she read it back to him. He thanked her and wished her a good day.

With a smile on his face, he hurried back into the kitchen and opened the refrigerator door. *What do I want? What do I want? I think I'll make myself a cheese omelet with beacon, toast and coffee. That's a substantial breakfast for a starving artist.* Singing *Hallelujah* as loud as he could, he proceeded.

When it got to making the coffee, he realized there was no sugar. What to do? What to do? With empty cup in hand, he went into the hall and knocked on his neighbor's door. When Jack Johnson opened the door, J.R. introduced himself and asked for some sugar.

Jack, a tall, lumbering man in his mid-seventies, dressed in a robe and pajamas, invited him in and offered him a chair at the kitchen table. While he poured sugar into the cup, J.R. noticed the high quality of craftsmanship that had gone into the making of Jack's kitchen cabinets. "Where'd you get those cabinets?" J.R. asked. "They're beautifully made."

"I made them," was the response. "That was my trade. Carpentry."

"Well, you're a master."

"I used to be."

"Thanks for the sugar," J.R. said walking to the door.

"By the way, I thought I heard Carl's voice out here earlier. Did he come to see you?"

"He sure did."

"He didn't spin any tales on you, did he?"

"Tales?"

"He's much better now, but he has a problem telling the truth."

"He told me he had a master's degree.

Jack clucked his tongue and shook his head. "There he goes again. Telling those fibs. He can't help it, you see. He's sick. He's got something called . . . I can't remember exactly." Jack scratched his head. "It's not schizophrenia, but something like it.

"Could it be schizothymia?"

"Yeah, that sounds like it. They said it was a mild form of schizophrenia. And that he's introverted and likes to stay to himself a lot. He's been in and out of mental institutions for years."

"He also told me that he suspected Molly of killing her husband."

"The truth is Mr. Miller died of natural causes."

"Why did he lie?"

"Because that's what he does. He makes up stories about people. And himself. He can't help it. Twice a month he goes to Roosevelt Hospital for psychiatric group therapy."

J.R. shook his head and said: "It doesn't seem to be helping much."

"Don't worry about Carl," Jack said, opening the door. "He'll be all right."

"Thanks for the sugar."

After brunch, as he called it, J.R. put his laptop on the old secretary desk that sat in a corner of the living room, near a window. For snacking purposes, J.R. had placed diet Coke and peanut butter sandwiches on a little end table next to the desk.

The first order of business was research. He entered "Information regarding Sex Addiction," and was amazed at the amount of information available. *This is going to be an almost-all-nighter,* he thought.

CHAPTER 4

About three o'clock the next morning, he climbed into bed, exhausted but exhilarated from hours of intensive work. Before falling asleep, he thanked the Lord for all his blessings, vowing to spend the rest of his breathing days as the best father he could possibly be to his children. With a P.S., he added that he'd be the best grandfather, too, if he had grandchildren.

At nine the next morning, feeling strong and refreshed, he climbed out of bed, grabbed his robe, and headed for the bathroom. Hanging the robe on a hook behind the door, he stepped out of his pajamas and into the shower. He turned the water on and in a matter of seconds the water turned to an almost steaming temperature. J.R. yelped and fumbled with the knob trying to adjust the heat. When the icy cold water hit his skin, he again let out a holler, but this time he determined to surrender to its therapeutic effects.

Splashing his body with water, he started singing. Within minutes his body relaxed and the coldness of the water seemed to have a calm and mollifying effect on him. As he rubbed his chest with body wash, he began to hum. Before long, he was belting *Singing in the Rain* as loud as he could: *I'm singing in the rain, Just singing in the rain . . .* Even as he dried himself, he continued to sing loudly. So loudly, in fact, that Mrs. Molly Miller upstairs started banging on the pipes. He had disturbed her sleep, and she wanted him to know it.

The next thing he knew someone was banging hard on his door. He called out "Who is it?" She banged again. Wrapping a towel around his waist, he stormed down the hall shouting "Who is it? And why are you making so much noise so early in the morning?"

"If you open this door, Mr. Cronyn," she yelled, "I'll tell you why!"

My goodness, he thought. *It must be Mrs. Miller. I wonder what's got her dander up this morning?* He opened the door. There stood a woman of average height in her mid-sixties, with curlers in her hair, wearing an old, faded pink robe adorned with what looked like a vine of red roses that climbed zigzag from the bottom hem up to the frayed collar that she clutched tightly at the throat. Her face was a ghastly red, probably affected by her anger, or perhaps too much alcohol, or both.

What drew J.R.'s attention to her were her eyes. They were wild and aflame with anger. He took a deep breath waiting for the inevitable outburst. And it came quickly and with a venomous sting that caught him off guard. "You sir, are a menace to this household." Her strong alto voice thundered through the hall. J.R. was sure Carl could hear her on the third floor.

Now, as she spoke, she shook an angry finger in his face. "Mr. Cronyn, your shouting and yelling in the bathroom this morning was so bothersome to me that I was unable to sleep. I am going to tell you this once and only once. I am not to be disturbed early in the morning; I work the late shift at the bank and I need to get a full eight hours of sleep starting at eight o'clock. Is that understood?"

"Understood," he said meekly, trying to smile.

"I hope so," she snapped.

"I'm sorry; it won't happen again."

She scowled and crossed her arms. "It better not happen again. If it does, I will be forced to call the owner of the building and let him deal with it."

The woman's unreasonable. She's . . . J.R.'s thoughts were interrupted by Carl's voice: "What's going on here, Molly? For God's sake."

As though by magic, Mrs. Miller's attitude changed in an instant. Putting a large smile on her face, she turned and greeted Carl with outstretched arms.

"God woman!" he yelled, grabbing her hands, "your voice can be heard all over the house."

"My dear," she said sweetly, her deep alto voice mellowing, "you know you shouldn't use the Lord's name . . ."

"It's all my fault, Carl," J.R. chimed in. "I made a lot of noise in the shower this morning and Mrs. Miller wasn't able to get to sleep. I apologized. I think it's all settled now. Isn't it Mrs. Miller?"

Ignoring J.R., she put her hand on Carl's arm and cooed: "I'm going up now. Would you like to join me for a few minutes before I go to sleep?"

"Not now." Carl snapped, turning away. "I'm going for a walk; I have a lot of thinking to do." Seeming not to like Carl's answer, Mrs. Miller scowled, clutched the collar of her robe, turned, and hurried passed him. Carl mumbled something under his breath and hurried down the hall to the front door. "Women!" he yelled, slamming the door hard behind him.

Standing alone and half-naked in the doorway with nothing more than a large bath towel wrapped around him, J.R. crooned: "Ahhh. Ain't love grand!"

J.R. dressed and ate a light breakfast. Before starting the long and difficult writing task ahead, he decided to pay a visit to the local pound to pick out a young dog. He looked at a lot of dogs, but the one that caught his eye was a long-haired mongrel the color of mud. The dog's large, brown eyes drew J.R. to him. And when he called him Puddles, the dog responded by barking loudly, wagging his tail, and running in circles around the cage.

Back home, he let Puddles loose in the garden. He chased butterflies and, when he was tired, he slept soundly in the shade of the old maple tree and dreamt of burying bones.

J.R. started the SEX article three times before he was satisfied with the opening. After having consumed a number of peanut butter sandwiches and downed large quantities of diet Coke, he was satisfied with the amount of work he had accomplished. The time was twelve-twenty. He figured he could finish the article by six in the morning, if he stayed up all night, or he could go to bed, get some rest, and finish it on Sunday. Before he could make up his mind, he heard Puddles whining. He went to the kitchen and found the dog scratching on the back door.

"Poor Puddles," he said. "Daddy's ignored you and now you have to pee. Well, come on, boy. Let's go for a walk. I need some exercise anyway.

By the time they got back to the apartment, J.R. had made a decision; he was going to bed. He shut down his computer and turned off all the lights in the living room. After donning pajamas, he knelt beside the bed and recited the Lord's Prayer. When he had finished, he folded his hands and looked up. "Dear Lord," he said aloud, "I felt you here with me while

I worked, and I believe so strongly that you guided my hand. Thank you. Amen."

While J.R. slept, Puddles curled up at the foot of the bed and dreamed of chasing cats in a large garden filled with leafy cattails and showy orchids known as cattleyas.

Sunday morning, J.R. was up bright and early. After putting water on for coffee, he fed Puddles, and sat down at the table and ate a bowl of breakfast oats.

With a cup of coffee in hand, J.R. went to the bedroom and dressed casually in jeans and T-shirt. He sipped the hot liquid and sat at the desk ready to work.

Two hours later, Puddles came and sat by J.R. holding a leash between his teeth. He looked up at his master with large, soulful brown eyes.

J.R. looked at him and laughed. "Are you crying?" he asked.

When J.R. said *crying*, the dog whined as if on cue, and pawed his leg.

"What a ham you are," he said, getting up. "Come on. Let's go for a walk. I'm at a log jam here anyway. Maybe some fresh air will clear my brain."

J.R. and Puddles were home no more than five minutes when there was a knock on the door. When he opened it, he was greeted by a middle-aged woman dressed all in white and wearing a white nurses' cap. She smiled broadly and said, "Are you Mr. Cronyn?"

"Yes. How can I help you?"

"My name is Ruth Jones, and I'm a nurse with the Good Samaritan Society. We're a non-profit organization that provides nursing services to shut-ins. I'm here to see Jack Johnson."

J.R. looked surprised. "I didn't know Mr. Johnson was a shut-in. I saw him yesterday in the hall. He'd just returned from shopping and he looked just fine."

"Yes, I'm sure." She smiled, revealing a row of yellowed teeth. "When Mr. Johnson got out of bed this morning, he lost his balance and fell."

"Did he break anything?"

"No, thankfully not, but I have to leave him for a few hours, and . . ."

"You want me to watch him while you're gone?"

"Could you, would you, Mr. Cronyn? I'd be so thankful."

"Can't he take a nap while you're gone? He'd probably sleep for several hours, wouldn't he?"

"The problem is he just woke up from a long nap, and . . ."

"Never mind, Ms. Jones, I'll look in on him."

"Oh, thank you so much. I'll call you as soon as I'm ready to return." With a little wave, she hurried down the hall.

"Wait a minute," J.R. called. "I need your business card."

"It's on the table in the kitchen," she said, opening the door. I'll be back before you know it. Bye."

J.R. rapped a few times on the door and called: "Mr. Johnson, this is J.R. May I see you?"

"I'm in here, J.R.," he said. "In the bedroom.

J.R. walked through an archway into a darkened and musty-smelling room. The first thing he saw was an unmade four-poster bed that sat in the middle of the small room.

"Over here, J.R."

"Do you have something against light?" J.R. asked, feeling his way around the foot of the bed. Mr. Johnson reached over to a table lamp and turned it on.

A not very bright light cast unflattering shadows onto the old man's face.

"That's better." *My God, he looks awful.*

Johnson, dressed in an old fashioned knee-length night shirt, looked gray as he slumped in a small wooden chair next to the bed.

"You don't look good, Jack," J.R. said, standing at the foot of the bed. "How do you feel? Nurse Jones said you fell."

"Jones doesn't know what she's talking about." Jack brushed her off with a swift wave of his hand.

"Then you didn't hurt your knee?"

"My knee's just fine."

"Well, I'm glad to hear it."

"The woman talks too much."

J.R. looked around. A photograph on top of the dresser caught his eye. "Who's the good looking couple in the photo, Jack?"

Jack smiled. "That's my wife Ethel and my younger son, Chris. I may be a good craftsman, but he was an *artist.* That picture was taken when he was about sixteen in front of our house in Coney Island. The other photo is George, my older son; he was born there in 1971, and Chris came along a year later. We had money then, and life was good."

"They're both good looking kids, Jack."

"Go into the living room, J.R. and take a look at the carvings on the fireplace. That's his work. Look at the detail."

J.R. entered the room. "It's dark in here."

"The light switch is on the wall to your left."

J.R. reached over and clicked it on. A warm light from a bold-colored Tiffany-like ceiling lamp illuminated the room. J.R.'s eyes immediately found the ornate fireplace with its carvings and one of the biggest framed beveled mirrors he had ever seen. It reached almost to the ceiling.

"Now *that's* the work of a true artist." Jack's voice was loud and proud.

My God, Jack! He walked to it slowly letting his fingers touch the intricate carvings of cherubs in a lavish garden with climbing vines of leaves and flowers: roses, tulips, crocuses, daisies, and wild flowers.

"It's magnificent, Jack." He turned and saw the old man holding his face in his hands. "Are you all right?" he asked, sitting on the bed. He didn't answer. "What happened to your son?" Still no answer. "Would you like me to go, Jack?"

"No, no, it's all right," he murmured, as tears welled up in his eyes. "I can talk about it." He wiped the tears away with a dry towel. "He died three years ago right there, in the living room, from an overdose of drugs.

"I found his body on the floor in front of the fireplace. He was only twenty-five." He hesitated, trying to catch his breath. "It's hard to talk about it sometimes because he was so young. He was Ethel's boy; she adored him, doted on him, spoiled him.

"She loved him so much. "She was in the hospital at the time; I couldn't bring myself to tell her. Not at first. She'd suffered a stroke and her heart wasn't strong. I figured she didn't have to know until it was time.

"He was a good boy, really, and he had dreams. You know. Dreams of success as an artist and of having a family of his own. But he left home early and got caught up with a group of young people who had a bad effect on him.

"They got him hooked on drugs, and, of course there was a young woman. Never knew her name, but she came to the burial ceremony at the cemetery dressed all in black with a scarf over her head. She was small and dark and pretty. She looked a lot like my Ethel, in a way. She left before the ceremony was over. We never saw her again.

"Ethel took it hard, real hard. She never got over it. She mourned him for a year and then she died. Her heart failed. I told the doctor she died of a broken heart.

"And now I'm left with only memories of him and Ethel. My big regret is that I didn't get to tell him I loved him. He got away from me before I could.

"After his death, strange things began to happen here in the apartment. I heard noises late at night coming from the living room. When I went to see what was causing it, I found the room empty. Nothing to see; nothing moved.

"This went on for months until one night I couldn't take it no more. I fell to the floor in front of the fireplace and prayed to God. I begged him to free my son; I begged him to take his restless soul and heal his pain and sorrow." Jack wiped his brow and took a deep breath. "Take him home, dear Lord," I cried. "Take him home.

"The next night I sat up in bed and waited. All was silent. Not a sound. I lay down and went to sleep and didn't wake up until eight the next morning, the first full night's rest I'd had in a long time.

"When I got out of bed I could see light under the double doors, and when I opened them sunlight flooded the room. There was a bright glow around the fireplace.

"I clasped my hands together and said a prayer of thanks to the Lord. I knew Chris was free at last and in the arms of God.

"I was about to turn away when I saw something on top of the mantel. I remember I gasped; for a moment I couldn't breath."

"What was it?" J.R. asked, deeply moved by the story.

"Right there, in the middle of the mantle, was that photo of Ethel and Chris. It was just sitting there. I had no idea how it got there, but it was there all right as plain as anything.

As I walked slowly to it, the sunlight hit the silver frame and it glowed and glistened, if you like, and I had to shade my eyes against its glare. When I reached the mantel and was real close to it, and I was about to pick it up, I saw something else. Right there, on top of the mantel was some writing in the thick dust that had collected there. It was hard to read but I managed to make it out. Just four words but the message made me cry out like a baby."

"What Jack? What was the message?"

"The message was: *I love you dad!*"

J.R. was so touched, he could not speak.

After a long moment of silence, Jack spoke: "You know, J.R." he began slowly, "I'm feeling much better. No pain at all. As a matter of fact, I think I want to join you for a walk. What do you, say?"

"I'd love to, Jack," he answered. "But do you mind if I take a rain check on the walk? I have a lot of work to do today."

"Sure, J.R.."

"How about tomorrow morning when I take Puddles out for a walk?"

"Perfect."

J.R. tried to work on the article, but he couldn't. His mind was preoccupied. All he could see was the message on the mantel: *I love you dad.* It was tragic that he lost his young son, but at least Jack can take comfort in knowing that Chris loved him. Does Bobby love me? Has he forgiven me for all the years that I was absent from his life? I pray to God that he does love me and that he will forgive me.

CHAPTER 5

*S*unday. Puddles ran on ahead while the two men walked in silence. Finally, Jack spoke: "My older son, George, loved to play ball and he was good at it too. He could've been a player, but, I don't know, he didn't like the city and the crowds. Every time we went out to visit the relatives in Jersey he didn't want to come home. He loved the country. Now he lives in the country."

He chuckled. "George's Brooklyn girlfriend moved with her family to St. Louis and she'd write to him almost every day. She told him about a farm for sale and why didn't he come out so they could get married and live on the farm. She said it would be a great place to raise a family."

"So . . . ?"

"So—he went to St. Louis and they got married. They bought the farm, and now they live there with two children, a boy and a girl. He says he loves farming; wouldn't want to trade it for anything else."

"It sounds like a good life, Jack."

"Yes, it does, and I'm sure he's very happy."

"Do you hear from him often?"

"No, not really," he answered, a look of sadness crossing his face. "It's been a long time. You know, I was thinking the other day: wouldn't it be nice to spend the holidays with them? I've never seen the kids, you know. Except in pictures."

"Why don't you call him?"

"Yeah, I've thought of that. Maybe I will; maybe I will call him."

Puddles was getting tired; he looked up at J.R. and barked his *pick me up* bark, and J.R. immediately obeyed.

"Jack," J.R. began, "about the power of prayer. Do you realize that you have experienced, directly, that power? You told me that beautiful story about how you, in your moment of grief over the death of Chris, got down on your knees and prayed to God.

"You beseeched him to take your young son with him to his spiritual home. He answered you. He did what you asked. I can't think of a better example of the power of prayer."

"You know, my Ethel would agree with you. She prayed all the time. The problem was, she did little to help herself. The Lord can do a lot, but He can't do it all by himself. You've got to help him."

"True," J.R. said. "That's why I exercise every day and watch what I eat. I stay slim and fit."

"How long do I have to walk?"

"I suggest you start out walking every day for about fifteen minutes. Then, over time, increase that to twenty minutes until you reach one hour. You'll lose weight and gain strength. You're welcome to walk with me any time you want to."

Jack was hesitant. "Oh, J.R. I don't know."

"What do you think your son would say?"

Jack gave J.R. a curious look. "You mean Chris?"

"Yes. What would he say?"

"He'd say you were right."

"Maybe your wife was right too."

"Yes, I guess she was," Jack said, chuckling. "I was just too *stubborn.*"

"That's a perfectly good word, Jack."

Jack gave him a side glance: "You know something J.R.?"

"What Jack?"

"You're a royal pain in the ass!"

J.R. ate a small lunch and got back to work on the article. It went so well that he worked through dinner until he neared the end. Then he got stuck. He realized, as written, that the article offered classic examples of sex addiction, its cause and effect, without so much as hinting at a positive outcome. Since he was interested in writing a follow-up article entitled SEX ADDICTION, *The Cure,* he decided, therefore, to end the piece on that note.

Two hours later he was finished. He knew the article was lengthy, but he decided to send it just as it was.

To celebrate his endeavor, he treated himself to a dinner at Mario's Bistro around the corner from the apartment on Second Avenue. He dined on veal scaloppini, salad, and red wine, topped off by a delicious chocolate mousse. He went to bed that Sunday night a happy man.

Monday, he thought, *would be a transitional day in his life—the day that he sent his first article off to a magazine.* He believed that, if the article sold, it might very well signal the beginning of a long and successful writing career.

Monday. Today was the big day. *Reunited with Bobby* he kept saying over and over to himself. *If he doesn't call by noon, I'll call him. But what if he doesn't want to talk to me? God, J.R., don't even think it!*

He showered and dressed and downed the usual eggs and bacon breakfast before putting Puddles in the back yard with a bowl of fresh water and his favorite dog bites. Grabbing the large manila envelope from the desk, and his cell phone from the kitchen table, he walked in brisk manner to the post office just three blocks away.

After posting the envelope with a clerk, who stamped it and dropped it on a conveyer belt, J.R. watched as it moved along among other envelopes and small packages and disappeared behind a partition. He smiled to himself.

"Can I help you with something else, sir?"

"Uh? Oh, no," J.R. mumbled. "Everything's just fine."

On his way home, J.R. decided to stop by the local grocery store to buy food for lunch and dinner. He checked his watch; it was almost ten-thirty. *Plenty of time,* he thought.

At the checkout counter he moved in behind a woman who was scrounging through her purse looking for money. He couldn't see her face but he observed that she was dressed, top to bottom, in oversized sweats.

"I can't imagine what I've done with my money," she said. "It was right here . . ."

The moment she spoke he knew she must be English; he was swept away by the lovely lyricism of her voice. Obviously embarrassed, she tried to explain to the cashier that she must've left her wallet at home and that she had no money. At the same moment, she glanced over her shoulder at J.R.

He was immediately struck by her loveliness. He figured she was in her late forties or early fifties; but she looked years younger. He smiled as he stared unashamedly into glistening eyes as blue as the water of an island lagoon. Shimmering waves of red hair framed and caressed a delicate oval face. Full, lightly tinted lips parted for just a moment as if she were about to speak.

"Please," J.R. said, reaching for his wallet. "Let me help you."

"Oh, no," she said, turning away from him looking into her purse. "I'm sure I can find some money in here . . ."

While she rummaged for money, J.R. handed the cashier a ten dollar bill. "It's all right," he said.

"You're very kind, sir," she said accepting change from the cashier. When she offered him the money he told her to keep it. Thanking him, she grabbed the money, dropped it into her open bag, picked up her groceries, turned, and started for the door.

"Wait!" J.R. implored, as he paid for his groceries.

The woman stopped and turned to J.R. "I'm sorry, sir, but I'm late for work. You can reach me at the Westside Boys & Girls Club." With that, she turned and hurried through the door.

In his effort to pursue the woman, J.R. grabbed the plastic bag with such force that the handle broke and three cans of dog food fell to the floor and rolled away from him. Retrieving the cans as fast as he could, he shoved them back into the torn bag, held it close to his chest, and pushed his way through the door.

Once outside he spotted the woman walking fast on the other side of the street. He yelled to her to wait for him, but she kept walking as if she hadn't heard him. He tried running a little until he was opposite her. He called again and she stopped, glaring at him.

Sir," she began, "I told you . . ."

But I need to know your name," he said.

"Don't worry, sir, you'll get your money."

"I don't care about the money. I just want to know your name. I think you're beautiful."

The woman smiled. "My name is Kathryn Mayfield."

J.R. couldn't believe his ears. "Are you called Kate?"

"Oh, no, sir," she said, shaking her head. "Never Kate. I'm *always* called Kathryn."

"I want to see you again," he yelled.

"You can find me at the Boys & Girls Club." Waving, she turned left at the corner.

Watching her he thought: *This Kate is going to mean a lot to me in time.*

When J.R. got home, he put the groceries away and hurried out to the garden. He was greeted by a happy dog that wagged his tale and yapped until his master picked him up.

He scratched Puddles behind the ears and put him down. His mind was elsewhere. Not able to sit, he paced around the yard, with Puddles following close behind.

It's getting late, he thought. *The suspense is beginning to get to me. If Bobby doesn't call me in the next few minutes, I'm going to call him.* He walked around the garden again. *Okay, that's it.* He reached into his pocket and pulled out the piece of paper with Bobby's phone number on it. But, just as he was about to make the call, his cell phone buzzed. He froze. *Oh, my God! What am I going to say?* It buzzed again. He pressed the call sign and said, "Hello?"

A woman's voice asked if he were J.R. Cronyn. He said that he was and she introduced herself as Bobby Cronyn's secretary. She explained that Mr. Cronyn's car had been rear-ended an hour earlier, and that the released air bag had broken his nose. "He's in a great deal of pain," she said, "but he wanted me to tell you that he's been waiting for this call from you for a very long time. He plans on making a trip to New York City very soon. He'll be in touch."

J.R.'s spontaneous outburst of joy sent Puddles running for cover.

CHAPTER 6

Tuesday Evening

Journal entry: *Of course I couldn't wait to see Kathryn (Kate) again. Today, I called the Boys & Girls Club to find out if she were at the Club. She was and I asked where I could find her. "In the music room," was the answer.*

I wore sneaks and jeans and a plain sweat shirt and walked the entire twelve blocks to the Club. It was good exercise.

As I was walking down the hall to the music room I felt a sudden urge to stop, turn, and go home. I had a sudden attack of the old cold feet. How absurd is that?

What's there to be afraid of? I thought. Nothing, you silly old fool.

Just then I heard a piano playing Chopin. I listened; it calmed me. When I reached the music room, I took a deep breath, opened the door and poked my head in.

There she was in all her loveliness, dressed in leotards and standing in the middle of a group of eight, nine, and ten-year-old girls, all dressed in tutus, and all pirouetting around her while she encouraged them to "Keep your heads up."

Just as I was about to make a reasonably quiet and unobtrusive entrance, one of the little girls, a blonde, saw me and screamed: "There's a man there!"

Everything came to a halt except me. My body moved forward and I felt myself losing my footing. Fortunately, I managed to regain my composure and, with a little grace, and, I might add, strength, I landed on two feet.

When I looked up I noticed that several of the girls were smiling; a few covered their mouths and giggled, and Kate stood poised with both arms crossed observing me with the most enchanting smile.

The next thing I remember she and I were sitting in a corner booth in a sandwich shop and she was ordering coffee for two. We talked for hours.

She took me home and we talked some more and she made good old fashioned English fish and chips. Delicious!

After dinner we talked for about two hours or more. Then I went home. It's after twelve and I'm getting sleepy . . .

So, to the best of my ability at this late hour, I'm going to write down everything we talked about.

Kate told me little about her life except to say that she was born in London, studied Ballet and danced with the Royal Ballet.

I told her about my marriage and my children, Bobby and Elizabeth, both of whom I hadn't seen for years. But I let it drop, casually, of course, that my son was the same Bobby in Bobby Computers. She was impressed.

However, she was not impressed by my admission that I had not seen my children for almost thirty years. I explained that I had been on the wrong path and that I'd become an agnostic and had lost my belief in God. I was young and foolish and expremely arrogant.

That arrogance failed me and brought me to a dark and ominous place. It almost killed me.

But I know God's not through with me yet. I know that. He - and a brave young doctor in a Manhattan hospital - decided to give me a second chance.

That's why I'm here in Brooklyn. I'm starting over. On a journey of spiritual renewal,. A journey that will reunite me with my children. They may reject me. But that's a chance I must take. I have no other choice.

Kate's reaction to my tale of redemption was understanding and kind. And she tried to reassure me that my children would forgive me. I wanted desperately to believe her.

Then she asked me if I wanted to call her Kate. I said I did and she smiled and said it was all right, and that I could call her Kate.

I showed my delight and appreciation by kissing her hand.

She rewarded me with a sweet smile, kissed me gently on the cheek, and sent me on my way.

Out side, on the porch, I watched as she switched the lights off and disappeared into the shadows of the hall.

I couldn't help but wonder if I'd ever see her again.

Several days passed and still no word from Kate. Every time he called her cell phone he found it full.

Right after breakfast on Thursday, he took Puddles and went for a long walk through the streets of Brooklyn to the one spot where he might find out where she was: the Boys & Girls Club. When J.R. and Puddles entered the club, a gray-haired lady standing next to the reception desk glared at them over large, bejeweled glasses. "Oh, sir, you can't bring that, that mutt in here," she said, waving them away. "It's not allowed."

J.R. decided to stand his ground. "Madam," he snorted, "I'll have you know this Puddles dog is a pure bred; he comes from the most northern regions of the Andes. He's very rare. Only a handful of Puddles exist anywhere in the world. And I'm lucky enough to own one."

"Oh, sir, I'm so sorry. I had no idea he was so rare."

"That's all right."

"How can I help you?"

"I'm looking for Ms. Kate, the dance teacher. Is she here?"

"No sir. I'm sorry. She's not here. She had a family emergency."

"Oh?"

"Her mother I think."

He thought for a moment. "That means she must've gone to England."

The old lady didn't answer.

"She is coming back, isn't she?"

"Oh, yes, sir, she wouldn't leave her girls for very long."

"Don't I know," he mused. Unsmiling, he brought Puddles up and held him against his chest.

The old lady, now mesmerized by the dog's constant stare, removed her glasses and put her face close to his.

J.R., amused by the exchange, leaned in and whispered: "His eyes are strange, aren't they?"

"Yes," she answered softly. "And large, *very* large.

"All the better to *see* you with."

Realizing she'd been had, she snorted her disgust, shoved her glasses back on her face, and spun around on her heels. J.R. watched, smiling, as she disappeared behind a floor-to-ceiling glass partition.

It was late on a Sunday night. J.R. was lying on the sofa with pages of the *New York Times* spread out over his body and on the floor beside him. He sighed deeply, and closed his eyes.

He hadn't heard a word from Kate and he was sure he had lost her. When his cell phone buzzed, he sat up straight and picked it up. He said *hello* several times before he realized there was a man on the other end of the phone. He said he was sorry, that he was expecting someone else. "If you're selling something," he said, "I'm not interested."

He heard a soft chuckle then a strong baritone voice: "Hello, Dad. This is Bobby calling you from California."

Bobby? From California? I can't believe this. "Bobby Cronyn?" he asked after a moment. "Is that really you?"

"Yes, Dad," he said, "It's really me, Bobby Cronyn."

All J.R. could think of to say was "How's your nose?"

"What can I say about a nose? It grows and grows and grows." He chuckled. "It's just fine, Dad. How about yourself? What've you been up to?"

As succinctly as he could, J.R. told his son about his savage attack and how, after being beaten and stabbed numerous times, he was left for dead. But he was recuperating now and living in Brooklyn, he told him. He explained that he was healing and growing stronger every day. And that he felt confident that his pursuit of a new career as a writer would be successful.

"I'm so proud of you, Bobby," J.R. said. "And so happy to be talking to you after all these years.

"I feel the same, Dad," he said. "By the way, the reason I'm calling is to tell you that I'll be in the Big Apple in two days and I want to see you. Around six, I'll send a limousine to pick you up; it will take you to the heliport where you'll board a helicopter and fly to the penthouse. We'll dine on a delicious meal, drink champagne and talk until midnight. You do want to see me, don't you, Dad?"

"Of course I do. I was just afraid you wouldn't want to see me."

"Oh, Dad, I realize you did the best you could under the circumstances. I've got to go now. The baby's crying and I've got to feed him. It's a boy, and yes, you're a grandfather. Four times over. I love you. God bless."

"And I love you, too, Bobby." No answer. "Bobby?" His son was gone. "God bless you too."

He put the phone down on the kitchen table and walked through the apartment in a kind of daze, running his fingers through his hair and smiling, and then laughing and repeating his son's name over and over again.

When the phone buzzed a second time, he thought it might be Bobby calling back. He rushed to the kitchen, snatched it up and said loudly: "Bobby? Bobby? Is that you?"

A woman said: "No, sir. This is the overseas operator. Will you accept a call from a Kathryn Winfield?"

"Will I?" He was ecstatic. "You bet I will!"

"J.R., this is Kate. It's Kate. Who's Bobby?"

"Oh, Kate, Kate, I've missed you so much. Is this really you?"

"Yes, it's really me. And I've missed you too. Who's Bobby?"

"He's my son. He just called me from California. He's coming to see me—after all these years. I'm so happy . . ."

"And I'm happy for you too, J.R."

"It's a baby boy. I'm a grandfather!"

She was silent for a moment. "That's wonderful. A life is born. And a life . . . I'm in London and . . . . Oh J.R. I buried my mother yesterday."

"Oh, Kate, I'm so sorry," He said. "When are you coming home?"

"Soon. Very soon."

"Thank God. I thought I'd lost you."

"Oh, no." J.R. sensed that she was crying. After a moment she said: "I need you. I need your shoulder to cry on and your arms to hold me. I need your warm words of comfort to calm me and to bring me peace. I'm coming home, J.R., and I'm never going to leave again."

Minutes after he got off the phone, he sat down and wrote Kate's final words in his journal: *I'm coming home, J.R., and I'm never going to leave again."*

He read the words to himself over and over. He wrote: *These sweet words will be with me for the rest of my life. However, even at this moment, we are already family. I will cherish them, all of them, forever.*

I know Bobby will love Kate as much as I do. This is the happiest moment of my life, and I will thank God for blessing me with the greatest of treasures: family.

CHAPTER 7

They met in the garden under the spreading branches of the great maple and embraced, neither one wanting to let go.

Kate sat close to J.R., and held his hand. She told him about her mother's devotion, her love, and her sacrifices as a young woman coming out of the Second World War in London.

In 1945, her mother's first husband was killed in the war and she and two children struggled to survive the destruction of their modest row house. Thanks to the generosity and love of relatives they were given shelter and sustenance to survive the horrors of war.

In 1954, Kate's mother met and married a handsome army veteran, and just a year later Kate was born. Her father later went on to become an honored member of the British parliament.

Kate spoke for hours as the morning sun took center stage in its high place in the sky. She spoke of her childhood days and her first dance when she wore a pretty party dress with pink ribbons around her slender waist. She spoke of her first ballet class and how she dreamed of becoming a famous ballerina one day. In sad tones she described her American husband whom she'd met in Paris. She returned with him to his home in Dallas, Texas.

She hated Dallas. To placate his unhappy wife, her young husband promised her that she could pursue a dancing career. However, just after two years he broke his promise. He was making money as an advisor and manager for a large financial firm, and he announced one day that he wanted to buy a larger house and start a family and that she was to give up her dream of becoming a ballet dancer.

To his way of thinking, motherhood was the supreme and only role for a woman. If she wanted to dance, she could, but only after the children were older. Then, if she desired, she could open a small dance studio and teach ballet to the neighborhood children. Disillusioned and broken hearted, Kate fled to New York.

After her husband divorced her, she worked hard and became a featured dancer with the New York City Ballet Company. She married a ballet dancer and they toured South America and the continent. During a stay in Paris, her young husband was killed in an automobile accident. She returned to London where she discovered that she was pregnant. She gave birth to twin girls.

With the help of her mother, she raised the girls while she continued to dance and teach ballet to young dancers. When the girls were grown, she moved back to New York City where she continued to teach. After several years, she retired and bought a house in Brooklyn, and one day volunteered at the Boys & Girls Club. She liked it so much she decided to stay and teach ballet to eight, nine, and ten-year-old girls. Kate was silent. J.R. looked at her; tears were welling up in her eyes. Before he could say anything, she said firmly: "I'm a realist. I know it's too late for me now. I've dreamed my dream and I've lived it the best way I could. Now . . ." She paused. Taking both of J.R.'s hands in hers, she said, "Tell me it's not too late to dream another dream."

"Of course it's not too late." He looked deep into her eyes. "It's never too late to dream a dream. I believe everything's possible when you turn to the light."

"To Him."

"Yes."

"I want my own dance company, and I want to start it right here, in Brooklyn with my talented girls and boys from the Club. I pray with all my heart that He will grant me just one wish before I die. It's a dream . . ."

"Wait, wait, wait." J.R. put his hands up as a signal for her to stop. "Wait." He looked at her for a moment. "I think you may be a little confused about something.

"We don't ask God to grant us wishes, as in a fairy tale. This is real life time. We can ask God to give us the strength and the courage to go forth to try to attain something that might fulfill a dream."

"But what of the light, the spirit you talk of? Is that not God?"

"According to the great Tolstoy, He is *The spirit within—that real divine self which lives in every person.* To answer your question: I think the light I saw as a child was a physical materialization of my divine self, of the spirit . . ." He stopped and stared at the large maple at the end of the garden. It brought him back to Brooklyn to memories of that little child again. "Kate, Kate . . ." he murmured. "I've just experienced a revelation. That's what I'm seeking, Kate, that divine self that is the spirit. That's my *real* purpose in this life. To find that light again, that spirit that I knew as a child . . ." He turned to look at Kate. His eyes were wide with wonder and delight.

"Oh, Kate." He kissed her hand. "You have a dream, as we all do. My dream is to become a successful writer. I just finished my first article about sex and sex addiction. My fate is now in the hands of the publishers. Your fate is a lot simpler because there's little doubt that you can make your dream happen. And it's a wonderful dream. All you need is a whole lot of money."

She laughed. "And a whole lot of prayers . . . and faith."

"Speaking of faith, Tolstoy said that when he lost his belief in the existence of God, he did not live, and he would have killed himself a long time before had he not had some dim hope of finding Him. He goes on to say that he lived, really lived . . . only when he felt Him . . . A voice exclaimed within him: *What more do you seek? This is He. He is that without which one cannot live. To know God and to live as one and the same thing, for . . . God is life!*"

"God is life," she repeated. Dearest J.R., you and Tolstoy shared a great thing. A great experience. You both saw the light and you both lost it. But you can regain it. You can find it again."

'Yes, I can," he said, his eyes wide and bright with the joy of confirmation. "But I cannot live without God!"

Feeling his pain, she moved slowly into his arms to comfort him. He sighed. "The love that I feel for you right now, Kate, will help me succeed in my quest. I have not doubt of that."

"You feel love for me?"

"Oh, Kate, don't you know I fell in love with you the moment I saw you?

She smiled. "You expect me to believe in love at first sight?"

"Don't you?"

Pressing a finger against his lips, she said: "Hush you, and walk me home. We can talk."

They walked in silence for minutes while Puddles busied himself by sniffing the sidewalk. Kate held his arm and when she put a hand to her forehead, J.R. asked: "A headache?"

She nodded.

They walked the next couple of blocks in silence to Kate's one-hundred-year-old Victorian that stood tall, proud, and singular on a large corner plot.

At the gate, Kate turned to J.R. and said: "I miss my mother so much. Her favorite perfume was Chanel No. 5. She wore it all the time. A few nights ago I was in the kitchen, standing by the sink when suddenly the air was filled with her perfume. I know it so well. I know she was there in the room with me. I was ecstatic. I felt her presence, her spirit, and I called out her name. But, sadly, in seconds, she was gone."

"She'll never be gone, Kate," he said *sotto voce*. "She'll always live in your heart."

"You dear, sweet man," she said, opening the gate. "Let's sit on the porch for a while. I'm feeling better.

As he followed her up the path, he said: "Are you feeling well enough to hear about my children?"

"How many children do you have?"

"Just two. Elizabeth Cronyn and . . ."

"Bobby," she said, interrupting. "I remember. Bobby Cronyn." She looked at him and frowned. The same Bobby who owns Bobby Computers and is probably worth hundreds of millions of dollars?

J.R. smiled and nodded.

"Well," she began, her face lighting up, "if it's that much, come . . ." She took his hand and led him up the path. "Let's sit on the porch and talk—*philanthropy.*

When they had settled in on the top step, Kate sat close to J.R. and spoke softly in his ear. "We'll have to put his money to good use . . . doing a lot of good work."

"Any suggestions?"

She took a deep breath, and said: "Oh, J.R., there are so many things I want to do for the hundreds of wonderful children at the Club. For instance, for the holidays I was hoping to put on a production of

"Nutcracker Suite," but it's so terribly expensive, and the cost of costumes alone, well . . ."

"Do you have a theatre?"

"We usually use the auditorium of the local high school. But it's totally inadequate for a production of *Nutcracker.*"

"Well, perhaps you could talk him into renting a theatre for you."

"But you're his father. I think you should ask him."

Bobby told me that when he gets here, he'll send a limousine for me that will take me to a heliport where I'll take a helicopter to his penthouse in Manhattan. I'm sure you could do a much better job of persuading him to help you than I can. What do you say? Is it a date?

Of course I'll go, "she said softly. "I wouldn't miss this reunion with your son for anything."

CHAPTER 8

From the time they left Brooklyn in Bobby's stretch limousine to the moment they landed on the copter pad on top of a penthouse apartment overlooking Central Park, J.R. and Kate were without words.

The houseman, dressed all in white, greeted them: Welcome to the home of Mr. Wright."

J.R. glanced at Kate, then looked back at the houseman. "Mr. Wright? I don't know any Mr. Wright. Isn't this the home of . . ."

Kate stopped him with a sudden elbow nudge.

When he looked at her she shook her head and said: "Isn't it just possible Bobby took his step-father's name?"

"I thought his name was Taylor."

Kate glared at him.

"He's still my son."

"This way sir." The houseman waved them forward. They followed him through a doorway and down a winding marble staircase to a large ornately carved iron door.

He pressed a button, then turned to them, bowed, said it was a pleasure serving them, then turned and hurried down the marble stairs to the floor below.

Soon the door opened and an Oriental man, about forty-five, and almost as big as the door, smiled broadly at them and welcomed them to Wright House.

They followed him into a wide hallway that was eclectic in its décor featuring priceless antiques mixed with contemporary furniture and museum-quality artwork.

The houseman took their coats and gently laid them on an old bench that Kate recognized as French Provincial at least three hundred years old and worth, well, more than she could afford.

The walls were covered with paintings and drawings by the likes of Van Gogh, Rembrandt, Cezanne, Goya, Klee, and many others.

"This place is a living *museum*."

"We won't be living too much longer if we don't get a move on. Our tour guide looks like he wants to do us bodily harm."

"Let's go." J.R. winced. "I wouldn't want to have to wrestle with him."

"If you did, you'd lose."

"Tell me about it."

Without another word they quickened their steps and joined the houseman at the double doors.

When the big man opened them, J.R. and Kate stepped into the Great Room. What they saw made them stop, and stare. J.R. was struck by the sheer size of the Great Room, while Kate, who gasped, thought she had just stepped into one of the most beautiful rooms she had ever seen.

A strong male voice quickly brought them back to the reality of the moment. "Hey you two," it intoned. "Just don't stand there. Come on in."

J.R. was the first to respond to the voice. When he looked into the room he saw a young man, about six-feet three or four and weighing approximately two hundred and fifty pounds coming toward him fast with both arms outstretched.

His first instinct was to flee the scene as fast as he could, but he knew the young man must be Bobby and that he wouldn't hurt him, so he smiled as broadly as he could and approached Bobby ready and fortified for what promised to be one of the biggest, and strongest, bear hugs he had ever received.

With a huge smile on her face, Kate watched the warm father/son welcome with a sense of glee she had not felt in a long time. And when they hugged and continued to slap each other on the back, or shoulder, she was delighted. It was the best show in town, she thought.

After introductions were made, and drink orders were taken by big Son Fu, Bobby announced that he was also the head chef. He had owned a famous restaurant in Hong Kong and had been brought back to the states by Mr. Wright, who, as it turned out, was not Bobby but Will Wright, a good friend, who had insisted that Bobby use the penthouse to entertain his father and friend.

"Wright's an old friend of mine, and while he's flying all over the world in his jet, looking for fun, and whatever, he's allowing me to use this place for entertaining friends and family. Anyway, he owes me."

Taking a deep breath, he expanded his chest. "My name is Cronyn," he proclaimed. "Just like my dad. I'm proud of it. And I'm proud of my dad. Look where's he's been and look where he is now. I predict he'll become a famous author one day."

"Well, I don't know . . ." J.R. began.

"Well, I do know," Kate said, interrupting. "You should be proud of your dad. He's a good man, a very good man."

During an exquisite seafood dinner perfectly seasoned with exotic oriental herbs and spices, they talked of family and the future.

With typical fatherly pride Bobby produced photographs of his new son. "Look at the size of him. He was almost nine pounds when he was born."

"How old is he?" Kate asked.

"Just two and a half months old."

"He's certainly a healthy looking boy," she added. "What's his name?"

"Will Cronyn."

"That's my father's name," J.R. interjected.

"Yeah, I know."

"Your grandfather would be so pleased.

"Don't you think he looks like a Cronyn, dad?" he asked. "Look at that face. That's a Cronyn face. He's got your blue eyes, dad." There was silence for a moment. Bobby became quiet, thoughtful. J.R. and Kate looked at one another.

J.R. shrugged.

Then something unexpected happened. Bobby was curious about something, and, although he wanted to talk about it, he was reluctant. Before J. R. could say a word, Bobby blurted it out. "I had a dream . . . and God spoke to me." He looked at his father and Kate for a reaction, but they were mute, as if waiting for more. "Didn't you hear what I said?"

"Oh, I heard you," J.R. answered. "I'm just waiting for more. What did God say to you?"

"You don't think it's odd?"

"Not at all. If you believe He spoke to you, then he did."

"Well, I guess I'm on the right course, but . . ." Bobby hesitated, shaking his head, looking uncertain.

"But what, Bobby? What? What did God say to you?"

"He told me to give my money away . . ."

J.R. laughed.

"What's so funny?" Bobby asked.

"I think it's *wonderful.*"

"Wonderful?" Bobby asked, looking troubled. "I can't just give my money away. *That's* crazy."

"What's crazy about it?" J.R. asked. "It's called philanthropy. Rich people, like yourself, do it every day."

"I know, but . . . it seems so . . . *irrational.*"

"Listen, Bobby" J.R. began, his voice strong and stern, "I've been reading a lot lately about the spread of AIDS throughout the world. There are forty million AIDS cases and ninety-five percent of those live in developing countries like South Africa. And almost one half, or twenty million cases, are women and children. I find those disturbing facts *irrational!*"

"I had no idea."

"Bobby, when the Lord asked you to give money away he didn't mean *all* your money. He meant a percentage of your money. How many millions do you have?"

Bobby grinned. "I don't have millions. I have billions."

"Billions?" J.R. glanced quickly at Kate who was staring at Bobby with an open mouth. Turning to his son, his eyes large with excitement, he said: "In that case, can you afford to spend . . . two billion a year?"

Bobby laughed. "Of course I can."

"Listen, Bobby, listen," J.R. said, "this is very important." Leaning forward, he gestured as he spoke to make his point: "There's a drug called Nevirapine that reduces prenatal transmission of HIV by forty-one percent at eighteen months of age in a breast-feeding population. Think of it, Bobby, this drug is now available at a relatively low cost. We can save the lives of thousands of South African babies. But time is of the essence."

Bobby's large brown eyes shone. "This is so exciting, dad." He quickly got to his feet and began pacing back and forth in front of the table. "This is big, dad. We'll have to think this out carefully."

J.R. glanced at Kate; she was beaming. "We'll have to form a foundation," J.R. offered.

"Of course," Bobby agreed, clapping his hands together. "We'll call it *"The Bobby Foundation."*

"Sounds good," J.R. offered.

"It *is* good, Bobby," Kate offered. "But wouldn't something more like: *The Bobby Children's Foundation* be more to the point?"

Bobby thought about it. "Yes, I like that a lot. What do you think, dad?"

"I think it's fine, but what happens next?"

"A lot of planning, dad. A whole lot of planning." He stopped at the head of the table and turned to J.R. and Kate. "What do you think of this: You and Kate get your personal business and affairs in order and return with me to California. We'll work on this together."

J.R. shook his head. "I can't leave New York now. I have things to do. How long will this take to form a foundation and get it up and working?"

"Great question, dad. I'm not sure. But the process takes time. I'll get my lawyers in California on this right away. They'll get started drawing up papers, and . . . ."

"Bobby," J.R. interrupted, "why can't they come to New York? Surely you must have offices here in Manhattan where we can do the job without going all the way out to the coast."

Bobby thought for a moment. "It's possible," he said. "It makes sense. I have a few sales offices in the city, but we need more. I've had my eye on a great old twenty-story building in lower Manhattan for years. I think this is the time to take action. All right, Dad. You got your way. Now, let's seal the deal by drinking a toast."

He poured three glasses of champagne and offered a class to each of his guests. Then, holding his glass up high, he was about to speak when J.R. asked: "What is this?" he asked. "It's delicious."

"Well, Dad, for your information, this is a very special champagne. It's a Krug Clos D'Ambonnay 1995."

"Oh," Kate said, looking at her glass. "I had this only once before—at a very special party in Paris. It's *very* expensive."

"How expensive?"

"Oh, thousands, I think."

"In dollars?"

"Yes, in dollars."

"Approximately four thousand dollars, Dad."

J.R. started to laugh.

"What's so funny, dad?"

"Oh, I was just wondering how much money this single glass costs."

"I'd guess about three hundred and ninety dollars."

"Oh my," J.R. said, catching his breath. "Well, son, you'd better make that toast pretty good because I intend to sip this champagne very slowly."

"Here's to us, the three of us . . ." Bobby began, "and to this great philanthropic adventure that . . ."

"Hold it." J.R. said, sipping the bubbly.

". . . we're about to embark upon . . ."

"Hold it! J.R. sipped the champagne.

"Are you done, dad?"

"I think so." He picked up the bottle and poured three hundred and ninety dollars worth of champagne into his glass. "Okay, I'm ready for more.

"I'm done, dad."

"Oh." J.R. looked disappointed. "Kate, say something nice."

"Well," she began, "all I can say is that I'm very proud of you two, and I know you'll both be very successful, and . . ."

"Wait!" J.R. cut in. "I just thought of something, son. And I don't think you're going to like it."

"What, dad? What?"

"Well, Bobby, do you realize that when word gets out about you're great philanthropic endeavor, you'll become a hero. You'll probably sell thousands of Bobby Children Computers. Who knows? Maybe you'll sell *millions!*"

When his brain had computed the news, Bobby realized that immediate action needed to be taken. "Holly—!" he cried. "Excuse me you guys, I have to go; I have to make a call to California right away." He turned and dashed out of the room.

As soon as Bobby was out of sight, J.R. and Kate began to laugh almost simultaneously. It was contagious. Before long, they were laughing so hard they couldn't stand. Together they collapsed onto the leather couch, and when the laughing had subsided, J.R. looked at Kate and Kate looked at J.R.

J.R. knew the time was right. As he moved to take her into his arms, she helped the process by reaching up with her right hand and gently pulling his head down until his eager lips found hers. Their deep passionate kiss symbolized the spiritual oneness of their love.

CHAPTER 9

S till somewhat hung over from the great Krug and moon-eyed from Kate's first kiss, J.R. maneuvered about his little apartment the next day making every effort to get his affairs in order. After giving Puddles his morning meal, his cell rang: The call was from Bobby.

"Hi dad," the big voice said. "Break any plans you might have for lunch because I'm bringing it. Okay?"

"Well, Bobby, I don't know . . ."

"You got a date with Kate?"

"No."

"Then I'm bringing homemade lasagna and a bottle of your favorite champagne. What do you say now?"

"How can I say no? Sounds great."

"See you around noon. Bye." The phone went silent.

"Bye." Smiling to himself, he pressed the "End" button and headed for the shower.

After he had dressed, J.R. leashed the dog and away they went for a long brisk walk up the avenue. When they returned to the apartment house, J.R. checked his mailbox and found a single envelope. It was the letter he was so eager to receive.

Once inside the apartment, he ripped the envelope open and read the contents. The first few words of the editor's letter were enough to assure him that his article on *SEX and Sex Addiction* had been accepted for publication. Not only did the editor like it, he accepted J.R.'s proposal for a follow up article dealing with various cures.

The garden. At noon, when the sun was directly above, J.R. opened the umbrella on the old metal table so that he and Bobby could enjoy their lunch of Yu's home-made lasagna. When Bobby arrived at exactly five after twelve, J.R. hurried him into the back yard where he gave the editor's letter to him. After he read it, Bobby exploded with a holler that J.R. was sure echoed all the way to Staten Island across the river.

Grabbing his father around the waist, Bobby waltzed his father around the garden. When they reached the table, they each collapsed in a chair and laughed until they hurt.

"Pouring Krug, Bobby made a toast: "Congratulations, Dad, for your great accomplishment. Here's to a long and prosperous career." They drank.

"Now," said Bobby, "let's enjoy Yu's fabulous lasagna."

"Is there anything he can't make?"

"Yu's a genius," Bobby said. "You name it, he'll make it."

Bobby raised his glass and made a toast to J.R., Kate, Geri, his wife, their three girls, Suzy, nine, Sandra, eleven, and Sally, thirteen. At that point, out came pictures of his wife and the kids, including his new baby boy. "We waited forever for a boy. We even prayed for a boy."

"And it paid off," J.R. offered with a smile.

After lunch, more champagne was poured and J.R. voiced his interest in knowing how Bobby's business originated and how it got started. "You must've been some kind of computer whiz with a new idea," He said.

Bobby laughed, slapping his knee. "Not at all." He reached for his glass of champagne. 'I think you must have this romantic idea of a rags-to-riches story." He sipped the champagne, and looked at his father. "That's not how it happened, Dad."

"Then how did it happen?"

Bobby shifted his weight and thought for a moment. "I'm not an innovator, dad, I'm a entrepreneur. Just like Mark, my stepfather. He was a business wizard, a gambler, and a builder. "He made millions in the real estate business. There was nothing he couldn't build. So, when I went to college, I studied business and got my degree from Berkeley in business administration."

He told J.R. the story of how he met two young men when he was not quite twenty-five. They were computer "geniuses" who had an idea for a new computer but who needed someone to back them financially.

Ironically, around this same time, Bobby's stepfather, who was coming home from a night at a casino, and who had been drinking heavily, crashed his car into a telephone pole. He was taken to a local hospital but died two hours later from his injuries.

Mark left Bobby and his sister, Elizabeth, fifty million dollars each. Bobby took the money and invested in a fledgling computer company that within five years grew into a successful business that covered, not just the west coast but reached across the Pacific Ocean to Hawaii, Australia, New Zealand, Africa, Japan and finally China.

The Bobby Basic Computer earned the company millions. But with the addition of the Bobby Children's Computer, when Bobby was still in his thirties, the company's bottom line soared—like its fledgling that had morphed into a strong, courageous and keen-sighted *Eagle*!

"The slogan we use for our Bobby Children's Computer is *Soar and be Great!*"

"I like it," J.R. responded. "And I think Kate will like it too—for the Boys & Girls Club."

Bobby slapped J.R. on the back. "I think she's a swell lady, and she's welcome to use it," he said, stretching his long arms high above his head. "How about a brisk walk, dad? I feel a need to get some exercise."

"Can I bring Puddles?"

"Sure," he said, heading for the door. "You get him and I'll meet you outside." The door slammed behind him.

J.R. went to the bedroom window and looked out. He couldn't believe what he saw. Puddles was chasing a large gray cat around the garden. The strange thing about it was the dog wasn't barking. Just as Puddles was about to catch up with the cat, the feline hopped the fence and disappeared.

J.R., laughing, scolded the panting dog for being a poor cat chaser. "You won't get your *Cat Chaser* medal this month."

But Puddles wasn't interested in J.R.'s opinion or medals; ignoring him, he jumped up at the fence several times, barking the whole time.

J.R. shouted: "Puddles! Puddles! Come on. We're going for a walk!"

As soon as the dog heard the word *walk*, he turned away from the fence and scampered to the pathway that led to the back door.

J.R. hurried to the kitchen door and, as soon as he opened it, the dog darted into the room and ran directly to his leash which hung on the closet door knob.

When J.R. and Puddles caught up with Bobby, he was talking in animated fashion with someone on his cell phone.

Grinning, he spoke loudly. "He's right here. Yeah. I swear it. Hold on." Bobby pressed the phone against his chest and turned to his father. "There's someone here who wants to talk to you, dad."

"Who is it?"

"It's my sister and your daughter."

"Liz? Is it really Liz?"

"All the way from Hawaii." He raised his voice so that Liz might hear. "She heads up our Honolulu branch office where sales are in the *millions.*" Smiling, he handed J.R. the phone.

Before J.R. could say a word, Bobby leaned forward and said into the phone: "How was that for a build up, sis?" J.R. listened. She said that was fine, Bobby, and that you're crazy. Bobby laughed, putting his big hand under Puddles and lifting him high in the air. J.R. responded to his daughter by saying that if Bobby was crazy, he was *wonderful* crazy."

The warm but breezy day was perfect for walking and talking on a cell phone. Liz talked a lot and J.R. listened. There was so much she wanted to say to her father. She told him she was absolutely thrilled and excited about their plans to fight HIV/AIDS in South Africa and that she wanted in on the plans. J.R. assured her that she would be.

She was married to a jerk, she said, but she had twin boys, Mark and Matthew, who were the light of her life. They loved Hawaii and . . . "You must come to Honolulu for Christmas, dad," she said. "Bobby will no doubt fly you over on one of his jets. He's so crazy-cool, isn't he, dad?" Before he could answer, she continued: "You will come, won't you, dad? Please. Please."

Of course he would come if they could work it into the schedule. After he said it, he thought about Kate. *I won't go without Kate. I've got to convince her to go with me—children or no children.*

The smell of salt air wafted through their nostrils as J.R. and Bobby leaned against the iron railing looking across the waters at Staten Island.

After a moment of reflective silence, Bobby spoke: "Dad, when a person is on the path, or journey as you call it, does he have to struggle and suffer in order to find truth and fulfillment?"

"The journey can take a lifetime, or it can take but a moment out of time. So many of us tend to make our lives so difficult that we miss the simple and the obvious. God doesn't want us to suffer; he wants us to be content, to find fulfillment and a purpose, by coming to him with an open heart. God knows you've found a purpose, son, and you should be proud."

"But doesn't all this money keep me from finding true fulfillment?"

"Do I detect a sense of guilt? If so, put it aside. The rich have a duty to perform and you are performing it in a most magnificent way . . . in a *spiritual* way.

"Remember what Kriananda said: *". . . money is merely a symbol of energy. One can use energy wisely or foolishly, generously or selfishly, or with greedy attachment. To use it rightly is to perform a useful, even a spiritual, service . . .*

"Of course you're worthy." He put his hand on Bobby's arm. God has spoken to you and you have listened and you have agreed to His terms. And soon you will embark on a great adventure that is destined to change your life forever. That is the spirit, Bobby. You've been chosen and you've been blessed.

"That's all very nice, dad." He sounded skeptical.

"You don't think this is all some kind of fluke, do you?"

Bobby took a moment, then smiled: "Divine intervention?"

"Yes," J.R. sighed. "Divine intervention." Turning to Bobby, he opened his arms wide and said: "I need a hug."

Bobby laughed and wrapped his large arms around his father. "I don't think any of this is a fluke, dad," Bobby said, taking his father's arm. "But I don't believe I've been chosen yet to be included in the company of such august persons as Tolstoy or Mother Teresa, and especially Gandhi, who, by the way, just happens to be one of my heroes."

J.R. smiled. "Well, maybe not yet, but soon. Maybe as soon as tomorrow."

"Speaking of tomorrow, dad," he said, "I must fly to California to take care of some business, but I'll be back in several days."

They walked home in contemplative silence while Puddles, who seemed to understand, tagged along behind them without so much as a whimper.

CHAPTER 10

The day began with a light drizzle. Scaffolding hid the structure's facade, but over the main entrance to the building, a sign printed in large black letters announced:

WELCOME TO THE HOME OF THE BOBBY CHILDREN COMPUTERS FOUNDATION FOR THE FIGHT AGAINST HIV/AIDS

A black Mercedes sedan pulled up in front of the building. A man in his mid-forties, wearing a dark blue suit and carrying a raincoat, umbrella, and leather briefcase, stepped out of the car and approached the front door.

Smiling to himself, the man entered through an automatic revolving door into a lobby decorated with larger-than-life photographs of children dressed in colorful costumes from around the world.

As he stepped into the elevator, he was aware of a strong odor of fresh paint. *Let's see. The executive suites and conference rooms are on . . .* He checked a small black notebook he took from his coat pocket. *Oh, yes.* He pushed number 18 and watched as the numbers passed by in the overhead window. He thought: *This is the old elevator; Bobby rebuilt it to its original glory, and that's the paint I smell. I love it!*

He walked the long hall to the last door on the left: *Conference Room.* Before he entered the room, he placed his umbrella in one of several metal stands and hung his raincoat along with about a dozen other coats on a large portable coat rack.

Brushing himself off and putting a hand through his hair, he tucked the briefcase under his arm, took a deep breath, and opened the door.

As soon as the gentleman entered the room he was confronted by an ebullient Bobby who, smiling broadly, and with outstretched arms, welcomed the man to the first official meeting of the Bobby Children's Computer Foundation meeting.

Standing tall at the far end of the eighteen-foot antique oak meeting table, Bobby announced: "Ladies and gentlemen, it gives me great pleasure to introduce to you the handsome, the distinguished, the world renowned doctor and international attorney and statesman, Dr. Jason Lord." This elicited spontaneous applause from eleven attendees.

Smiling, Lord nodded to one and all as he took a seat at the near end of the table. He opened his briefcase and removed a few papers which he placed neatly on the table in front of him. Closing the case, he put it on the floor next to his chair.

When the applause subsided, Bobby introduced Lord to his father, J.R., who was sitting to his right, and finally to his sister, Elizabeth, who was seated to her brother's left.

Continuing introductions, Bobby introduced three visiting board members: his personal financial advisor and friend, Board President, Ralph Barton, of Barton & Barton, Secretary, Mrs. Joyce Maynard, also of Barton & Barton, and finally, his personal legal advisor, David Cross of Cross, Draper & McCollum of San Francisco.

At this point, Bobby poured himself a half glass of cool water and drank it all. Looking down the table at every face, his eyes rested on Dr. Lord. He smiled.

"Good Doctor Lord, I just want to take a few moments before you speak to introduce you, and the others, to four doctors who are sitting two to your left and two to your right; they are Dr. Paul Doherty, Dr. Bart Gruber, Dr. Sarah Landy, and Dr. Gary Miles. They are all talented and dedicated pediatric practitioners with years of experience, specializing in HIV/AIDs in mothers and children.

"They have agreed to come with us when we go to South Africa in a few months. They're leaving lucrative practices and their families to become members of the team.

"We thank them, and my father and my sister thank them. They are our heroes and we welcome them as we all go forth on a journey that will change, not only the lives of HIV/AIDS ravished women and children, but our lives as well. The change, I'm sure, will be profound and life altering."

Gesturing to his distinguished guest, Bobby said: "Ladies and gentlemen, I give you Dr. Jason Lord."

"Thank you, Bobby," he began. "Thank you for what you've done and are about to do. Ladies and gentlemen, this man, my friend, Bobby Cronyn, has spent a great deal of money to fight a disease that has, to date, killed hundreds of thousands of women and children the world over. Governments, whole countries, have not done what this man is about to do. I know that from personal experience.

"To give you some history: earlier this year I had become a key advisor to several developing countries, most notably South Africa. Quite simply, I tried to make deals to buy drugs to fight HIV/AIDS and was met with a wall of indifference from the United States pharmaceutical lobby, the United States Trade Representatives, or USTR, as well as other wealthy nations. Of course the losers in all of this were the millions perishing from AIDS because they could not afford the drug treatments that would save their lives. The truth is the drug companies were arbitrarily keeping drug costs at an artificially high level."

Lord picked up a piece of paper and began to read: "In June 1999, when Mandela passed the torch of national leadership to his deputy, South African denial would come to be identified with a new face.

"It belonged to Thabo Mbeki. The son of a prominent dissident family, Mbeki was groomed for leadership from an early age. He was selected to lead a prominent student political organization forced to spend much of his adult life in exile, in England, where he received a master's in economics from Sussex University.

"Western-trained and very well read, Mbeki was cerebral, and did little to downplay his image as an urbane intellectual. He was also fiercely anti-colonial, espousing an 'African Renaissance' as the bedrock of his governing philosophy. The mantra was: African solutions for the African people.

"Through 1998 and part of 1999, Mbeki appeared to be emerging as the strongest continental leader on the issue. From 1994 to 1999, the Health Ministry had in fact increased condom distribution from six million to ninety-eight million.

Mbeki had publicly castigated western pharmaceutical companies for keeping drug prices too high for Afrikcan consumption.

Unfortunately, Mbeki remained resolute and refused to stiffen his resolve to formulate an independent viewpoint on HIV/AIDS. In his research on the subject, he stumbled onto a series of individuals known as AIDS 'dissidents' who argued, among other things, that AIDS was caused by 'lifestyle' factors such as poverty or malnutrition, not the HIV virus, which they contended was a harmless 'Passenger virus.' Finally, Mbeki made the following comment: *The reality is that the predominant feature of illnesses that cause disease and death among black people in our country is poverty.* That was the spring of 2000.

"Sad to say that, even after the United States dropped its opposition to the South African Medicines Act, and some pharmaceutical companies had agreed to drop their drug prices by ninety percent or more, the South African government still refused to help provide its people with the lifesaving drugs. Particularly egregious, Mbeki's government refused to help make Nevirapine, a drug with a very strong rate of success in reducing mother-to-child transmission, available to pregnant mothers.

"Fortunately, however, the South African Supreme Court had to overrule the administration. By the late 1990s, it was clear that something of an unprecedented magnitude was afoot. Twenty to thirty percent of the adult populations of most nations in South Africa were infected with a lethal, insidious disease that would lead to their demise in a few short years. The sad fact is: as many as ten million children had been orphaned by the disease.

"But, by the middle of 2001, African leaders would finally call upon the United States to enter the fray and to help combat the pandemic. The US would respond with a recalibration of its effort. The initiatives, from both sides of the Atlantic, demonstrated that leadership need not have come so late."

Dr. Lord looked about the room and smiled. "I wish I could go with you. I see you like soldiers embarking on a mission into the land of a ferocious enemy, a disease so vile, so terrible. But you will defeat and slay it with your wiles and your vast ammunition of drugs.

"God bless you all. When we meet again, we'll celebrate your great victory over the enemy with a bottle of George's spectacular champagne."

The moment was interrupted by a burst of laughter and spontaneous applause.

Bobby got to his feet. "Before we adjourn, ladies and gentlemen, I'd like to take this moment to give credit where credit is due. It was my father's vision and inspiration that brought us all here today. I love him very much, and I'm proud to present to you my dad, the honorable, J.R. Cronyn."

Instantaneous applause as people got to their feet. J.R. smiled and stood. All he could manage to say was: "Thank you." With tears welling up, he looked at Bobby and said, "I love you too, Bobby. Very much."

CHAPTER 11

Two weeks later, the great room was decorated with large blue and white balloons each bearing the adage: *DOCTORS FIGHTING HIV/AIDS*

Yu had prepared a great feast, served buffet style, for about fifty guests, including foundation board members and their families, the pediatric doctors and their families, Elizabeth, and her husband, Mark Stoford, Dr. Jason Lord, and, of course, Bobby, J.R. and Kate.

Servers, dressed in blue with white aprons, moved among the guests offering wine and soft drinks. The Krug Clos D' Ambonny 1995 was being held in reserve for that moment at the end of the evening when Bobby proposed a toast.

Taking Kate by the hand, J.R. gently urged her toward the balcony so they could be alone for a moment.

"Oh, sir, where are you taking me?" she asked, turning her face aside and placing a limp wrist on her brow.

Staring at her with eyes wide open, he spoke in the voice of a villain that was about to seduce the maiden: "I can no longer contain my composure, my sweet." He tweaked an imaginary moustache. "I want to take you out on the balcony and smooch."

"Oh, sir, I never smooch. I only . . ." She whispered something in his ear.

"Oh, madam, you are beyond propriety . . . and I *love* it."

Sitting but a few feet away, the twenty-one year old daughter of a United Nation's ambassador, heard what J.R. said, and began to giggle.

Embarrassed, J.R. took Kate by the hand and led her closer to the balcony. As he reached out to open the French door, Kate held him back.

"J.R. Wait. Look over there. Who is Bobby talking to?"

"Where is he?"

"By the bar."

"Oh." He glanced at Kate. "I told you who that was."

"I've forgotten."

"That's Dr. Jason Lord."

"Oh, yes. What do you suppose they're talking about?"

"Well, I don't know, but, by the looks of that open notebook Jason's holding, I'd say they're probably discussing our entire itinerary. That man has to be the most organized person in the world." He chuckled.

"I'd love to meet him."

"Not now darling. Now, I want to take you outside and . . . smooch."

Bobby handed Jason Lord a glass of champagne. "Krug, Dr. Lord?" Lord smiled. "My weakness," he said taking the glass. He took a sip of the champagne and put the glass down on the bar. Then he opened the notebook and looked at Bobby. "I think we should go over the itinerary just one more time."

"Is it really necessary, Jason?" Bobby asked. "I think I know it all now by heart."

"It'll only take a minute, Bobby. And it won't hurt, you know."

"All right."

Lord checked his notes. "First, I just want to note that with the event of the new drug, Nevirapine, and its proven efficacy in reducing the odds of the virus's transmission from pregnant mother to their children, the question still exists *What will happen to the rest of the family?* It was becoming very clear that without the potential for treatment, there's little incentive for people to get tested. And, of course, as we all know, the lack of treatment is keeping the virus underground, where it spreads most effectively, and, in turn, is crippling prevention efforts. But treatment must not be separate; it must be an integral element of a comprehensive prevention campaign.

"Now, I have listened to you very carefully, Bobby. And I realize that you have an innate ability to see things through to a comprehensive and substantive conclusion. I have taken your advice, as you know, and have contacted our Ambassador in South Africa. He, in turn, and maybe has by now, contacted Mbeki's people in the hope of spurring on a massive prevention campaign. This should be going on as we speak.

"By the time you arrive in South Africa, in just two weeks from now, with all the proper drugs at our disposal, the people will be ready and waiting for treatment. And, hopefully, there will be a huge turnout."

"I hope to God you're right," Bobby said, taking a sip of champagne. "I have already heard from Mbeki's Ambassador to the United Nations."

"You have?" Lord looked surprised. "Why isn't he here tonight?"

"I'll tell you why. Mbeki wants to meet me when I get to Africa. He wants to make a proposition."

"Proposition? What kind of a proposition?"

"He wasn't specific, but he intimated that the President wants to make a deal and it concerns Bobby Computers. It's a kind of *Economic Growth Improvement* deal, as he put it."

"Oh." Lord looked deflated. "I don't like the sound of that."

"I don't either, Jason." He took a slug of champagne.

"When did he contact you?"

"This morning."

"Still. I wish he were here. I'd like to talk to him."

"You can call him at the U.N. tomorrow. There's a meeting of the Security Council; I'm sure he'll be there."

Jason nodded in agreement as he sipped the champagne.

The night air was chilly, but Kate kept warm as she snuggled close to J.R. Together, they looked across the vast expanse that was Central Park and dreamed of the future.

"I wish I were coming with you," she whispered. "We could get married."

J.R. looked at her. "You want to get married in South Africa?"

"Why not?"

"You know, we could get married in Durban in October. I understand it's a beautiful city, and . . ."

"I don't know if I want to get married in Africa," she interrupted.

J.R. was curious. "Because?"

"Because, dear sir, your wonderful, generous, loving son has done something uniquely marvelous. Only *he* would think of it."

"What are you talking about?"

"I'm talking about our new performing arts center to be built on that vacant piece of land next door to the existing Boys & Girls Club."

"He bought that land?"

"No, he talked to the President of the Boys & Girls Club in Atlanta, and asked him to buy the land. He said that if they did, he would build the center, and they agreed, and they did, and presto! We're going to have a new performing arts center at the end of next year. Merry Christmas, darling."

She tried to kiss him, but he held her back. "Why didn't you tell me?"

"Well," she began, "I tried to, but I promised . . ."

"I think I see." He held her at arm's length. "You promised my son that you wouldn't spill the beans. Is that it?"

"That's it, in a bean shell. Oh, J.R. you won't tell him, will you?"

"Of course I won't."

"I like your children so much," she said after a moment. "Bobby, of course, but Elizabeth . . ." She paused. "We haven't talked much but I think I know her. On the outside, she's beautiful and stately like a lady. She looks stunning in that black and white couturier gown . . . And that black pearl and diamond pendant . . ."

"And on the inside?"

"Oh." She sighed. "On the inside I think she's a tough and a no-nonsense kind of gal. I like her."

"I like your assessment."

"I don't know about that husband of hers though. Those heavy-lidded gray eyes are cold. When Liz introduced him to me for the first time this evening, he didn't offer his hand and he mumbled something that sounded like *hello* and headed straight for the bar. Sorry, I wasn't too impressed."

"I wasn't either," J.R. began, "but I don't think he's happy."

"And to tell you the truth, I don't think Liz is happy either, despite the pretty and confident façade."

"Bobby won't say anything about his sister except that she's a great lady and terrific business woman, and so forth. He refuses to talk about Mark except to say that he's a successful CPA. I'm convinced, however, that there's something not quite right in paradise."

"Why don't I have little talk with Liz later—woman to woman."

"Good idea."

Kate laid her head on J.R.'s chest and snuggled up to keep warm.

While J.R. stroked Kate's hair, she pressed her ear against his chest trying to hear the beating of his heart.

"I'm listening to the beat of your heart but I can't hear anything."

"That's because I'm dead."

"Oh you." She hit his arm with the flat of her hand.

After a moment, he asked: "Did you meet Martin Reyes, Bobby's Vice President of Production?"

"Of course I met Martin Reyes," she said, looking up at him. "He explained to me that he was going to be the team captain of the second HIV/AIDS Mobile Clinic unit that will cover areas in western South Africa."

J.R. smiled and asked: "Who's the team captain for the Mobile Clinic for eastern South Africa?"

She hesitated. "Uh . . . you?"

"No," he answered, "Bobby's the team captain. My job is to work with laypeople who go out into the communities and bring women and children back to the mobile clinic for tests and treatment."

"That's a very responsible job, J.R.," she said.

"I know," he said. "I think that's why they gave the job to me—because I'm so responsible."

She guffawed and hit him playfully on the shoulder.

Their silence was suddenly interrupted by a piercing scream. They both got up quickly, looking around.

"Where did that come from?" Kate asked.

Another scream. J.R., now on his feet, looked into the great room. "It's the Ambassador's daughter! Oh, my God!"

When J.R. swung open the French door and entered the room he saw Elizabeth's husband, Mark, in a drunken assault, grabbing inappropriately at the Ambassador's daughter. She was crying and begging Mark to stop.

Before J.R. could make any move on Mark, Martin Reyes rushed forward, grabbed Mark by the coat collar with two hands and pulled him off of the frightened girl and let him fall face-down on the carpet.

Entering the scene, Elizabeth, with hands firmly placed on her hips, yelled at her husband. "Mark, you owe these people an apology."

Mark mumbled something that sounded like "I'm sorry." Covering his face, he began to cry.

Angry and disgusted, Elizabeth said: "Say it again, Mark, we can't hear you. Stand up like a man and apologize to this nice young lady."

"No," the Ambassador said, taking his daughter by the arm. "That won't be necessary. We're all right. I'm very sorry about all this, but, well, it's just one of those things that can happen." As he started to lead her away, Bobby approached and they had a few words. The Ambassador smiled at Bobby, shook his hand, and escorted his daughter out.

Turning to Martin, Bobby asked him to put Mark on the leather sofa. To his sister he suggested that she could sleep in the guest room. She smiled, thanked her brother, and turned away.

"Liz," Kate said, walking up to her. "Are you all right?"

"I could use a drink, Kate."

"Come with me," she said, and taking her arm, escorted Elizabeth to the bar.

Bobby put his arm around his father and tried to apologize for the unpleasant interruption. J.R. admitted that it was unfortunate, but that it didn't dim the enthusiasm of the guests who were there to have a good time and to get to know one another.

He expressed interest in spending some time with the experts and asking them questions that he had about HIV/AIDS.

Bobby laughed and brought J.R. over to a gathering of doctors who were sitting together and announced that his father had some questions for them.

Dr Gruber piped up: "If it's about impotence, I have nothing to say."

J.R. laughed.

"And if you have a big pain in the neck," Dr. Doherty offered, "I say get rid of her."

"OOhhhh," J.R. said, groaning.

"And if you have a big pain in the butt . . ."

"Never mind, Dr. Miles," J.R. said, laughing. "I'll leave quietly."

"No, don't go," Dr. Sarah Landry, an attractive blonde, said. "Sit here, J.R., and I'll explain the facts of life to you from the point of view of a horny ape."

"I don't want to know about horny apes, I just want to know something about AIDS."

A long silence. The doctors looked at one another. Finally, Dr. Gruber spoke: "In that case, J.R., sit there in the middle of the group and listen. Ready?"

J.R. nodded.

"Once upon a time . . ."

"Doctor, I'm not a child."

Dr. Gruber glared at him for a moment, then: "J.R., you must remember that we are all pediatricians. We specialize in children's diseases, and in the case of HIV/AIDS, it has a long history. It's one that's fraught with misery and the pain of death, on the one hand, and one that is filled with joy and the victory of life on the other. Do you understand?"

J.R. could not speak. He could only nod his understanding. He sat on a padded foot stool and waited.

"You know, we were only joking," Gruber said finally.

"What you just said was no joke; it was serious."

"It was meant to be serious."

"I feel like a little kid sitting here."

"You're a good sport, J.R." Dr. Gruber shifted his weight. "Are you ready for some more serious talk?"

"I'm ready."

Liz, fortified by several strong drinks, a desire to vent, and a willingness to talk, told Kate in great detail all about the early days of her marriage to Mark when life was good and sex was even better.

Things began to change, she explained, after about seven years of marriage when Mark announced one evening that he wanted to quit his CPA job and stay home and take care of the kids, who, by then, were five and six respectively.

After the heat of anger cooled, Liz suggested that if Mark wanted to stay home it was all right with her, on one condition: he could not quit his job. He would have to conduct his business from home. He agreed.

About that time, Bobby offered Liz a job at Bobby Computer in Honolulu. She accepted, and, after one year on the job, she was promoted to regional manager. As her time away from home increased and her salary more than doubled, she saw less and less of her husband.

Two years later when she was sitting at her desk she got a call from her then eight year old son. His voice was shaky as he explained that daddy was sick and passed out on the floor. He said that there was an empty bottle of Vodka on the coffee table and should he call a doctor?

She told him to do nothing and that she was on her way.

Liz paused. Taking a deep breath, she looked at Kate. "Well," she began, "that was the moment I turned from a trusting and loving wife and mother, *working* mother, into a goddess of anger and war."

Kate chuckled.

"I'm serious"

"Oh, I know you are."

Liz's ultimatum to Mark was quite simple and to the point: he was to quit drinking, join AA, concentrate on his job, or she would throw him out bag and baggage and file for divorce. He had just two weeks to prove himself worthy of her trust and love. "Well, he was panicked," Liz said. "It scared the crap out of him."

"It worked?"

"It worked." She sighed, looking away. "At least for a while, until he found a substitute."

"Which was?"

"Sex." She almost choked on the word. Fighting back tears, she said: "He's been very good . . . until tonight . . ."

"He's unhappy, Liz."

Liz looked at Kate for a moment. Then, taking a sip of her drink, she settled back in her chair and took a deep breath. "Kate, before I became a registered nurse, I studied Carl Jung. While I know that Tolstoy is dad's guru, if you will, Jung is mine. He believed that we are all extensions of the one and only *Atman,* or God, who allows bits of himself to forget his identity, to become apparently separate and independent. In a word, to become *us.* But we are never truly separate. When we die, we wake up and we realize who we were from the beginning: God."

"Much like J.R.'s belief that we are one with God."

"I didn't know that," she said, looking away for a moment. "Hmmm, I must talk to him about that." She smiled at Kate. "Anyway, to get back to Jung. He speaks of archetypes; but there is no fixed number of archetypes. There are many. But one comes to mind that definitely does *not* fit Mark.

"It's the hero, the mana, or spiritual power, who is the defeater of evil dragons. He's the one who rescues the fair maiden, fights the monster, and captures the bad guys. He's Superman. He's Batman. He's those and much more.

"When Mark was young, he was a momma's boy; he adored his mother. All he knew about his father was that he was a professional soldier who was rarely at home. But he knew he was a hero because he fought the battles, killed the bad guys and returned home with a chest-full of medals.

"*He* was Mark's hero. But, unfortunately, Mark grew up more like his mother. He followed her advice and became a CPA because it paid well and the job was steady."

"I see where you're going with this, Liz, but how do you change a momma's boy into a hero?"

"It's not easy, but it's not impossible either."

Bobby's big voice boomed through the room: "Okay you guys. This is supposed to be a party, not a requiem. We have a lot to celebrate and I think it's time for a toast. And you all know what *that* means, I hope. It means . . ."

He waited for a response and it came loud and clear: "Krug Clos D'Ambonnay 1995!"

On that cue, each server popped a cork of sparkling champagne.

Laughter and applause.

When all the guests had a glass of Krug, Bobby stepped forward and raised his glass. "Here's to all of us and to the mission.

"Here's to South Africa and to its people and to all the thousands upon thousands of mothers and babies who suffer with HIV/AIDS. We're coming! The BOBBY HEALTH CLINICS, two mobile hospitals on wheels, are coming to help you! We pledge to do our best to cure you and to restore your life. We pledge not to leave your beautiful country until we have completed the mission . . .

"We pledge to stay for one year and we will return, if necessary; you can depend upon it;

"We promise this and we pledge to you that we will be victorious;

"We pledge all of this . . . in the name of the Lord."

"Cheers!" They drank.

More applause.

As Bobby poured more Krug into his glass, he looked out at his guests. "Thank you all for coming. Please stay as long as you want. There's plenty of food and drink and I want you to have a good time, because, when we get to South Africa, there's going to be a radical change in your life styles. But you all knew that. Right?"

All the guests concurred except one: Dr. Gruber who said, "Radical change? I thought we were traveling first class."

Bobby laughed. "Yeah, first class . . . all the way to Cape Town where we'll spend one night at the magnificent Manchester Manor. But, after that, it's on the road, mobile living, and catch as catch can. Maybe you'll get lucky and find a first class hotel room here and there, but don't count on it. Be prepared to rough it. Is that all right, Doctor?"

Smiling, Gruber answered: "Sounds good to me, boss."

Bobby, smiling, waved to his guests and said: "Good night, every one. I'm off to bed and I'll see you next week. One last word: please, *please* don't miss the plane. Good night." He left the room with his glass of Krug.

On the balcony, Kate and J.R. held each other close to keep warm. Kate spoke: "I love your Liz. She's a fabulous gal and so smart. It's going to be wonderful having her as a step-daughter. I wish you'd been there when I was talking to Liz. She's so into Carl Jung. And Hinduism. They believe that our individual egos are like islands in a sea: Above the waterline, we look out at the world and each other and think we are separate entities. The part above the water is the ego, or *jiv-atman* which means individual souls. What we don't see is that we are connected to each other by means of the ocean floor beneath the waters. That is called the personal unconscious or . . ."

"The collective unconscious," J.R. offered, cutting in. "I know that *Atman* is God and that when we die, we wake up and realize who we were from the beginning: we were God. But Liz forgets that the Hindu God and the Christian God, if you will, are one and the same . . ."

"Oh, you!" she said. "You knew . . ."

He looked up at her and smiled. "Do you know what time I'm leaving for the airport on Friday morning?"

"You're leaving at ten."

"That's right. And don't be late."

"Oh," she sighed, "we're starting rehearsals for *Nutcracker* on Friday morning, and I'm a bit nervous. My assistant is ill and we may have to replace her for the duration. I don't know where I'm going to find someone who is, not just a good dancer, but someone who's experienced in teaching ballet to young children."

"Are you telling me you might not make it on Friday morning? I couldn't leave without saying goodbye to you."

Oh, darling," she said, stroking his hair, "of course I'll be there to say goodbye. I'll be there rain or shine. I promised to pick up Puddles. Don't you remember? I'm taking care of him while you're gone." When she looked at him, his eyes were closed. She had to regain his attention. "J.R.," she said, nudging him. He opened his eyes and smiled at her.

"You remember that your original question was: Are we getting married in New York or Durban, South Africa? Well, J.R., I really do want to get married in Durban. Liz could be my bridesmaid and Bobby could be your best man. What do you say?"

"I say fine," he said sleepily. "Let's do it. Just as soon as possible."

"We can't do it as soon as possible, you silly." He didn't answer. She looked at him. "J.R.? Are you asleep?" Seconds later, she heard the throaty sound of a snore. Smiling to herself, she kissed his cheek and pulled the blanket up around her shoulders. "Goodnight my husband," she whispered, snuggling close to him. "See you in my dreams."

CHAPTER 12

J.R. was up with the sun on Friday morning. To fortify himself against *the rumbles,* as he called it, he ate a hearty breakfast consisting of eggs, bacon, and pancakes covered with melted butter and plenty of rich maple syrup.

At seven, someone knocked on his door. "Who's there?" he asked, approaching the door.

"It's Carl."

He opened and door and welcomed his friend in. "I'm happy to have this opportunity to say goodbye to you. How are you this morning? Everything all right?"

When Carl didn't answer, he asked: "Is something wrong, Carl?" He shook his head. "Well come in and have a cup of decaf coffee with me. I just made a fresh pot."

Without a word, he followed J.R. into the kitchen and sat at the table.

"What is it?" J.R. asked as he put a mug of coffee in front of Carl. "Help yourself to sugar and cream."

"I've been a bad boy," Carl looked uneasy as he poured a little cream into his coffee. "And I've come to apologize for lying to you about Molly's husband. He wasn't murdered; he died of natural causes."

"It's all right, Carl." J.R., said, sitting across from Carl. "Speaking of Molly, did you make up with her? She's really a very nice lady, you know."

"Molly's got a cold."

"Have you been in to see her?"

"Yes. She wants me to take care of her.

"And?

"And so, I guess I'll take care of her."

"Good boy."

Carl shook his head. When he spoke he didn't look at J.R. "I also lied to you about my book. I mean, I'm not going to write a book about universal consciousness. It's way above my head; I'm just not smart enough to write a book like that. But, but I am going to write a book." He paused, looking at J.R.

"I hope you'll believe me now when I tell you that I heard from the Lord. I mean, he spoke to me and he told me what my purpose is. I was so excited because I know you talk about having a purpose but I never really grasped the concept. Now I do."

"What did the Lord tell you, Carl?"

"Last night, as I was getting ready for bed, he spoke to me. I was about to say a little prayer when I heard a voice. The voice told me that I was to write a book about this house—a kind of history, I guess. I was to tell the story of all the people who lived here over the years. He even gave me a title for the book. He said that he wanted me to call the book *Humanity in a Jar.*"

"What do you think it means?"

"I think it's a metaphor for life. By writing the human stories of all those people who lived, and live, in this house I will be preserving that history for an age or more. And when you preserve something, what do you do with it; you put it in a jar."

"Hence, the title, *Humanity in a Jar.*" I think it's great, Carl. The Lord could not have chosen a more worthy person than you to complete such a task. Aren't you excited?"

"Yes," he answered, smiling. "At last I have a purpose. I have something important to do. And I'm not just doing it for myself. There are hundreds of stories to tell about the people who lived here. And they're all important. It's a daunting project but I think I'm up to it." Carl rose from the table and walked to the door. "I hope you'll help me," he said. "Maybe act as my editor?"

"I'd be honored, sir," J.R. said, following Carl to the door. "I'm so proud of you."

Before they said their *goodbyes,* Carl asked J.R. if he had been redeemed. J.R. assured him that he had been redeemed, and reminded him that . . .

"In true faith a person seeks one thing alone: to learn to please God. Love dwells in the spirit, and whoever unites with it, is happy."

With tears in his eyes, Carl admitted that when the Lord spoke to him he didn't feel afraid; instead he felt a sense of pure joy. He had never been happier. Putting his arms out he said: "I think I need a hug."

J.R. responded immediately. He put his arms around Carl and gave him a big bear hug.

Before Carl left, J.R. promised him that he would keep in touch with them as often as he could and that he would be thinking of them every day.

When J.R. closed the door, he smiled to himself. He knew now that it was all right for him to leave. These people weren't just neighbors; they were friends. No, they were family.

8:30 a.m. Friday. Kate's bedroom.

Burdened with the responsibility of finding a replacement for her sick assistant, Kate had to deal with Bertha, the Club's elderly secretary. "Tell me again, Bertha, what was her name?" She listened. "Please, Bertha, slow down and take a deep breath . . . Yes, I know you're excited, but I can't understand a word you're saying. Are you sitting? . . . Good. Now, say it again. What's her name, and where does she come from?"

"Spell her first name. I-r-i-n-i. Irini? All right. What's her last name? . . . Petrovich? No? Spell it please . . . P-e-t-r-o-s-o-v-i-t-c-h. Petrosovitch . . . No, I've never heard of her. Where's she from? . . . Brooklyn? Oh, she lives in Coney Island? . . . She came to the states from Russia?

"The what? . . . The Russian Ballet? Are you sure? . . . I don't care. Even if she just danced with the Corps de Ballet I'd be excited. She did? Well then, when can she start? . . . Good. How long can she stay? . . . Six months? That's okay. I can work my schedule around that. Can she start next week? . . . What? You're waiting to hear from her? . . . I can't wait that long . . .

"All right, here's what we'll do. When you speak to Irini, tell her she has the job and that she can start next Wednesday at two o'clock. Mrs. Wagner has the schedule and she'll work closely with Irini. Call Joan and see if she'll assist Irini. . . . She will? You're an angel. Then it's all set. I couldn't be happier. (She glanced at her watch).

"Oh, Bertha I must run now. I have to see a friend off on a long journey and pick up a dog. I probably won't see you until eleven. Thanks for everything you've done. Goodbye."

She looked at her watch again; it was 9:15. She tried to reach J.R. on his cell phone, but he didn't answer. There was a sound of thunder. When she looked out the window, lightning struck and it began to rain.

Feeling somewhat stressed, Kate made the decision to leave and walk to the apartment before the storm worsened.

It was 9:30.

Friday was no ordinary rainy day. Large pellets of water fell from the sky and exploded on the pavement with such fierce force that everything it touched was either drenched or swept away by rushing rivers of rain.

Puddles, out for a walk with Jack, broke loose and ran off. Jack tried to catch the dog, but the rain and slippery pavement kept him from doing so.

Kate struggled to keep her footing, but she was loosing the battle. Her rain hat was a victim of strong storm winds, and when her umbrella was threatened by collapse, she lowered it to keep it from taking off.

That created a problem. It prohibited her from seeing a foot in front of her. She almost tripped over a low fence and stumbled into a wet and muddy garden.

The sound of a far-off bark made her stop, look, and listen. There it was again. A dog barking. And not just any dog. It was Puddles!

She followed the sound until she came to a narrow alley between two apartment buildings. As she slowly made her way between garbage cans, she called Puddles by name. About half way down the alley she saw a cardboard box to her left. She called his name and he barked. When she reached the box, which was turned on its side, she saw Puddles; he was crouched in a corner. He was wet and shivering but his furry little tail was wagging and he barked loudly when he saw Kate. He was happy to see her.

She scooped him up, leash and all, and sheltered him from the rain by tucking him in under the broad lapel of her raincoat. When she turned to leave, she saw the outline of a man standing at the entrance of the alley. Thinking he might be J.R., she hurried along as fast as she could. When she got close she realized it wasn't J.R. at all. She recognized Jack Johnson. He was smiling and holding out his hands to receive Puddles.

"I'll take him, Kate."

The dog barked, and Kate handed him over. She smiled. "I thought you might be J.R."

"I'm sorry, but I think he's gone."

Kate almost stopped breathing. "What?" she gasped. "He's gone? He can't be; it's not ten o'clock yet."

"It's a few minutes past ten."

Kate glanced at her watch. "I have nine fifty-five," she said. "I still have five minutes. I've got to make it. I promised J.R. I'd see him off."

"In that case, you'd better get a move on."

"Thanks Jack," she said, pulling the collar of the raincoat up around her neck. "I'll pick up Puddles later," she said, hurrying away.

Fortunately, as the rain let up, she was able to close her umbrella. But, as she neared J.R.'s house, she lost momentum. There was no sign of the limousine.

It was gone.

She wanted to sit on the wet stone stoop and cry, but she wasn't ready to give up just yet. She was convinced that J.R. was out there somewhere looking for her.

Perhaps he got my message and is heading back to my house this very minute.

The notion gave her renewed energy. She hurried across 88th Street and headed down Second Avenue as fast as she could to 87th Street. There she turned left and headed up the street toward Third Avenue.

Then again maybe they're half way to the Airport by now. Oh, I mustn't think like that; it's much too depressing. I must keep a positive attitude.

The rain was a mere trickle by now. She closed the umbrella and quickened her pace. She wanted to get to her house before J.R. arrived. *Oh, Kate, really. What are you thinking? For all I know they're probably at the airport getting ready to take off. The thought of it makes me unhappy, depressed. But I must face the truth. I must be realistic.*

And that Irini whatshername! I don't know anything about her really. I've never heard of her. For all I know she's a second rate dancer who knows little or nothing about teaching choreography to little children, especially something as intricate as the Nutcracker! For all I know, she might be incompetent. She might even be a fraud! God help me!

Engrossed as she was in her own thoughts, Kate was completely oblivious to the long black car that had pulled to the curb on the opposite side of the street and stopped. The sound of a familiar voice calling her name made her stop. A moment, then she heard it again: "Kate! Kate."

She turned. And, when she saw J.R. standing by the open car door, she ran across the street to him as fast as she could. "J.R.," she cried, as he wrapped his arms around her.

"Kate, Kate, my Kate." He picked her up and kissed her face, her hair, her neck.

They stood smiling at one another. "How'd you find me?" she asked. "Why did you come back?"

"I had to," he said, holding up his cell phone. "I finally got your message. Anyway, I had to find you. I couldn't leave without saying goodbye." He explained that he tried to call her several times but that he couldn't get through."

Oh, J.R." Kate threw her arms around his neck. "I'm so happy, and I'm so in love with you."

J.R. was ecstatic. "Oh my dear, sweet Kate." He put his arms around her waist and pulled her to him. Their lingering kiss brought Bobby out from the back seat. Without saying a word, he opened the door to the front seat and climbed in.

"Oh, J.R." Kate pulled back, looking at her watch. "I have to go. It's almost ten-thirty and the girls will be waiting for me. But, and I know this is a bad thing to say, but I want to go with you. Will God punish me for saying that? For not being good or measuring up?"

"Kate, it's not about being good or measuring up. God's not testing you. He just wants you to follow your heart and do what's right. If He measures you by anything it's not by being good, or by what you say; it's by what you *do*. He measures by deeds. It's that simple."

She smiled. "That reminds me of something Mother Teresa once said: *If you can't feed a hundred people, then feed just one.*"

"And she might've said: *If you can no longer dance, then teach the young how to dance.*"

"Oh, J.R." She pressed close to him, "I know that's my purpose and I welcome it gladly, but I also want to feel that spiritual light that you speak of. I want to feel that God is with me."

"He *is* with you, Kate." J.R. gently held her face in his hands. "I can see the light of the Lord in your eyes. They shine with his love."

At that moment Bobby got out of the car to remind his father that if they didn't get a move on they'd miss the plane.

"My girls and I have a ballet to put on December eighteen. I wish you both could be here."

"We'll be there in spirit, Kate," Bobby said, putting an arm around her.

Before Kate left, she instructed J.R. to call her at least once every day. He promised to do so and kissed her one last time. Before getting back into the car, he told her that he loved her very much and that he'd see her again in Durbin.

With the engine roaring, the big limousine slowly pulled away from the curb; the skilled driver maneuvered the difficult U-turn in the narrow street and headed back toward Second Avenue.

Kate waved at the car as it sped off. Taking her cell phone out of her coat pocket she hurried off in the same direction. When she reached the corner of 87th Street and Second Avenue the light was against her; she dialed the Boys & Girls Club and waited for someone to answer.

"Bertha? Yes this is Kate. I'm on my way to the Club right now . . . What? Irini can't come in on Wednesday; she's got a cold?"

"Will she be in on Monday? . . . Maybe? . . . Yes, I'm here, Bertha . . . No, I'm not coming in. I'm too depressed. I'm going to get Puddles, and . . . What? . . . You know Puddles? . . . Yes, he's the dog with the big eyes . . . What? He's one of a kind? Who told you that? . . . The handsome man with the beautiful blue eyes and gray hair? Would his name be J.R. by any chance? . . . That's the one. That's my love . . . That's right. You know what, Bertha? I've changed my mind. I'm coming in after all. So tell the ladies to tighten their corsets because it's going to be a bumpy ride!"

As the big black limo made its way through city traffic on its way to LaGuardia Airport, J.R. speculated about the future; to him it looked bright. He was excited about the foundation and their mission and he was grateful for the opportunity to be a part of a great humanitarian endeavor.

When he took a moment to look back on his life's journey, and his search for personal truth, he realized he had a lot for which to be grateful.

After a moment of silence he closed his eyes and prayed:

Oh Lord, what a journey this has been;
What a sea of troubles I've endured;
Only through your devotion, patience, and love
Have I come to realize that the only way is through the light of
your love;
Oh, Lord, I've passed through the door;
And I've been blessed;
You have given me an extended family that I
        have come to revere;
You have given me my son and my daughter;
You have given me the love of a woman whom I will treasure
forever;
She now owns my heart and we are as one;
Oh Lord, dear God, we feel so close to you.
Amen

CHAPTER 13

Cape Town, South Africa
CTIA—International Airport

The British Airlines jumbo rolled easily into the arrival port at the Cape Town International Airport and stopped. In the first class section of the jumbo, Bobby addressed his two teams. To minimize time, he suggested that they remain seated and let the majority of the passengers disembark.

He explained that a Mr. Trobak, an Indian diplomat, was in the terminal and ready to escort them to the International Flight Office where they would be given VIP treatment and processed as quickly as possible.

After processing they would be taken by limousine to their hotel, the Manchester Manor.

"Any questions?"

Dr. Gruber raised his hand.

"Yes, doc?"

"What's the present situation regarding our mobile units?

"I'm assured that they are both in the warehouse down at the docks and will be brought to our hotel early tomorrow morning, probably sometime around five."

"So early?"

"We must all be up and ready to leave tomorrow morning at six."

"Any other questions?"

Again Gruber: "Who's going to drive them?"

"I, for one, will drive the Mobile through Eastern Africa; the Western driver is a highly experienced South African man who has driven, not only buses, but big rigs and trailers. He has been fully documented and background-checked. I have not yet met him, but I'm assured that he is in perfect health."

"Bobby," J.R. piped up, "what about all these press releases I have? Do you want me to distribute them to the media?"

"Yes. There has been a lot of pre-publicity so there could be a handful of press, or there could be twenty or thirty; I don't know. But whatever it is, get rid of those releases as quickly as you can and make your way to the international office. Be sure to ask Trobak how to get there."

Liz raised her hand and said: "I'm so excited to be here."

Bobby looked around the group and asked: "How many of you are excited?"

No one raised their hand.

Bobby frowned: "If I tell you there's champagne waiting for us at the hotel, how many are excited now?"

All hands went up.

Bobby shook his head and laughed.

After most of the passengers had disembarked, Bobby, with his arm around his father, led his two teams into the air bridge that connected the plane with the terminal. When they approached the entrance to the terminal, a small dark-haired man with dark eyes and a long, neatly trimmed beard, stepped forward. This was Mr. Trobak who was holding a hand-printed sign that announced . . .

The Bobby Group

Dr. Gruber saw the sign and exclaimed: "The Bobby Group; we're rock 'n roll stars." Without missing a beat, he began to sing and play an imaginary guitar. *"We're here to rock. And we're gonna make it right . . ."*

Dr. Doherty took up the lyric: *"We're here to roll. And we're ready to fight . . . the dreaded H.I.V. slash, the dreaded H.I.V. slash AIDS. Oh, yeah . . ."*

Spontaneous applause as Mr. Trobak waved the sign back and forth.

Bobby, cool and silent, smiled at Mr. Trobak, gently took the sign from him, and, with a pen, crossed off the word *Group* and printed the word *Team.*

Mr. Trobak's face fell. "But it was good, don't you think?"

Bobby's one word answer: "Brilliant."

Trojak tried to apologize, but Bobby was in no mood; he was in a hurry and nothing or no one was going to stop him.

"Mr. Trobak, did you see any press people in the terminal?"

"Uh, no press . . ." he began.

"No press? No media people?"

"Oh, yes," he said, smiling. "Lots of media. Out there." He pointed to the terminal. "Standing out there behind, uh, . . .

"Behind a rope?"

"Yes. Behind a rope."

"Good." Bobby took a beat. "Now, Mr. Trobak, can you tell my dad here how to get to the office?"

"Yes. You go down the hall that way until you get to next building. Go in and walk down hall until you get to a door that says *International Flight Office.* Then you go in."

"Got it, dad?"

"I got it."

"Get rid of those press releases as soon as you can and then get the hell out of there. Okay?"

"Okay."

Giving his father a hug, Bobby turned and hurried away.

J.R. opened the portfolio he was carrying and removed the stack of press releases. Taking a deep breath, he started down the ramp that led into the main terminal. He passed the outgoing flight desk and looked left and right for the press people; he saw no one.

When he turned the corner to the left he found himself in a large hallway with windows on both sides. At the end, the hallway was roped off, and twenty to thirty media representatives started shouting and waving their hands at J.R.

Quickening his pace he took the press releases in his right hand ready to thrust them into the first hand he could grab. As he got closer camera flashes blinded him. He stumbled forward and almost fell on the floor. A young woman reached out and grabbed his right arm. "We want to see Bobby," she said loudly.

"Bobby's not here but he has asked me to give you these press releases. They'll tell you everything you need to know about our mission."

The young woman grabbed the releases. "There's nothing here. Not even any photographs."

One young man, who pressed hard against the rope holding them back, demanded to know who he was.

"I'm Bobby's father, J.R."

"Hey everyone," he shouted. "This is Bobby's father."

There was an uproar. And someone yelled. "Get his picture."

Cameras exploded with flashing light bulbs and J.R. was blinded.

Dropping the portfolio, he turned and started running down the hall.

Shouts of "Let's go," and "Let's get him," rang in his ears.

As he neared the flight desk, the voices were getting closer and he knew they were chasing him. Instead of going straight ahead, he took a right turn down a hallway with windows on the left and office doors on the right. He thought he might find the Flight office soon, but, when he got to the end of the hall the only door left was the MEN'S REST ROOM.

He pushed the door open and entered. He pulled up short when he found himself in the company of a couple of pilots who were standing at sinks along the left wall. They were in the midst of shaving. But, when J.R. entered, they glanced at him as if he were a crazy person. Trying to catch his breath, he smiled at them, and entered a stall and locked the door behind him. He sat on the seat and waited. He heard the pilots talking but he couldn't understand what they were saying.

He waited a few minutes before leaving. Then he opened the stall door and peeked out; the place was empty. He went quickly to a sink and glanced at his face in the mirror; he thought he looked haggard.

Walking as quietly as he could to the exit, he put his ear to the door. Silence. Taking a deep breath, he slowly opened the door and, much to his surprise, he found himself looking into the face of a young man, about twenty-one, an eager reporter from a local newspaper who wanted an exclusive.

"I can't give you an exclusive now, but, uh, . . . What's your name? Do you have a card?"

"The name's Tim Warren, and yes . . ." He took a card from his shirt pocket and handed it to J.R..

"I'll make a deal with you. You let me out of here and I promise to call you tomorrow morning, say about six-fifteen, and give you an exclusive. Is it a deal?"

"Are you sure you're Bobby's father?"

"Do you know Bobby's last name?"

"Sure. It's Cronyn."

J.R. reached for his wallet and opened it so that his driver's license was facing Tim.

Tim looked, and his face lighted up. "You *are* his father."

"Well, is it a deal, or not?"

"It's a deal, sir."

"Can I go now?"

"Yes, sir. Of course sir." Tim opened the door and stepped to one side.

"Where are the others?"

"Oh, they're all gone."

"You sure?"

"Positive."

"Thanks, Tim," J.R. said. "Talk to you tomorrow."

"I can't wait."

When J.R. finally entered the International Flight Office he found the room virtually empty, except for a handful of airport personnel and security guards and Mr. Tropak who welcomed him.

"Mr. Cronyn, where have you been? Mr. Bobby has been worried about you."

"I lost my way," he said, looking around. "Where is everyone?"

"They are all waiting for you outside."

"Then I must go," he said starting for the door."

"Oh, no, Mr. Cronyn," Mr. Tropak said. "You must take picture first."

"Where do you want me?"

"Stand right there and look at camera. Good. Now smile. Take picture please. Good. Now you may leave Mr. Cronyn."

"Do you have my papers, sir,?" J.R. asked.

"Oh, your papers," he began, "I gave them to pretty tall lady."

"Elizabeth?"

"Yes, I think so."

Thanking him, J.R. turned and hurried to the door.

"Goodbye, sir," Trobak said, "and may God bless your journey."

J.R. stopped and looked back at the smiling diplomat. "I really appreciate your kind words, Mr. Tropak. Thank you."

"Dad," Bobby called as he hurried toward his father. "What happened to you? We've all been waiting."

"I had to go to the bathroom."

Taking his father's arm he asked: "What did you get? A shower and a shave?" J.R. kept silent as his son escorted him to the second of the two limousines waiting at the curb.

"Dad?"

J.R. stopped. "To tell you the truth, I promised a young reporter a phone interview tomorrow morning. I'm sorry, Bobby, but I really had to do it."

"Well, if you promised, dad. But . . . why?"

"He kept the mob off me. You should have seen them, Bobby. I turned and ran down the hall and they ran after me, twenty, maybe as many as thirty, yelling and screaming, and, well . . . I—I opened the first door I could find. It was the men's room. I stayed there for about five minutes and when I opened the door to leave, he was standing there, right in front of me—a young man about twenty-one or twenty-two.

"He thrust his card in my face and introduced himself as Tim Warren, a cub reporter for a local newspaper. He promised to keep the pack of wolves, as he called them, off of me if I promised to give him an exclusive. I told him I'd call his office in the morning about six-fifteen. He seemed to be satisfied, and I went on my way."

Bobby smiled. "Well, it's not so bad, dad. You don't have to call him tomorrow if you don't want to."

"Oh, but I do want to," his said. "It's the only right thing to do."

"Dad" . . .

J.R. opened the rear door, stepped into the limousine and closed the door.

Shaking his head, Bobby opened the front door and climbed in next to the driver and asked him how he was to signal the other limousine. The driver said he was to flash his lights.

"Okay, flash your lights and let's get the hell out of here."

The two long cars pulled away from the curb and moved slowly and smoothly into the early evening traffic.

CHAPTER 14

*B*obby on speaker phone: "Okay guys, listen up. We're heading into Cape Town, and pretty soon you'll see the famous Table Mountain if you look off to your left. "You'll notice that Table Mountain is flanked by Devil's Peak on the left and Lion's Head on the right."

In the back seat of the limousine, Dr. Paul Doherty, took up the slack as he read from a visitor's guide that he confiscated from the IFC Office. "Table Mountain is a flat-topped mountain forming a prominent landmark overlooking the city of Cape Town . . ."

"It reminds me of the ex-wife," Dr. Gruber said, straight-faced.

The other doctors chuckled.

Elizabeth frowned and said: "Why is it that every time men look at a mountain, or anything that might resemble a mountain, they have to compare it with the female form?"

"Are you kidding?" Gruber asked. "What else would tall peaks remind you of?"

"Well, the top of your head, for one thing."

Dr. Sarah Landry chuckled; Doctors Doherty and Miles tried to suppress a snicker, while Gruber stared at Elizabeth who was sure the shoe was yet to fall. When it did, however, Elizabeth was surprised.

After just seconds of silence, Dr. Gruber responded with two words: "Touché, Elizabeth."

As the car turned on to Western Boulevard, Bobby picked up the inter-vehicle phone and spoke into it: "Everyone look to your right; that's the great harbor of Cape Town and that big span of water out there, in case you don't know it, is the Atlantic Ocean. We'll be arriving at the hotel in about ten minutes. It's now almost six. When we reach the hotel, check in and go to your rooms.

"Your luggage will be brought to you. Take time to do whatever it is you do to get ready for dinner. And be ready to dine at seven-thirty in the main dining room. There will be a short meeting after dinner in Conference Room #1 at nine. Any questions?"

"When do we get to play?" Dr. Gruber wanted to know.

"You get to play as soon as the meeting has adjourned."

Bobby waited for his reaction, which was an enthusiastic "Whoopie!"

Smiling to himself, he shut the phone off.

The Manchester Manor, a perfect example of original Cape Dutch architecture, was situated along the Sea Point Promenade overlooking the ocean. Over the years it earned the reputation as Cape Town's *iconic* and leading sea front hotel among local and international guests.

The ceilings were high and vaulted and a huge crystal chandelier that hung from its center, was the obvious focal point. Four square floor-to-ceiling marbled columns set the perimeters for several seating areas. Groups of chairs and sofas in muted colors of gold and blue offered guests comfort and understated elegance.

As members of the two teams entered, Bobby, who was standing near the entrance with J.R., told everyone to check in.

When Dr. Gruber entered, he stopped, looked around, and grumbled: "This is all very nice, but if my suite doesn't face the ocean, I'm canceling my reservation." With that he tossed an imaginary scarf over his right shoulder and hurried to the check-in window.

Bobby chuckled: "Where do you think the great pediatric doctor Gruber gets his sense of humor and child-like mischief?"

"I think he gets it from the children," J.R. responded, smiling.

"God knows he's a jokester."

"Humor's important in their lives, especially when there's so much stress involved."

"God knows there's a lot of stress in Gruber's job. But I'll tell you something, dad, the word from his peers is *professional.* He's the consummate professional. He may enjoy fun and games, but not on the job. There he's dedicated and deeply devoted. And he's a no nonsense kind of leader. He'll make a great team captain."

J.R. looked at his son and asked: "How'd you get him, Bobby?"

"I almost didn't get him," he answered. "He's one of the best pediatric doctors in the country and he was offered a position at a hospital paying twice what I was offering him."

J.R. frowned. "And? How did you get him?"

Bobby looked at his father and smiled: "I made him an offer he couldn't refuse."

They laughed and headed for the check-in desk.

CHAPTER 15

The elegant dinner offered *starters* that consisted of a choice of Thai Prawn Risotto, Oyster Mushroom Salad, Turkey Breast 'Tonato' with capers, and Henry's Nicoise Salad with dukka spiced sashimi tuna.

The *main course* offered seafood platters including Atlantic crayfish, linefish of the day, prawns, mussels and calamari; Foccacia & Pesto Crusted Kingklip on tagliatelle and roasted vegetables served with tomato beurre blanc; and, finally, Cape Malay Sea Food Casserole with basmati rice, grilled vegetables, sambals and papadoms. If you didn't like fish, you could have Chicken Supreme. No one ordered the Chicken. Most went for the Cape Malay Sea Food Casserole.

The popular deserts were White Chocolate and Tonka Bean Fondant served with piña colada ice; Chocolate and Black Cherry Fondant served with an orange crème anglaise and a beetroot parfait; Pecan Nut Tart with vanilla ice cream; and a Crème Brulee of the Day.

After dinner, all the doctors got up, stretched, and went for a walk on the promenade.

Bobby and J.R. challenged Elizabeth and Martin to a game of pinochle.

In the conference room later that evening, Bobby talked about each team's schedule for the year but stressed the point that they were subject to change. "For instance," he said, "my team's first stop is Littleberg, a city of 150,000 people. The rural areas around the city probably have an additional 50,000 people. We're scheduled to stay there for one month.

But, if our job is not completed in that time, then we'll stay longer. We'll stay as long as it takes."

He began talking about Littleberg and its inhabitants. He explained that it was important for them to know and understand why he chose this particular city. "I wanted to find a place where poor villagers lived within walking distance of well-administered drugs, and where nobody need die for lack of medical care.

"I wanted to find a place where people were staying home and dying of HIV/AIDS. I wanted to know why they were doing so. Those are a few of the reasons I chose Littleberg. No matter how far they live from antiretroviral (ARV) treatment, no one need die for lack of medical care.

"It is a chronically poor place, where people have been dying for want of decent care since long before the HIV virus.

"In 2002, *Doctors Around the World*, in partnership with the Eastern Cape Department of Health, administered ARV treatment in the district's rickety and neglected primary health-care clinics. When they arrived nearly one in three pregnant women was testing HIV-positive.

"I never saw any mention of Nevirapine. At least one person a day was dying of AIDS at the hospital on the outskirts of town. A depressing fact is that there are still people who live close to a clinic but are staying home and dying.

"Dr. Charles La Barre, the DATW program director, has been in touch with me. He has assured me that there's good news. He told me that the clinics are up and running and staffed by a cohort of laypeople and ordinary government nurses. Thousands of villagers are cramming the waiting rooms to test for HIV. And he said he would be very happy to see us—especially when I told him we were bringing Nevirapine."

"What is his association with us?" Dr. Gruber asked.

"None whatsoever, doctor," Bobby responded. "They have their mission; we have ours.

"Having said that, Mr. Bhalla, the Gov'nor of Littleberg, as he likes to be called, has promised to provide us with nurses, doctors, and laypeople. Laypeople are most important; many are bilingual, but most speak three and even four languages. They will be our translators. Not only that, but they are like public relations people. They go out into the neighborhoods and bring the sick directly to us for treatment."

"Were you to read Littleberg's economic data off a spreadsheet you might think it was a depressed inner-city zone. The majority of adults are unemployed or underemployed, and most households get their income either by cheap unskilled labor, or survivalist self-employment, or government grants."

At this point, Martin raised his hand for a question.

"Yes, Martin?" Bobby asked.

"What about Johnsonville where my team is going? Is it anything like Littleberg?"

"Yes, as a matter of fact it is. The population is slightly more, but it's a poor town with a large part un-or underemployed. The HIV/Aids epidemic is high and they are in dire need of medical help. They are ready to help you in any way they can. They have a well-equipped hospital and the city leaders are eagerly awaiting your arrival. As a matter of fact, they have planned a festival in your honor which is scheduled to take place . . . ." Bobby hesitated, looking through his portfolio.

"I can't find it, but . . ."

"I've got it," Martin said, scanning his schedule. "It's set for . . . tomorrow."

"Do you have a problem with that?"

"No, but . . . What about the schedule?"

"The schedule is flexible, remember? You'll start the next day."

"Who's the head guy in Johnsonville?" Martin asked, looking through papers. "I can't seem to . . . oh, here it is." He reads: "What? It looks like Schwartzenhogenburger."

"Perfect, Martin," Bobby said, applauding. "You deserve a medal."

'But I can't keep calling him that; it'll take all day." Martin rubbed his chin. "I know, I'll call him Schwartz, for short."

"I don't think he'll like it, but, well, you work it out."

"Oh, one more thing Bobby," Martin said. "Where's my driver?"

"He'll be here tomorrow."

"What's his name again?"

"Hugo, Hugo Warren. He's an excellent driver with years of experience. He comes highly recommended. I'm sure you'll like him."

Bobby looked around the table. Taking a deep breath, he said: "Well, I'm tired and I'm sure all of you are too. We have a long day tomorrow. So, unless there are more questions, I'd like to say a little prayer before we adjourn.

"Dear Lord," he began, "as we embark on this mission into South Africa, we pray that you guide us and bless us. Give us strength, dear Lord, to carry out our mission in a manner worthy of you. We do not expect to create miracles, but we do expect to work hard and to do the best we can in fighting the epidemic known as HIV/AIDS. In your name, we pray. Amen."

At 6:10 the next morning, Bobby found a table in a corner of the coffee shop that faced the ocean and settled in with a newspaper and a cup of coffee.

A few minutes later he was joined by J.R. who brought a cup of coffee with him from the buffet table. He was smiling.

"I take it you got the young man on the phone?" Bobby asked.

"Sure did."

"What happened?"

J.R. smiled: "When I asked him what he was working on, he said an article about you. That's not what I mean," I said. "What I mean is, what kind of *computer* do you work with and how old is it? Well . . . he stammered a little, cleared his throat and blurted out, 'I work on an old IBM electric.'"

"What?"

"Yeah."

"That's an antique," Bobby said, chuckling. "Did you tell him what I said?"

"I told him that you were going to send him a brand new Bobby computer."

"And?"

"He was ecstatic," J.R. answered, sipping his coffee. "And . . . there's more. He has started an article about you."

"Did he read it to you?"

"He's written the opening paragraph." J.R. reached in his coat pocket and pulled out a piece of paper. "I made notes. Quote: 'The great humanitarian, Bobby Cronyn, owner and CEO of the Bobby Computer Company, along with two teams of doctors, including his father, J.R. Cronyn . . .' I did not ask him to include my name . . ."

"I didn't say anything."

"I saw that look on your face."

Bobby smiled.

J.R. continued: "'. . . arrived by jumbo jet yesterday on a mission of immense importance. Tomorrow morning they will leave our city in two mobile clinics and embark on a year-long mission to fight HIV/AIDS in our country. We thank them for coming and we wish them well . . .'"

"Very good start."

"I wish we had a computer we could send him now."

Bobby scratched his head and mumbled something.

"What Bobby?"

"Well, I do have a new computer with me. I suppose we could send him that."

"That would be great, Bobby. He could write his column on it."

"Okay," Bobby said, getting to his feet. "I'll go get it, give it to the manager and ask to have it delivered as soon as possible. Do you have the address?"

J.R. handed him a piece of paper that he'd taken from his pocket. His name is on it: Tim Warren."

"I remember," Bobby said hurrying toward the door.

J.R. called to him: "You're a good man, Bobby Brown."

Bobby turned: "The name's *Cronyn*. Bobby *Cronyn*."

J.R. smiled to himself. *If you only knew, Bobby. You bring new meaning to the name . . .*

At around 6:30, when the two Bobby teams left the hotel at the east end of the building, they saw two, 45-foot long, white Bobby Mobile Clinics waiting for them.

The immediate reaction by each member of the teams was unanimous: they were in awe. Sheer size alone made an impact; large bold black letters spelled out:

THE BOBBY HIV/AIDS MOBILE CLINIC

Dramatic artwork featuring intermingled swirls of red and blue danced across the entire length of the mobiles from the driver's compartment to the rear.

A large "red" cross dominated the near-center of the mobiles. In addition, each mobile was equipped with a red, white and blue four-wheel drive vehicle attached to the back.

Dr. Gruber quipped: "Red, white and blue. Mighty patriotic if you ask me."

The group chuckled and Martin said proudly: "I like the look. Is there any reason why we shouldn't bring a little bit of our country to South Africa?"

No one spoke.

While the teams inspected the mobiles, Martin's driver arrived, ready to go to work. The tall, thin, but muscular black man, in his mid-forties, carrying a large duffle bag over his shoulder, approached Bobby and introduced himself.

"I'm Hugo Warren, sir, reporting for duty."

"Were you in the navy Hugo?"

"Yes. I was a young man. Many years ago."

"And you still have your duffle bag?"

His grin was wide and toothy. "Still have it, sir."

"You have all your maps?"

"Yes sir.

"Have you figured the miles?"

"I figured about 350 miles, sir."

"Does your map show that you go from the Western Cape, into part of the Northern Cape and eventually into the Free State?"

"Yes, sir, it does."

"Where do you leave us?"

"About fifty miles down the main highway."

Good," Bobby began, "let me introduce you to your group leader, Martin Reyes."

J.R. was initially impressed by the clinics scope and capabilities. To him it felt and looked like a small hospital; it had everything the doctors and nurses needed in their efforts to fight HIV/AIDS.

When Dr. Gruber appeared, J.R. asked: "Well, doc, what do you think?"

Smiling, he answered: "In a word *terrific*. It's got everything, including great pharmaceutical storage, fold-away seats, collapsing tables; it's even got handicap accessibility."

"I'm glad you approve, doctor."

Taking J.R. by the arm, Dr. Gruber led him to the exterior of the mobile.

"See that awning? Well, that's a wonderful feature. Once we get to our destination, we can roll out the tent awning and provide an outdoor examination area for the nurses. They can conduct basic examinations, take patient histories, and measure blood pressure."

"How can I help, doctor?"

"What can you do?"

"I can take blood pressure."

"Good."

"I think I'd like to work with the laypeople, those who are bi-lingual and who go out into the rural areas to bring women and their babies to the clinic for testing."

"Excellent. You know, there is much shame among the populace, especially among the men, when it comes to HIV/AIDA. They don't want to admit that it even exists. And, of course, Mbeki, their so-called leader, hasn't helped the situation any."

"I don't know about you, doctor, but I'm eager to get on the road."

"Right on, J.R," the doctor said, as they slapped their hands together in a high-five. "Let's get this show on the road, people" he yelled, waving his team to join him.

Bobby turned to Martin and his crew: Doctors Landry and Miles and driver Hugo Warren. He shook Martin's hand. "Good luck you guys. It's important that we keep in touch so be sure to call me every day. Do you remember your contact's name, Martin?'

"Oh, sure," he said with confidence. "It's easy."

"If it's that easy, what is it?"

"Oh, you want me to *say* it?"

"Yeah."

"Well, it's—uh—it's Scwartzenholgenbogger . . . or something . . ."

Bobby smiled. "You have a long drive ahead of you and plenty of time to learn how to pronounce his name properly. I suggest you use that time wisely."

"Yes, sir," Martin said, saluting his boss.

Bobby chuckled. "Let's get the hell out of here and hit the road."

CHAPTER 16

There was little traffic on the highway leading out of Cape Town east to the coast. J.R.'s only concern was that Bobby was driving. He had tried to convince his son to hire a professional driver, but Bobby insisted, saying that he had lots of real experience driving his own 50-foot mobile through most of the western states, across the wide state of Texas into Oklahoma.

Bobby's team of four settled back in comfortable leather chairs focusing their attention on the road ahead and the terrain.

"Who's got the time?" Bobby called out.

"I've got 6:45," J.R. answered.

Bobby was silent for a moment: "I figure we have about a four and a half hour trip to Littleberg, and . . ."

Gruber interrupted: "We should get their about noon, just in time for lunch."

"Always thinking about your stomach," Liz said.

"If I don't," he began, "who will?"

Liz smiled. "You got a point there, doc."

About an hour into the trip, the landscape changed abruptly. City trappings gave way to rolling hills, milkwood trees, and long stretches of nothing but wildness.

Around a bend in the road, Bobby noticed a sign reading *Johnsonville* with an arrow pointing northwest.

To signal the turn for the second team, Bobby pressed the horn button. The sound it made was like a blast of a trumpet; it surprised everyone and woke Gruber from a nap.

"What happened?" Gruber mumbled. "Are we there already?"

"Not yet," Elizabeth said. "Go back to sleep."

Gruber grumbled, turned in his chair, and closed his eyes.

Bobby checked the rearview mirror; he watched as Hugo, who returned the blast of his trumpet horn, turned the big mobile left into a wide, two-lane highway, and disappeared behind high hills.

Bobby found the intercom, switched it on and tested it. Elizabeth responded: "Hear you loud and clear, brother."

"Okay, sis," he responded. "Just want to remind you guys that Bhalla is our host for lunch. I have assured him that after that we will commit to spending five or six hours working with patients . . ."

"When do we sleep?" Doctor Paul Doherty asked.

"I suggest you guys get some sleep now," Bobby said. "We should be seeing signs of the coast in half an hour. After that, we're another thirty minutes from the outskirts of Littleberg."

Dr. Doherty scrambled out of his chair and headed toward the rear of the mobile. "Goodnight everyone," he said. "I'm going to sleep in the examination room."

Liz mumbled her 'goodnight,' turned in her chair, folded her arms and closed her eyes.

Gruber didn't stir.

Smiling, J.R. left his chair and moved closer to Bobby. "It's just you and me now, son."

When Bobby turned the wheel of the mobile hard on a left turn, the hills on the right gave way to flatlands, and a grand blue expanse of the Indian Ocean, framed by a dramatic stretch of coastline and a clear sky of floating clouds, came into view.

Bobby and J.R. were without words.

At a wide turn-out, Bobby pulled in and stopped the mobile. They stood in silence for a moment enjoying the view.

"Oh, Bobby," J.R. began, "so much beauty and wellness out there . . ."

"Make the most of it, dad," Bobby said, taking a deep breath, "because we're here to fight the ugliness and the sickness."

The sign read:

Welcome to Littleberg
Pop. 152, 472

Bobby shifted gears as the big mobile climbed the winding road up passed native villages flanked by wild forests, on one side, and deep green grasslands, on the other, where cows, goats and horses grazed together.

As the mobile took a sharp turn to the right, the view ahead commanded everyone's attention. Up ahead they could see villages perched on high cliffs that offered breathtaking views of the ocean.

Around the next bend the road leveled off, and they began to see more people as they approached the center of Littleberg. Native women, dressed in colorful beaded kaftans, or Boubous, as they are commonly called, walked along the side of the road carrying baskets of eggs, fruits, and an assortment of vegetables that they would sell at the main street's open air markets.

"What's that?" Gruber asked, sitting up straight in his chair.

"Looks like a motorcycle cop to me," Bobby answered.

As the mobile neared main street, more motorcycle police could be seen."

"There's a whole bunch of them," Gruber said. "We're done for. Mbeki has sent his goon squad to arrest us and throw us all in prison for our belief that HIV causes AIDS."

Bobby laughed. "You're paranoid Gruber."

Gruber pointed, saying: "Is that not the head goon walking this way right now?"

"I don't like the looks of this, Grub," Doherty said, sliding down in his chair.

Bobby, looking a little uncomfortable, opened the driver side door just as the motorcycle policeman appeared. He stepped up and bowed to the group. A handsome young black man, he looked at J.R., and asked: "Are you Bobby?"

"No," J.R. said. "The driver of this mobile is Bobby."

He looked surprised. "Why do you not have a driver, Bobby?"

"Because I like to drive," he responded. "I like the control."

"Ah,ha," he said, a smile on his face. "As do I."

"Uh-oh, here it comes," Gruber interjected.

"We're in for it, Grub," Doherty whispered.

"Let me introduce myself. My name is Makala Umbegati. But you can call me by my Christian name: John."

"Excuse me, John," Elizabeth began, "but are you a member of Mbeki's goon squad?"

"Pardon?" he asked, shrugging. "I do not understand."

"Never mind, John," she said, smiling. Just an inside joke."

"What can we do for you, John?" Bobby asked as he frowned at his sister.

John explained that he and his men were there to provide a motorcycle escort for the Mobile. He said that the Gov'ner was waiting to welcome them all at the far end of the main street and that hundreds of people were ready to cheer him. Like a parade."

"A parade?" Bobby asked.

"Just a little one. You, my men, and a marching band."

"It's a charade," Gruber mumbled. "They always play music just before they put you in chains and march you off to your bloody demise."

As he was stepping out of the mobile, John advised Bobby to keep the speed between ten and fifteen miles an hour. No more.

When John was out of sight Bobby turned to his people and said: "Well, people, it's been nice and peaceful up to this point, but from here on out, all hell's going to break loose. So hold on to your seats, because here we go."

The marching band, not yet in sight, began playing a lively rendition of *Stars & Stripes,* at the same time Bobby could see John drop his arm. Slowly *The Bobby HIV/AIDS Mobile Health Clinic* began to roll quietly into town behind the motorcycle escort.

As soon as the mobile came into sight of the crowd, they went wild. Hundreds, perhaps thousands of men, women and children stood in the road waving and shouting Bobby's name. Keeping the mobile at an even twelve miles an hour, a smiling Bobby responded by waving back.

Almost every boy and girl carried a sign that read: *Welcome Bobby.*

The town center was made up of a single market street that sold everything form food to the tin roofs over their heads. The rows of hawkers that pushed pedestrians off the pavements and into the street, were absent today, because it was a holiday made possible by the Gov'ner.

The huge crowd of people on the main street was not an unusual sight because every day, five days a week, eight hours a day, the street was dense with people, metal noise, and a cloud of carbon. The only things missing were metal noise and a cloud of carbon, because the Gov'ner forbid car owners to drive on the main street until seven at night.

Near the end of the main street, a large, ten-story hotel dominated the landscape. The bright morning sun caught its white façade transforming it into an object of brilliance, causing a dramatic statement of contrast to the hotel's rather shabby surroundings.

Green shutters accented the windows while the front entrance was enhanced by a green oval awning that announced in white the name of the hotel: *The Continental.*

Directly across the street from the hotel, Mr. Bhalla, dressed formerly in a black suit, white shirt and tie, stood on a raised platform with several city officials, patiently awaiting Bobby's arrival.

When Bobby appeared in the open door of the mobile, the crowd erupted. Women screamed and men and boys shouted his name over and over. Various signs read: *WE LOVE BOBBY! BOBBY'S OUR HERO! BOBBY FOREVER!*

One little boy, about five, standing close to his mother, held his own sign. It read: I WANT A BOBBY COMPUTER

Liz leaned over and shouted in her father's ear. "I've never seen anything like this. He's being treated like a rock star."

"Better," J.R. said, smiling. "It's like that sign over there says: *Bobby's Our Hero!*"

John approached and escorted Bobby to the stage and introduced him to Mr. Bhalla, an Indian man of average height and a pleasant demeanor. They shook hands, and when he presented the key of the city to Bobby, the crowd was hushed.

Bobby accepted it with a smile but said bluntly to his host: "I wish you hadn't done this, Mr. Bhalla."

Mr. Ballah returned Bobby's smile and said: "But I had to, Mr. Bobby. The people insisted."

"Oh," Bobby responded, a bit taken aback. "In that case . . ." He held the key high above his head, turning his attention to the people who seemed eager to hear what he had to say.

Stepping up to the microphone, he looked out at the crowd and said: "Thank you . . . to all of you . . . for this great honor."

There was applause and a few shouts of *Speech, Speech . . .*

"I'm not very good at making speeches, but this I can say: My mission and the mission of my team is to fight this epidemic called HIV/AIDS and to do all we can to save the lives of thousands of women and children infected with this dreaded disease. Too many are dying from HIV/AIDS and that need not happen. But we cannot do it, and we will not be successful, without your help. So please. Do all you can to help us. Thank you. And God bless you."

The crowd went wild, chanting Bobby's name over and over and over again.

Bobby and his team were the Gov'nor's guests for lunch at the City Hall, situated directly across the street from the Continental.

The old, grey building had its European charm, but it faded into the background when compared to its glistening neighbor.

A *bountiful buffet,* as Gruber called it, offered everything from fancy fish dishes to beef, chicken, and pork, along with fresh vegetable dishes and salads that seemed to include every conceivable thing *red and green.*

For dessert, the assortment was impressive: puddings of various flavors, chocolate mousse, five cakes, seven pies, six large plates of cupcakes, tortes, and cookies, and homemade ice cream.

Eight people sat at the large round table that was set with a white linen tablecloth, good quality porcelain china and silver-plated utensils. The drinking glasses were crystal.

Mr. Ghalla sat between his secretary and assistant, Mary Tagumba, a pretty middle-aged black woman with a warm smile, and Dr. La Barre, a local doctor and head surgeon at the town's only hospital, St. Luke's. A short, stocky, and energetic Frenchman, La Barre was eager to help the Bobby Team, and he was ready to start immediately.

Looking at Mr. Bhalla, Gruber asked him what he would do with all the left over food. Bhalla smiled, and said the office staff would be fed and then, if there was food left over, it would be sent to the local orphanage.

"Orphanage?" Gruber asked. "Where is it?"

Mr. Bhalla said that it was situated next to the hospital and that it was supported by contributions and governmental grant money.

J.R. leaned forward and asked Bhalla: "Are the children adoptable?"

"The healthy children are adoptable."

"Could a foreigner adopt a child?"

"Yes," Bhalla responded, "but they would have to be approved by the national government."

"What are the government's guide lines?"

"Most important, the person or persons must be of sound moral character, and financially able to provide a good and loving home for the child."

"Thinking about adopting a child, J.R.?" Gruber asked.

"Truthfully, I hadn't thought about it . . . until now."

"You know what *that* means," Doherty said, elbowing Gruber. "He's gonna do it."

"Yeah."

J.R. chuckled and shook his head.

During lunch, Ghalla offered the Bobby Team use of his home, a new, two-story house about a mile from the town center. He made a point of telling them that the house was completely surrounded by an electrified fence to keep the "bad element" out.

When Bobby asked if that so-called "bad element" was a large segment of the population, Ghalla explained that there was a small element only but that they all owned guns."

"Even small children have guns," Mary Tagumba offered.

"That's gratifying," Elizabeth said softly as she cut into a scallop.

No one spoke for a moment.

Gruber broke the silence with: "When does it ever get quiet around here?"

"It's quiet now, Grub," Doherty said, screwing up his nose.

"Not now, Doherty," Gruber said, slapping his friend's arm with his napkin. "I mean out there—on the street."

Mr. Bhalla smiled, and said: "I guess you all must know by now that the main street is dense with people and very noisy; it's like that five days a week, and eight hours a day. Only by seven in the evening is it quiet and empty."

Gruber glanced at his watch: "We've got almost six hours to go."

"Not all is negative, my friends," Mr. Bhalla said. "We have much to be proud of here in Littleberg. While the rest of South Africa was going to hell, fighting apartheid and so forth, we represented something else entirely. It's true that many of our men had to spend much of the year away from home at the gold mines, but they did so to gather the resources that nourished a way of life back in Littleberg.

"They lived alongside the graves of their forebears; they paid *brideswealth* to marry, and they sired children who bore their names."

"It was their quest," Mary Tagumba added, "to leave a legacy in this world after their deaths, the site of their humanity."

"But now, sadly, there is a cruel irony in our midst. We face a new scourge, a new threat to our very existence: HIV/AIDS. It is tearing our society to pieces; it is killing our people before it is time for them to return to their forebears."

"And that is why we are here, your honor," Bobby said. "We're here to stop the scourge."

"You will need a lot of help, Bobby," Dr. LaBarre interjected.

"That's why you're here, sir."

"Yes." LaBarre said, dabbing at his lips with a napkin. "We are prepared to provide you with two nurses and a doctor, if you need him. More important, we have recruited several laypeople, who, as you probably know, are most vital to the success of the entire operation."

"Will they be ready to start today, doctor?" Bobby asked.

"When do you need them?"

"Oh." He checked his watch. "In about ten minutes."

"You've got them," he said, rising quickly from the table. He thanked Mr. Bhalla for his kind hospitality, reaffirmed Bobby's request, and, with cell phone ready in hand, hurried out of the room.

As Dr. LaBarre exited, John, the motorcycle policeman, entered and hurried to whisper something in Bhalla's ear.

Standing, he smiled at his guests. "Ladies and gentlemen," he began, "the news is that there is a line of women and babies stretching from the front door of the mobile to almost all the way down the main street."

Bobby jumped to his feet, dropping his napkin on the table. "Thank you, Mr. Bhalla and Ms. Tagumba. Thank you for everything."

Bhalla smiled and said: "It was my pleasure."

"All right lady and gentlemen, are we ready?"

"Yes," was the unison response.

"Let's go fight HIV/AIDS."

As they hurried out, Bhalla called after them. "May God go with you."

CHAPTER 17

A strange thing happened when Bobby and his team appeared at the front door of City Hall and proceeded to the mobile: the noisy crowd went silent.

Even when Bobby greeted them, they remained quiet; a few of the younger children waved back at Bobby and called his name.

He opened the door of the mobile and fastened it so it remained open. The doctors and Elizabeth, looking serious now, entered the mobile and went about their business. J.R. and Bobby entered behind them and soon reappeared. Bobby opened the overhead awning to create a shady area, while J.R. set up a small table and a couple of folding chairs.

Most of the women, especially those carrying babies, worn down by the long wait and the hot sun, were squatting on the ground next to the mobile. In order to protect their babies from the glare of the sun they had wrapped their tiny heads with scarves or shawls.

One young mother approached Bobby. She looked exhausted and she was perspiring. She looked up at Bobby and held her baby out to him. In Afrikaans she said: "Take my baby, please. I am too sick and I . . ."

Before the woman collapsed, a large, square-shouldered woman, with broad hips and a stern face, suddenly appeared beside the young mother with the baby. Without saying a word, she took the baby from the mother, held it firmly in her left arm, and with her right hand took a firm hold of the woman and steered her to a chair where she sat.

Cradling the baby in her arms, she ordered someone to get the mother some water. "She is dehydrated," she said. "And this baby is dying." Without another word, she entered the mobile and disappeared.

Bobby followed her and returned with a cup of clean water which he gave to the woman; she gulped it down, held the cup up to Bobby and said one word: *water.*

When Bobby returned with the water, he was met by the doctor and two nurses La Barre had promised them. After he gave the water to the young mother, he turned to the trio and introduced himself.

"It's a pleasure to meet you," the young doctor said, shaking Bobby's hand. He was a tall black man with dreadlocks and a demeanor that suggested that he was a true and dedicated professional. Dressed all in white and carrying a small black leather satchel, he told Bobby that he was called Dr. Smith.

The two nurses, also dressed in starched white uniforms, were young and attractive black women in their twenties; they were called Naha and Sheena. Their smiles were warm and they appeared eager to get to work. Bobby directed Naha to report to Nurse Elizabeth, as she would become Elizabeth's assistant as well as the entrance clerk who keeps records of all patients passing through the clinic. Nurse Sheena was directed to report to Dr. Doherty.

Moments later, the mysterious black lady appeared followed by J.R., who smiled at Bobby, and introduced him to his head layperson, Kaila Taguma-Mu.

He shook her hand and thanked her for appearing when she did. "I think you're going to be a very valuable addition to our team."

"Thank you, Mr. Bobby," she said, smiling. Sternness turned swiftly to one of warmth and friendliness

"How're the baby and mother doing?" Bobby asked.

"Nothing to worry about, Mr. Bobby," she said. "The wonderful doctors have stabilized the baby and the mother is resting. Her condition is probably worse than the baby's in terms of infection. Her CD4 cell count is low and she has an infection called PCP, a type of pneumonia; it can be life-threatening. The ambulance has been called and she will be taken to the hospital, but she will be isolated from her baby. The baby has HIV and will receive Nevirapine when she is a little stronger."

"Excuse me," Kaila, J.R. said, "but can you explain to this layman how CD4 works and what guidelines are we using to describe the different stages of HIV based on clinical symptoms?"

"All right." Kaila said, taking a deep breath. "It's not too complicated. We are using the World Health Organization's method for treatment. Do you know what a T-helper cell is and the part it plays in the immune system."

"No," he said, shaking his head.

"To begin, the T-helper cell plays an important part in the immune system by helping to co-ordinate all the other cells to fight illnesses. That's important to keep in mind. Now, if there is a major reduction in the number of T-helper cells, this can have a serious effect on the immune system. HIV causes many T-helper cells to be damaged or destroyed; as a result, there are fewer cells available to help the immune system.

"A CD4 test measures the number of T-helper cells in a cubic millimeter of blood. Someone uninfected with HIV normally has between 500 and 1200 cells/mm. In a person infected with HIV the CD4 count declines over a number of years. You would definitely treat the patient if their CD4 test showed 200 or lower. Treatment is generally recommended when the CD4 test shows fewer than 350 cells/mm. The World Health Organization has a system called WHO staging system for HIV disease; it is useful for places, like Littleberg, that have poorly equipped medical facilities. Any questions, J.R.?"

"No," he answered, "that's very clear."

"One question, Kaila," Bobby said. "After patients have been treated here at the mobile clinic, will they return for follow up?"

"Oh, no, Mr. Bobby," Kaila began, "that's the job of the hospital and its staff. They will do follow up. Nurse Naha will be responsible for keeping all patient records and they will be turned over to the hospital staff the entire time you are here."

Bobby sighed. "Thank God."

"Yes," she said, "we must all thank God, and thank him for watching over us." She looked from one man to the other. "Gentlemen, this day is just the beginning of our work. Plan on being here in Littleberg for a very long time."

For almost a month, Bobby and his team worked eight hours a day on average in the mobile clinic. Records showed that more than fifty percent of their patients were affected with HIV/AIDS.

By noon of the thirty-first day the team had treated only five women and their babies.

After lunch, J.R., feeling queasy from an upset stomach, went to his hotel room in the Continental to take a nap. He had been up most of the night and he was exhausted.

He placed a call to Kate and they talked for half an hour; there was much to catch up on and Kate had a lot of gossip to share with him regarding his fellow housemates on 88th Street. "Don't ask me to tell you everything now," she said. "It'll take too long; I'll e-mail you as soon as I can. All I can say is that it's mostly good news. I will give you a tease though: it's just possible that a certain twosome might be headed for the altar."

J.R. laughed and said that he missed her and all his *old* friends at the house. When there was a lull in the conversation, he took the moment to ask when she was coming to South Africa.

She wasn't too sure, but she thought she could get away sometime in July or August, and she would love to join up with them in Durban.

J.R. was delighted, and, assuming it was a definite possibility, expressed to her how happy she would make him and that he couldn't wait to see her.

She assured him that she prayed every night for the success and well being of the Bobby team.

His last words to her were: "The Bobby team is incredible; they are doing God's work. Thank you for your prayers. And remember: I love you . . . always."

Holding his cell phone tightly in his hand, he curled up on the bed, and, sighing deeply, closed his eyes.

In just seconds, his phone began to vibrate. Glimpsing at the number he realized it was a call from Kaila.

J.R. sat up and pushed the *talk* button. "Hello, Kaila . . . I don't feel too well . . . Oh, just a upset stomach . . . something I ate, I guess . . . What? . . . Oh . . . Of course I can. How far is it? Two miles? Then I think we should take the four-by-four . . . you're in the lobby? . . .

Good. Just give me five minutes."

With obvious ease, the blue and white four-by-four made its way up the winding dirt road passed small villages that were flanked by wild forests. Cows and goats grazed on grass in pastures surrounded by wooden fences. Now and then farmers could be seen working in the fields; round mud brick huts with grass and bamboo roofs dotted the landscape. Now and then, when they passed a clearing in the forest, they would glimpse a view of the ocean.

J.R. remarked about the breathtaking beauty of the land and compared it to the stark contrast of its human reality.

Kaila said that it was difficult to remind oneself that its political economy is no longer rural, and that almost everyone you meet is either unemployed, or in a job that earns less than a thousand rand a month.

"How much is a rand?" J.R. asked.

"It's roughly equivalent to 140 U.S. dollars," she answered. She took a beat, then: "Through much of this century, these villages were home ground; they represented a way of life to defend and to cherish. The men spent much of each year away from home at the gold mines, but they had to in order to nourish a way of life back home.

"But the cruel irony of all of this is that by the time apartheid was defeated and the Transkei incorporated into a democratic South Africa, the two things of this world—work in the gold mines and a peasant economy at home—were both in a state of decline. And so was a way of life based on the land.

"And so with democracy brings us sex. It is the most life-giving of activities. And along with that we have AIDS; it has given rise to accusation. Where there is AIDS, there is blame. Nowhere is this more evident than with our president who has questioned with bitterness whether the dying was caused by a sexually transmitted virus after all, and who asked whether antiretroviral drugs were for the benefit of Africans or pharmaceutical companies.

"And his rage is here in Littleberg and in surrounding villages. The sick people are accused of having murdered loved ones by their promiscuity. And neighbors are blamed for using magic to infect the beautiful and the successful.

"The accusations of national politics are part of our life and indeed, are woven into the individual consciousness."

After traveling five miles, they reached the village of Ithica, situated on a cliff overlooking the Indian Ocean. J.R. entered the village by driving the four-by-four onto a narrow road; Kaila advised him to turn the van around so it faced the exit.

Kaila stepped out of the vehicle and looked around. She was wearing a green kaftan decorated across the bodice, down the sides and along the bottom hem and sleeves with red and white colored beads, and a matching turban with bead trim; she was carrying a large black, leather bag. Gruber remarked later that he thought she looked like a walking Christmas tree. When Kaila found out about his remark, she did not smile.

When J.R. joined her, she told him to stay close to the vehicle and look pleasant. "Don't say anything," she advised. "If they say something that sounds like *Haai or Hallo* you can answer. Both words are *hello* in Afrikaans. You may find that one or two of the young men around here know some English."

She explained that she was going to visit as many as a dozen huts that have been designated as homes of young woman with a baby or two. She said she would be gone for about thirty minutes.

"Did you bring your cell phone?" she asked.

He said he had and she advised him to keep it close . . . just in case . . .

Ten minutes passed when J.R. noticed two young men standing about 300 yards away; they talked together, and every now and then glanced his way. After a few minutes a third man joined the group, then a fourth and a fifth. Soon the group of five started drifting his way, talking amongst themselves and looking in his direction.

When they were about twenty feet away from J.R., the youngest of the group, a tall, thin black man of twenty took a step forward and said: "Hallo." When J.R. answered in kind, he smiled and asked: "Praat u Afrikaans?"

Figuring that he understood what the young man had asked him, J.R. answered: "No." He shook his had. "I don't speak Afrikaans."

The thin young man stepped back. There was silence as the young men looked at him, then at the four-by-four.

J.R. smiled and pointing at the vehicle said: "This van . . . uh . . . I'm with the team of . . ." Seeing that the men didn't understand a word he was saying, he decided to just talk about Bobby. Maybe they would understand the connection.

"I'm with Bobby . . ." he began. "You know Bobby? Bobby the computer man? Bobby? The Bobby computer?"

At first it didn't register, but then the young thin man smiled and said: "Bobby computer?"

"Yes," said J.R. nodding. "Bobby computer."

The thin young man turned to his friends and started jabbering in Afrikaans. At first they were smiling but soon a couple of the men became agitated. The oldest in the group, a stocky, strong-looking young man of about twenty-five shook his finger in the face of the young thin man and spoke in loud tones as if he were scolding or lecturing him.

The young man, angered by what the other man was saying, yelled something and pushed him. Before J.R. could say or do anything, the two men were rolling around in the dirt, wrestling and kicking at each other. The three other men danced around, clapping their hands and vocally urging them on. When one or the other landed a punch, the three shouted: "O! O! O!" or "Dis goed! Dis goed!"

In the midst of all this, Kaila approached leading a group of six mothers with their children. When she saw the commotion, she picked up her skirt and rushed forward hitting the bigger of the two men with her leather bag. He yelled something, grabbed his head and fell forward. In Afrikaans she yelled at them to get up and act like men.

Without a word, they did as they were told. Only the older man scowled at Kaila and shook his fist at her. He walked quickly to a young black woman who was holding a baby close to her chest. He yelled something in Afrikaans and tried to pull her out of the line.

She cried out and tried to resist him, but he was too strong for her.

Kaila—realizing that he must be the woman's brother whom she had said was unemployed and always angry—walked up to the man and got in his face. She yelled at him to release his sister and allow her to take her to a doctor.

With that, he jumped back, pulled a six-inch knife from his waist band, grabbed his sister, and put it to her neck.

Everyone froze with fear except two women at the end of the line. They screamed, and, holding tightly to their babies, ran off.

Kaila immediately stepped back. She raised her hands and said that they were not there to hurt anyone. If he didn't want his sister to go, that was up to him, but she had to tell him the truth.

He cursed at Kaila and said that she didn't know the truth and that if she didn't leave, he would kill his sister.

J.R. eased forward until he was within inches of Kaila. He wasn't feeling well but he was urged on by a surge of adrenalin.

After what seemed like minutes of sheer tension, Kaila asked the man with the knife what his name was. At first he said nothing; then he said Marjo.

Trying hard to compose herself, she said in Afrikaans: "Well, Marjo, your sister is very ill. She needs to see a doctor. If we don't get her to a doctor now, she might die."

"She won't die," the man said, his voice cracking.

Kaila took a deep breath, and said: "But if we don't take her and she does die, what will you do then? What will the baby do? Do you want that to happen? Would you leave her baby without a mother?"

Marjo took a long time to answer. He was perspiring and Kaila could see that he was weakening. She decided to make her move. Turning to J.R., she asked him to take the other women and their babies to the van and help them in.

When they were safe inside the van, Kaila turned to the young man and his sister and asked: "Well, Marjo," she began, "are you going to let her live? Or die? It's in your hands now. If you're the man I think you are . . ."

Before she could speak another word, Marjo dropped the knife, turned and ran off toward a wooded area that bordered the village along the eastern confines.

At first, Marjo's young sister was reluctant to leave, but after conversing a moment with Kaila, she changed her mind and went with J.R. to the van.

Seeing the knife laying in the dirt, Kaila stooped and picked it up. She looked at it for a moment then called the tall, thin young man over. When he approached she asked: "What happened to your friend, Marjo?"

"He has gone to be alone because his heart is broken."

"When you see him," Kaila said, handing him the knife, "please give this to him. And be sure to tell him that he did the right thing."

Taking the knife, he smiled at her and asked in Afrikaans. "Are you a witch?"

She patted his face and said: "I am whatever I must be."

CHAPTER 18

The next morning, J.R. was up early. He had made a decision: a daily routine of exercise was advised to maintain a healthy life style. From now on, he would eat a lighter and more nutritious diet, and he would walk every morning for at least two miles.

Donning a T-shirt, walking shorts, and sneaks, he wrapped a sweat band around his head, and, grabbing a bottle of water, headed for the main street.

Outside he glanced across the street at the mobile; the awning was still up but there was no sign of life. He checked his watch: it was 6:05. He looked down the street. It was deserted except for a few pedestrians and peddlers setting up their stalls along the sidewalk. He started to walk briskly in the direction of the hospital.

No cars could be seen except for a jitney that smoked its way noisily up the street. As it passed, he looked at it and saw a familiar face. It was Kaila. Waving, she smiled and greeted him with a spirited "Good Morning."

He waved and yelled: "I'll be ready to go at eight."

She yelled back: "You'd better be."

When Kaila got to the mobile she was met by Dr. Smith and the two nurses. They were there early to open the mobile and to prepare the clinic for the day's work load. Kaila set about opening the awning and setting up chairs and the small entry table where every person was required to fill out a patient information form before being seen by a doctor.

She was about to get herself a cup of water when she heard her name. She looked up and saw Bobby walking toward her. He walked with measured steps like a stride, but his hands were deep in his pockets and he looked troubled.

When he reached the mobile he slumped into a chair. "Oh, Kaila," he said, exhaling.

She looked hard at him before she spoke: "What happened to you, Bobby?" she asked. "You don't look happy."

"It's bad news, Kaila," he responded, not looking up.

On his run back, J.R. was side-tracked by a particular peddler's hawking: "Silk from the Orient! Beautiful silk from the Orient." He stopped at her stall to inspect the merchandise. There were rows upon rows of silk available in bolts. This was the real thing, he thought.

"How much?" he asked, pointing to a bolt of silk.

"Special price for you," she answered, lifting the bolt and handing it to him to inspect. "Pure silk from the Orient. Very special price for you. Only twenty dollars."

"For the whole thing?" He couldn't believe his ears.

"Yes," she said, "just for you."

That's a steal, he thought. Kate will love this for the kids. He took his wallet out, found a twenty dollar bill and gave it to her. He took the bolt of silk from her and strode up the street with a wide smile on his face, thinking that he had made the deal of the day.

When he got to the mobile he found Kaila sitting in a chair reading.

"Look at this beautiful silk," he said. "Isn't it something?"

"It's something all right," she said. "How much did you pay for it/"

"Just twenty dollars."

"You paid *dollars?*"

"Yes," he responded. "What's wrong with that?"

"Everything. You don't deal with the locals in dollars. You end up spending more every time. It's very nice silk of good quality, but you never pay dollars. You deal in rand and you always bargain. Let's see, you paid her about one hundred and fifty rand and this silk usually sells for about one hundred, sometimes less."

"That's not so bad," he said. "Anyway, for me, it's worth it. It will make Kate's girls happy."

"Kate? Your lady friend?"

"My lady friend and soon-to-be wife. We might get married in Durban later this year."

"I'm happy for you."

"Thank you." J.R. looked around. "Where's Bobby? Isn't he here?"

"No," she said, getting to her feet. "He's in the hotel coffee shop, waiting for you."

"Oh?"

"Not good news, J.R."

"What's wrong?"

"Go and see him. He'll tell you." As he started across the street, she called out: "Don't forget. Be back here in an hour. And J.R . . . ."

"Yes?"

"You have great legs—for an old man."

"Thanks a lot," he yelled. "I think."

J.R. found Bobby sitting at a small table near the window. As he approached, he noticed that his son's eyes were closed. Without saying a word, J.R. pulled back a chair and sat down. Bobby opened his eyes.

"Dad," he said softly, sitting up in the chair and rubbing his eyes.

"What's up, son?"

"Coffee, dad?" he asked as he picked up a porcelain pot.

"Yes, please."

He poured coffee into J.R.'s cup.

Putting the pot down, he again leaned back in his chair and cleared his throat. Taking a deep breath, he looked at his father and said: "Bhalla called me early this morning with a message from a Mr . . . . Hold on, I have his name written down . . ." He removed a piece of paper from his shirt pocket, opened it, and read : "Mr. Yablon Zograbyan is his name. He's an official with the present government. He told Bhalla that he wanted to talk to me about *a project of economic proportions.* Does that sound familiar?"

"Yes, I think so."

"The rub is that he wants me to fly to Pretoria and, of course, I told Bhalla I had no intention of doing so. He called Mr. Zograbyan and told him. Apparently he wasn't too happy but finally told Bhalla that he would fly here this morning and would meet with me at the hotel around seven-thirty."

"Seven-thirty," J.R. said, looking at his watch. "It's almost seven-sixteen."

"That doesn't leave us much time, dad."

"I've got to go, Bobby," J.R. began, "but please don't make any promises.

"Don't worry, dad, I won't. I've dealt with government types before. I know how to handle myself."

"I'll see you later," J.R. said, getting up from the table.

"I'm going to invite the entire team here for dinner tonight. We can discuss everything at that time."

"Good luck, Bobby," J.R. said pushing his chair in. "See you later."

As he started to walk away, Bobby called out: "You do have good legs for an old man."

J.R. turned: "What?"

Bobby laughed. "Kaila told me. I think she likes you."

"Well, of course she likes me," he said. "As a matter of fact, I think she loves me. I love her. And I'll tell you why. I love who she is and what she does. I think she's a great lady." With a slight salute to his son, J.R. turned, and quickly left the room.

"Wow," Bobby said to himself. "What a guy."

When Bobby reached the ballroom on the second floor of the hotel he found one of the double doors open. Standing in the doorway looking in he could not make out the size or shape of the room because of the lack of light. He took a few steps into the room.

"Hello," he said, "is anyone here?"

Seconds passed before a response. A cluster of crystal chandeliers that hung from the ceiling in the middle of the room, lit up, spreading a warm glow across the room. When Bobby's eyes became accustomed to the light he could see a man standing behind a table at the far end of the large rectangular room.

"Mr. Bobby," the man said, his deep, rich voice resonating around the room. "Welcome. Come and join me."

As Bobby approached, the black man stood and held out his hand. He was at least as tall as Bobby, but he was broad shouldered and slim. His head was bald and oval shaped. Dressed impeccably in a dark blue suit, shirt and tie, he was clean shaven except for a large, black moustache that covered half of his upper lip. His broad smile was warm and welcoming.

Bobby thought: *If I'd known this was going to be formal, I could've worn my dark blue suit too.*

Bobby shook his hand and said: "Nice to meet you Mr.—uh—. I'm sorry. How do you pronounce your last name?"

"It's Zog-RAB-yan, but never mind, Mr. Bobby," he said. "You may call me Yabby. All my friends do."

Bobby smiled and said: "And you may call me Mr. Bobby."

"Oh," he said, clapping his hands. "How rude of me. Thank you, Mr. Bobby."

"It's all right."

"Please. Sit. Make yourself comfortable. Would you like a cigar?"

"No, thank you," Bobby said, sitting in the soft comfortable leather chair. "I don't smoke."

"Do you mind if I do?"

"Go right ahead," he responded, getting to his feet. "I'll just move this chair back a little if you don't mind."

"Mr. Zograbyan lit a cigar and took a couple of puffs, careful to blow smoke away from his guest. "I understand your work here is going quite well and that you are helping a large number of our women and babies.

"Yes, that's right, Yabby," he said. "My people are experts in what they do and they are working very hard to save lives. I'm happy with the results so far."

"I'm sure you are Mr. Bobby," he said coolly. He took another puff of his cigar. "You understand that I am not here to judge you or to interfere. What you do here is a humanitarian endeavor and I, we, the government, accept it as such. However . . ."

Bobby sat quietly, watching, waiting for the final blow.

Mr. Zograbyan looked at Bobby for a moment, then, while he was thinking, contemplated the red glow of his cigar. Before he spoke, he flipped ash into a ceramic ashtray to his right. "However, the government is ready to compromise . . ."

"Compromise?" Bobby asked.

"Yes. Compromise." He puffed on his cigar. "We're allowing you to do something that, quite frankly, runs against the grain." He looked at Bobby waiting for a response, but he remained neutral. "I think you know what I'm talking about."

Bobby nodded.

"So, we want in return something only you can give us. It is something that will add to the success of our economy, on the one hand, and to the welfare of our citizens on the other. It is something so important and so vital that it will affect our very way of life . . ."

What is this all about? Bobby wondered.

CHAPTER 19

Later the same afternoon, J.R. and Kaila drove into town in the four-by-four with three mothers and their young babies and three pregnant women.

The women and their babies were helped out of the van and into the mobile. Nurse Naha welcomed them and helped each woman fill out the patient information form. Each pregnant woman was sent to see Dr. Gruber and Nurse Sheena in the first examination room, and each woman with a baby was sent to see Dr. Doherty and Nurse Liz in the adjourning pediatric examination room.

The first woman sent to Gruber tested negative for HIV, and was released. But the second and third pregnant women tested positive for HIV. They were treated with appropriate drugs to reduce the women's viral load and to lessen the risk of the each baby becoming infected with the disease.

In the waiting area the two pregnant women with HIV bowed their heads and cried. Kaila tried to comfort them with words of wisdom: "You must be grateful to God for this intervention. Without it, you might have died—you and your baby."

One lady blessed her for her words; the other, frightened and confused, voiced her fear that her husband would kill her and the baby. Her friend, the first lady who tested negative for the disease, sat down beside her and held her close. The woman wept.

In the pediatric examination room, Nurse Elizabeth placed a five month old baby on Bobby's special *Candy Cane* baby table complete with colorful graphics and features including upholstered end panels and beveled sides to prevent the baby from rolling off the table. After completing the test for HIV/AIDS she announced loudly to the doctor that the baby tested positive.

J.R. watched closely as Gruber, who was swabbing the inside of a patient's mouth with a cotton swab, asked for AIDS' treatment.

There was silence.

Gruber looked up. "Did you hear me, nurse?"

"I did doctor," came the response. "But I suspect there might be tuberculosis."

"Symptoms?" the doctor asked.

"Slight fever and mucous in the blood."

"Check."

"Test for TB?"

"Granted."

J.R. was fascinated. "What does she do now?" he asked.

Before Gruber responded to J.R.'s questions, he thanked the woman for her cooperation. He immediately put the swab into a plastic bag and closed it.

"What are you doing? Collecting DNA?"

"Yes."

"Why"?

Gruber got up and walked a few steps toward the examination room. He motioned J.R. to join him.

As J.R. approached he said that he had to test her DNA because she refuses to admit that the baby inside is hers.

"How did she get the baby?" J.R. asked.

"She said she found the baby one day last week outside her house."

"Isn't that possible?"

"Oh, yes, it's possible," Gruber responded. "But I have this gut feeling that she's not telling the truth. Something about her demeanor. She's very cool and just a little arrogant. I need to be sure."

Gruber turned, and approached the entrance to the examination room. Looking in, he asked:. "How are we doing, nurse?"

"Fine, doctor," Nurse Elizabeth answered. "Almost done."

J.R. stepped up and peered inside. "What's she doing?"

"She's doing a skin test for tuberculosis. It's a Mantoux test with five units of purified protein derivative, or PPD, as we like to call it. The test is read 48-72 hours later. Her baby has already tested positive for HIV, and if she's the mother, she's infected as well.

"But she denies being the mother," J.R. noted.

"We'll know for sure very soon," he said, holding up the plastic envelope.

"What happens now, doc?"

"Ambulance. We've got to get these people to the hospital." Turning away from J.R., he looked into the waiting room and called: "Ambulance please."

"Yes, Doctor," Nurse Naha responded. "Right away, doctor."

"Thank you."

J.R. checked his watch: it was almost six thirty, time to get ready for Bobby's eight o'clock dinner party. He'd invited everyone on his team, including Kaila, the two nurses, and Dr. Smith,

"What time is it, J.R.?" Kaila asked, approaching.

"Almost six-thirty."

"I'm excited about this evening."

"So am I," J.R. said. "All Bobby would tell me is that he had an interesting interview with Yabby, as he calls him, and that the news is 'big', whatever that means."

"Well," Kaila began, "since he didn't say 'good' or 'bad' news, I would assume that 'big' means important, substantial . . ."

J.R. began to laugh. "If you want synonyms, I can give you a whole bunch."

"Let's just say that whatever it is, there's a lot of it."

J.R. smiled. "I like that. I like your logic, Kaila." He hugged her, turned, and hurried out the door.

The woman who claimed not to be the mother of the baby, got up and said to Kaila in Afrikaans: "You must believe me; I am not the mother of that baby. Someone left him on my doorstep. Please believe me." With that, she pushed passed Kaila, and fled from the mobile as fast as she could.

Kaila called loudly for Doctor Gruber who appeared at the door of the examination room. He saw the look on Kaila's face and hurried to her. "What happened, Kaila? Are you all right?"

"I'm all right," she said. "It's that woman who denied being the mother of the baby. She's gone."

Doctor Gruber took a deep breath. "Oh, Kaila, don't worry about it. We can deal with it."

"But suppose she really is the mother?"

"I have a sample of her DNA."

Kaila looked at him and smiled. "You're a cool one doctor, aren't you? I should have known."

"You know where she lives?"

"Of course I do."

"Then we're okay." He patted her arm and started back to the examination room when Doctor Doherty appeared.

"Where're you going so early in the evening?"

"Nurse Sheena and I just made mad passionate love and now I'm going home."

Kaila giggled.

"You'd better be joking, doctor."

Doherty took a moment then shook his head. "Yeah I am . . . sadly speaking."

"Go on," Gruber said, "get out of here."

"Good night you all."

"Don't forget dinner at eight."

"I'll never forget *Dinner at Eight,*" Doherty yelled. "It's one of my favorite movies." With that, he bounded out the door.

Kaila looked around, smiled to herself, and patted the front of her dress to smooth it. Confident that she was ready to face the world, she opened the door and stepped out into the street. Looking around, she took a deep breath of the cool night air.

With the serving of hors d'oeuvres, Bobby picked up a glass of wine and stood up. Looking around the table at all the faces, he smiled and said: "I don't know where to begin." He paused. "I can tell you, all of you, that I am so impressed by you and the work you are doing. The level of professionalism is very high; your selfless dedication is beyond my words to express; that I respect and love each and every one of you is undeniable. I am so grateful.

"Having said all of that, I want to state for the record, right here and now, that I, Bobby Cronyn, have every intention of returning to this great country for as long as it takes to rid it of HIV/AIDS.

"I realize that that might take years. And I know that that commitment is mine alone and not necessarily yours.

"Today, as you all know, I met with a representative of the government. He was a cool customer—very smart, very savvy, and very eloquent." He smiled. "I think he must've been educated at Oxford."

The group laughed.

He continued: "He—we'll call him Mr. Z—told me that the government accepted the fact that what we do here is a humanitarian endeavor. But, in his next breath, he added that the government was ready to compromise. Compromise? What compromise?

"Then it became a little clearer to me when he said that what we did ran against the grain. We all know what that means.

"Anyway, not to keep you on tenterhooks any longer, I'll get to the point. The compromise he spoke of was quite simply this: the government wants the Bobby Computer Company to build a factory in South Africa."

There was silence. Then Gruber spoke up: "That's not a compromise; that's a shake-up."

Several guests seconded his opinion.

Nodding, Bobby agreed. Taking a sip of his wine, he looked again around the table and said: "I looked at Mr. Z and said that I was sure he understood that, although I was CEO and president of the company, I had no authority to agree to a proposal of such magnitude on my own. He said he understood and allowed me time to make all the calls I thought necessary. But, before I did so, he made it very clear that he needed an answer before he left.

"It took me hours to talk to everyone I needed to talk to. I even called Martin. By the time I'd finished calling everyone, a final decision was reached and it was unanimous." He hesitated, looking at Elizabeth. "I even called my sister. She agreed with my decision, and our compromise, if you will.

"The compromise I offered Mr. Z was this: The Bobby Computer Company will build a factory in South Africa on the following conditions: (1) that the government will provide the land; (2) that the government will provide all building materials; and (3) the government will provide all necessary manpower to complete the project. The Bobby Computer Company will provide all materials necessary to make the computers and it will be responsible for publicity and advertisement and the growth and formation of a country-wide retail outlet structure." He looked around the room.

J.R. spoke up: "Don't keep us in suspense, Bobby. Did Mr. Z go for it?"

"Not right away," Bobby answered. He frowned. "In fact, it took about another hour of negotiations. Mr. Z left me sitting in that stuffy old ball room while he went off somewhere to make phone calls. When he returned, he explained that the government was agreeable to just one condition: that it would provide the land. All other expenses and responsibilities would rest with the Bobby Computer Company.

"When I responded negatively to his proposal, he got angry and threatened to expel us from the country."

"What?" Kiala exclaimed.

"I can't believe it," the Gov'nor said.

J.R. raised his voice above the others: "They wouldn't dare," he snorted.

Dr. Gruber seconded his comment, adding: "They'd be scorned and laughed off the planet."

Bobby chuckled. "You guys are right," he said. "I got up the nerve to tell him that his government obviously didn't realize the scope and magnitude of my company's popularity and respect around the world. I reminded him that our present humanitarian effort in his country has and continues to receive world-wide publicity and support. And, all of that was made possible by the efforts of our mutual friend, Jason Lord, who, as you know, is respected worldwide for his intellect and diplomatic effectiveness . . ." He paused, as a sly grin crossed his face. "Mr. Z's eyes grew quite large, and he said in a kind of breathless manner: "You know Jason Lord?"

"Of course I know Jason Lord," I said. "He's a dear friend of mine. How else do you think we got here?"

"Without another word, Mr. Z. flew out of his chair like a rocket and ran to the nearest exit.

"Where're you going?" I yelled at him.

"Be back in ten minutes," he cried, as he disappeared behind floor-length drapes.

"About fifteen minutes later he returned, smoking one of his nasty cigars. He strode to the table like a stud in heat, and when he reached the big conference table, he turned, and looked down his long nose at me and said rather pompously: "After considerable consideration, my government has agreed to accept your proposition."

There was spontaneous applause and cheers.

Smiling, Bobby raised his glass: "Here's to you Jason, wherever you are." He drank. Looking around the table, he raised his glass again and said: "Let us drink to the new Bobby Computer factory in South Africa."

Everyone applauded, raised their glasses, and drank.

After guests enjoyed the last of the five courses, and they had relaxed with a liqueur, Bobby again rose to his feet.

Looking at his guests with admiration, he first addressed Gov'nor Bhalla. "Gov'nor," he began, "as you know the Bobby Mobile Clinic is leaving town the day after tomorrow and we're heading for a place called Batanga.

"But before we go, we not only want to thank you for your help and kindness and your dedication to the mission, we want to show our appreciation by giving to the city of Littleberg a newly paved main street *and* two brand new Jitneys . . ."

"Thank you, Mr. Bobby," he said, "from me and from all the people of Littleberg."

"You're welcome," Bobby said. He then looked to the doctor. "Doctor LaBarre, it has come to my attention that your hospital's emergency room is sadly lacking in up-to-date equipment. To rectify that problem, we have taken it on ourselves to purchase a completely equipped and most modern emergency room available.

"I don't know what to say," Dr. LaBarre remarked. "This is incredible. Thank you. We will dedicate the new unit to you and to your entire team. We will never forget this."

"Thank you, doctor."

Bobby looked at Kaila, and smiled. "What can I say to you, Kaila? We will never forget you. I think everyone feels the same about you: we love you forever, for your wit, your wonderful smile, and your profound wisdom. We will take that with us forever. And to show our appreciation for your unfailing support and indomitable spirit, it is our pleasure to present you with the keys to a new car."

To show her delight and appreciation, Kaila got to her feet, began singing an old African song, and swirled her way gracefully around the table. When she sat down, everyone applauded. She bowed her head and gave thanks.

Not to leave anyone out, Bobby quickly got to his feet and thanked Dr. Smith, Nurse Naha and Nurse Sheena with keys to new cars.

The reaction was spontaneous. Almost everyone got to their feet and, as Keila, sang a lively African song, they laughed and danced and hugged one another.

Bobby leaned back in his chair and watched. J.R., who was feeling the joy of the moment, turned to his daughter. She looked at him with tears in her eyes. She wanted to smile, but she couldn't.

"What is it, Liz?" he asked. "What's wrong?"

"It's my husband," she answered, wiping a tear away.

"Is he ill?"

"No," she answered. "*He's* just fine. He's having an affair. Can we talk about it later?"

J.R. nodded, and put his arms around her.

Bobby, feeling the happy spirit of the moment, started clapping his hands to the beat of the music. His heart was light and it was his time to play. He felt he had earned it.

CHAPTER 20

When J.R. saw his daughter walk through the door of the hotel's coffee shop the next morning, he was surprised to see a broad smile on her face.

She opened her arms to him and they embraced. Looking at her he said: "You look positively radiant this morning. Last night you were crying because you got news that your husband was having an affair. What happened between then and now?"

Chuckling, she sat down and, taking a deep breath, said: "I got an e-mail from him this morning begging my forgiveness because he really shouldn't have sent me an e-mail saying he was having an affair because, he truth, he wasn't really having an affair."

J.R. was baffled. "What?" he said, loudly. "Was he drunk, do you think?"

"No, dad," she responded, "he wasn't drunk. He was feeling lonely and abandoned, and, like any child, he wanted to punish his mother for leaving him."

"You're his mother?"

"The little boy inside of him *thinks* I am. Oh, dad, he has never really grown up. He's still a child, still the jokester. And I guess that's why I love him. The moment I saw him I knew I'd marry him. He was such a beautiful young man, a kind of Brad Pitt on steroids. I simply couldn't resist him."

"Well, I'm glad to see you're all right," J.R. said. "But, just because he said he didn't have an affair, how do you know he didn't?"

"I don't," she said quickly. "The fact is it wouldn't be the first time. He's had numerous affairs. They never last long, and he always comes home to me."

"He loves you."

"Yes." She smiled. "I think so."

"And, who know?" J.R. inquired. "Maybe one day he'll grow up."

Elizabeth laughed, leaned in, kissed J.R. and stood up. "I've got to go," she said, heading for the door. Turning, she added: "I can't believe this is our last day." She took a step toward her father. "You know, dad," she said, "I don't know about you, but this job, what I've been doing these last few months, has been the best time of my life. I can't remember anything else that fulfilled me so much.

"And, you know what? I feel proud of myself, proud of what I've done and what I'm doing to help people—helping women and little babies live again. How important is that?"

"There is nothing more important, Liz," J.R. said. "You have every right to feel proud; I feel proud of you, too, and Bobby, and everyone involved in this great mission of ours. But it's not over; and it won't be over until we eradicate HIV/AIDS forever."

She took another step toward him. "You're coming back next year?"

"Yes, I think so."

"But what about Kate?"

"I'll persuade her to come with me."

"And if she doesn't?"

"Well, then . . ." He smiled. "I guess I'll stay home and write a book."

"You can write about our experiences here in Africa. It will be a wonderful book."

"I think it'll be non-fiction," J.R. said. "You know, I keep a journal and I write in it every night before I go to bed. Already, I've written about one hundred pages."

"Well, let's see," she began, "you've written one third; all you need is two thirds more and by the time we finish with our mission you'll be done and back home and ready for the publisher."

J.R. smiled. "I wish it were that simple."

Elizabeth put her arms around her father and said softly: "I love you so much."

"And I love you, too," he said, "with all my heart, and I'm so proud of you and Bobby; my only regret is that I didn't find you sooner. I've missed out on so much . . ."

"You had your demons, dad," she said, stroking his face. "We all do. The main thing is that you're here now and we're all together. That's all that matters."

Batanga, a small village some miles from Ithica, was J.R.'s and Kaila's last destination together. He headed the four-wheel vehicle up winding dirt roads through landscapes of dense forests and naked hills.

From atop the tallest hills they could glimpse the Indian Ocean. After about twenty minutes of driving they found themselves at what looked like a dead end stymied by a barbed-wire fence.

Kaila told J.R. to take the road to the left. It was steep but it was the only road that would take them to the summit. The four-wheel drive car climbed slowly, steadily, swaying from side to side when progress was made difficult by the deeply rutted road.

At the top, a wide valley, surrounded by green hills, clusters of mud huts and square, tin-roofed structures appeared. The sight was so sudden, so unexpected, that it took J.R.'s breath away. He stopped the vehicle to get a better look at the village and its surroundings.

"See the river flowing through the basin?" Kaila asked. "You can see that it bisects the village. To visit a neighbor you have to take your shoes and socks off and just wade across."

"I see that the cows and goats and pigs drink from it," J.R. added, smiling.

"Everyone drinks from the river," Kaila said, stepping out of the vehicle with her little black bag. She walked to an opening in the fence and looked down into the valley.

"Do you want me to stay here?" he asked getting out of the vehicle.

"Oh, no," she said. "I want you to come with me. Be sure to lock the car and take the key with you. We'll take that path over there. If you listen closely, you'll hear children's voices echoing across the valley.

"The hills surrounding the compound create an acoustic amphitheater. You can't always *see* the children, but you can hear them. Sometimes it's so loud that you think you're surrounded by a crowded and very noisy schoolyard."

Once at the river side, J.R., who wished he had brought ear plugs, sat on a large flat rock and watched as Kaila waded across the river at it narrowest point. When she reached the other side, she turned and waved back at him; he lost sight of her when she entered a wooded area that surrounded a cluster of huts and tin-roofed houses.

Above the din, he heard what sounded like a trumpet. Then he heard the beat of drums and more trumpets. The music was similar to jazz, he thought. *A jazz band here in Batanga? Why not? How great!*

He was just getting used to the melody when it stopped. All was quiet. Then he heard children yelling and their voices were joined by the voices of men. The voices together made no sense to J.R., just a loud but unpleasant and steady sound that echoed over and over through the valley.

Then, something happened that caused J.R. to jump to his feet. On the other side of the river several young women appeared; their heads were covered with shawls and two of the women were carrying young babies. They moved as fast as they could toward the river. J.R. noticed that they were already barefooted. The pregnant woman, who looked no more than twenty, led the group across.

J.R. was concerned. He looked about but saw no sign of Kaila. He called her name, but there was no answer.

Meanwhile, the boys and men kept up a relentless kind of chant that got louder and louder and echoed through the valley.

Just when J.R. was about to go in search of Kaila, she and another pregnant woman appeared. Kaila, who had her arm around the woman, hurried her to the water's edge.

After J.R. had helped the first three women out of the water, he called out to Kaila: "Do you need help?"

"No," she said. "Take those women up to the van."

"I can't leave you like this."

"You must," she yelled. "We've got to get out of here fast."

He turned to the three women and motioned to them to go up the hill. They stood silent and did not move. They looked frightened.

"They don't understand me, Kaila."

In Afrikaans, she yelled to the women to hurry up the hill and get into the van. When they hesitated, she yelled at them: "Maak gou! Maak gou!" which meant *Hurry up! Hurry up!*

The women obeyed her orders and began to climb the stone steps as fast as they could.

As soon as Kaila and the pregnant woman reached J.R., he gave her the keys to the van and told her he'd stay behind as long as he could. In

Afrikaans, Kaila told the woman to hurry up the hill. After she warned J. R. not to stay too long, she started up the hill.

When J.R. looked across the river he saw about eight men and boys; they walked out of the wooded area carrying sticks and what looked like baseball bats. He decided to stand his ground; he didn't move. He stared across the river at the men and boys. Several of them shook their fists at him and waved their weapons in the air. Two boys caught his attention. They weren't armed, at least not with sticks or bats; the smaller boy, about age ten, was waving something about that shone of metal . . . like a gun.

Slowly, J.R. lifted both his arms in the air to show that he was unarmed, and meant no harm. While the men conversed amongst themselves, J.R. glanced over his shoulder; the women had reached the top. He figured that the women must be in the vehicle by now and ready to go. He thought: *If I make a run for it, will I be able to reach the van, start the engine and get it rolling down the hill fast enough before those men and boys reach it?*

Looking across the river one last time, it appeared to him that the men had made a decision. Jumping up and down, they started shouting as loud as they could and shaking their clubs at him. The chorus of voices that echoed through the valley sounded like hundreds of screaming fans rooting for their team. It was ear-splitting.

J.R. knew he must make a quick decision because the tension in the air was palpable and he was convinced the men and boys were about to attack. He decided to count to three and make his move;

One, two, three . . .

Turning, he ran for the rock-steps and, with a shot of adrenalin running through his veins, he scrambled as fast as he could up the slope. He dared not look back over his shoulder, but he could hear the loud male voices screaming at him and getting closer and closer. It reminded him of that fateful night in New York City when he fled down Forty-third Street, and he heard screeching sirens of police cars that he thought were in hot pursuit of him.

Oh legs, he thought, *don't fail me now.*

When he reached the top, his right leg cramped and he fell against the fence for support. Looking back he saw that the men were almost half way up the hill.

With a quick glance at the van he noticed that he was only about thirty feet away and that the door was open. Taking a deep breath, he hopped, skipped and practically jumped into the driver's seat, closing the door after him. He put the key in the ignition, started the engine, shoved the car into gear, and put his foot to the pedal.

The vehicle lurched forward and started rolling down the rutted road leaving most of the men behind. Only one young man was able to do some damage; he smashed a stop light with a stout club.

The sound of breaking glass frightened the young women; they screamed and covered their heads with shawls.

Kaila tried to calm them, but they didn't respond.

When they reached the bottom of the hill and J.R. was about to turn off onto the main road, he glanced in the rearview mirror and saw about six men wielding clubs running down the hill after them.

He mentioned it to Kaila and she immediately got on her cell phone with Bobby.

She explained the situation to Bobby telling him about the men chasing them, and suggested that he call the hospital and ask that they send an ambulance; then, she suggested that he call the police and advise them of the present situation and ask that they provide police presence at the mobile . . . just in case.

Minutes later, when they were within three miles of Littleberg, J.R. saw the four-wheel drive police van speeding up the hill toward them. As they passed, Captain John honked the horn and waved.

"Where are they going?" he asked.

Shifting her body around so she could see out the back window, Kaila said: "My guess is that they're looking for the men who were coming after us."

"Do you see anything?"

"The road back there looks deserted," she answered. "But I can't see all the way up the hill; the road near the top turns sharply to the left. They could be up there."

CHAPTER 21

B ack in Littleberg, J.R. parked the four-wheeler, and, as he and Kaila helped the four women into the mobile, the ambulance arrived, its siren blasting.

All the noise and commotion had attracted large numbers of curious onlookers who crowded in front of the hotel, the city hall, and the mobile.

While the doctors and nurses were testing the women for HIV/AIDS, Captain John entered the mobile to bring them all up-to-date on the situation. After searching the area around Batanga thoroughly they could find no sign of men with clubs. They decided to drop the search and return to Littleberg. It was his opinion that the women were safe, but he and his men would remain in the area to insure their safety.

Captain John and his men returned to the police van and drove off.

Each woman tested positive for HIV/AIDS. The younger of the two pregnant women, a nineteen year old, was frightened. She began to cry, explaining that she didn't dare go home because, if she did, *they* would kill her.

Bobby tried to comfort her saying that she didn't have to go home and that they would take care of her. First she would go to the hospital for a complete examination; then she would be treated with retroviral drugs that will also help to protect her unborn baby.

Further, he explained that she would then be taken to a Safe House where she would stay until her baby was born. After that, the city would provide care, food, and housing until she was strong and well enough to return to her village.

J.R. watched as Dr. Smith helped the young woman out of the mobile; he noticed that she wiped tears from her eyes. When she saw all the people, she smiled at them.

Standing at the open door of the mobile, J.R. was surprised to see so many people; many waved but most of the crowd was quiet as they watched the young woman start across the street to the waiting ambulance.

When she and the doctor got about half way across the street, J.R. noticed a boy of about ten, pushing through the crowd; he looked familiar to him. All at once, the boy took something shiny from his pocket and waved it in the air. At that precise moment, J.R. realized where he had seen him. Just as J.R. stepped out of the mobile, the boy took aim at the young pregnant woman and shot at her, not once but twice.

The first bullet hit her in the left thigh; she screamed and looked at her assailant. Recognizing him, she reached out with her right hand and called his name: "Isaiah . . . Why? . . . Why? . . ." He watched as she collapsed.

The second bullet slammed into the side of the mobile.

While Dr. Smith went to the aid of the injured woman, J.R. watched as the shooter turned and tried to push his way through the crowd. J.R. took off running, yelling at the people to stop the boy. The bystanders, mostly women of various ages, screamed and yelled. Frightened by the gun, which the boy waved menacingly in the air, they parted to let him pass.

J.R. joined a couple of men and ran up the street passed the hotel to an alley way. At the far end they could see the boy scrambling over a high wire fence. Two of the younger men ran to the fence, but, by the time they got there, the boy had disappeared.

Back at the scene of the crime, J.R. saw Captain John and a photographer taking pictures of the young woman's wound. When they were finished, Captain John leaned down and spoke to the woman who was lying on a stretcher. She smiled up at him and he bent down and kissed her on the cheek.

When he stood up, two young ambulance attendants put the injured woman on a stretcher and carried her to the waiting ambulance. At that moment Captain John got a call on his cell phone. Approaching him, J.R. could hear part of the conversation.

"We've got one down, a pregnant woman, shot in the right thigh . . . It's a small hole; my take is that the bullet's from a 9 mm . . ." Seeing J.R., he turned away. "Yes, I do . . ." After about a minute, he shut the phone off.

"I'm sorry, J.R.," he said.

"I'm sorry, too, Captain John."

A beat then: "You know, don't you?"

"I know that you know that young woman who was shot."

"Yes," he said sadly. "She's my sister-in-law."

"And the boy? The shooter?"

"He's her brother."

"And he was trying to kill her because . . . ?"

Captain John looked at J.R. for a long moment but did not speak.

"Let me answer your question, J.R.," Kaila said, approaching. "Through denial, confusion, timidity, and, yes, even egos, our people believe that if one of our own has HIV/AIDS they disgrace the family, and there are other reasons as well. We do not realize, out of ignorance or confusion of thought, that the disease is trying to teach us something. I know that sounds strange, but it's true. To beat this pandemic—it is no longer just an epidemic—we must wake up and learn; we must teach our people the truth through knowledge and fact, not from voodoo and myths, about the very real horrors of the disease.

"We must have vision, will, tolerance, sacrifice, cooperation, and humanity. These are the ingredients of a successful response. And if we do not respond in kind, we will certainly fail. And tens of millions of lives will be lost and another million children will be left orphans in a cold and hostile world."

On the morning of their departure, Bobby, J.R. and Doctor Gruber met with Doctor LaBarre in his office at the hospital. LaBarre told the trio that the young woman who had been shot by her brother was resting comfortably and that he was confident she would have a full recovery.

"What about a radiograph, doctor?" Gruber asked. "Was she fully examined?"

"Yes," LaBarre answered. "The radiograph showed a small bullet lodged in the soft tissues of the upper lateral thigh. But there is no fracture of the bone, nor is there any swelling or bleeding." He took a moment before continuing. "Having said that, I decided to call down to Port Elizabeth early this morning. I talked to the gunshot expert at the hospital and he offered to examine her himself. He's due here in a few hours."

"I think that was a wise move, doctor," Gruber said. "Gunshot wounds can be very tricky."

"He's my insurance."

Gruber chuckled.

"Well, gentlemen," LaBarre said, getting to his feet. "What more can I say to you? You've done an incredible job here. And the records show it." He picked up a white envelope and handed it to Bobby. "The figures show that you treated more HIV/AIDS patients than any previous attempt—including the famous Doctors International—by almost fifty percent. *That's* impressive. And you should be very proud of yourselves."

Standing, Bobby reached out and shook LaBarre's hand. "Thank you, doctor," he said, smiling. "We are proud of what we've done, but more than that we are grateful to you and to all of your young professionals who worked so tirelessly, sometimes into the late hours, to help us fight this pandemic that threatens so many lives. We also want to thank all the laypeople who worked so hard for so little and especially to Kaila who made us all better for having known her.

"We'll never forget you and we'll always be grateful."

CHAPTER 22

On the road again . . .
Destination: Harwood, approximately 100 miles up the coast highway.

After traveling about fifty miles, it began to rain, lightly at first, but by the time they went sixty miles, it poured. Dense gray clouds ahead gave proof to a long downpour that was likely to last for hours, perhaps even days.

Bobby got on the phone with Harwood's General Hospital. Its spokesperson explained that it had been raining in Harwood for days, and that the weather report promised that the rain would not let up for days.

Fortunately, the road to Harwood was paved and the only obstructions on the road were streams of mud. Here and there large rocks made driving somewhat hazardous. They made it to Harwood on time and were welcomed by a throng of enthusiastic citizens and government officials. The amenities were better than average and the general hospital was equipped with the latest equipment.

The team stayed for only one month due to heavy rains. Few people came to the mobile, and travel to the villages was made impossible due to muddy roads. Additionally, the local weather bureau predicted that the rains would continue off and on for at least two more weeks.

August: Durban

A bright warm sun and cloudless blue sky welcomed them to the sprawling city. Elizabeth, with tour book in hand, marveled at its beauty. "Listen to this, guys," she said, reading from the guide: *Durban's beaches are characterized by soft, golden sand, palm trees and the warm waters of the Indian Ocean.* Oh, Bobby, can't we go swimming? Just for a little bit?"

"Sorry, sis," he answered, "we have to keep moving."

"But why?" She asked. "We need some free time, Bobby."

"You'll get plenty of free time later."

"But we need it now," she countered. "Just listen: *The main beaches are shark netted and patrolled from sunrise to sunset by trained lifeguards who have an impressive track record in beach safety . . .*" Her voice trailed off at the end.

"What's the matter, Liz?" Gruber probed. "The shark got your tongue?"

J.R., who was reading a guide book, cut in: "You know, guys, we're no longer in the Eastern Cape; a little while back there we entered into KwaZulu Natal.

"I hope they speak English here," Gruber interjected.

"Yes," J.R. said, "a little more than thirteen percent speak English. Eighty percent speak Zulu. Oh, Kaila, where are you now that we need you?"

"What's our destination, Bobby?" Elizabeth asked.

"We're headed for a city called Dudleyville, which is about a hundred miles up the coast."

"I've got it," Elizabeth chimed in. "*Dudleyville is a city of historical importance. With a population of three hundred thousand, it offers visitors modern amenities and friendly hospitality. The surrounding countryside offers the most picturesque landscapes in the country; sweeping hills and knotty rock formations pepper the rolling plains and valleys of northern terrain.*"

When the team arrived in Dudleyville, the local HIV/AIDS data suggested that between 1997 and 2004, the death rate among men aged 30-39 more than doubled, while that among women aged 25-34, the rate more than quadrupled. The death rate among babies, one to five months, was even higher. So moved were they by these bleak statistics that they stretched their work hours to the limit. Working twelve and more hours a day they managed to dispense a record amount of antiretrovirals and nevirapine to young women and babies.

On October first, the team, their body's strained and exhausted, their spirits revived and renewed, drove away from Dudleyville knowing in their hearts that they had done their very best.

October/November
Destination: Chesterton

Chesterton, the third largest city in the province, is second only to Pietermaritzburg, the capital city.

"Its population is around four hundred thousand, and, by comparison to other cities like Littleburg, Chesterton is a large, modern city. It has many hotels and restaurants. The roads are paved and it is home to several colleges. There is a large, fully equipped hospital, the Chesterton General, and . . ."

"What's the government?" Doctor Doherty interjected.

"Well," Bobby began, there's some dispute about that. The way I understand it is this: there was some argument about whether a place called Ulundi should be the provincial capital or Pietermaritzburg.

"Just recently the dispute was resolved and the African National Congress, or ANC, and the Democratic Party, decided to make Pietermaritzburg the sole capital of KwaZulu-Natal."

"Bobby, do you have any HIV/AIDS statistics for this area?" Doctor Gruber asked.

"Among South Africa's provinces, KwaZulu-Natal has the highest of HIV infections—approximately thirty-nine percent."

There was silence.

The Bobby HIV/AIDS Mobile left the lowlands of the coast and climbed into the interior provinces where the scenery gave way to grass-covered rolling hills. At seven miles up the mist cleared, revealing a rich, fair valley where grass and bracken, a large fern, grew, and where the forlorn song of the titihoya, a bird common to the veld, could be heard.

A few miles beyond the hills gave way to vast flatlands that spread for miles north and south and where horses and cows and goats grazed, and where little mud houses and rough-hewn shacks had been replaced with attractive, modern-looking ranch houses. Some were made of brick; others were made of wood and other building materials.

When the mobile got within ten miles of Chesterton, Bobby picked up the intercom to address his audience. "Okay you guys," he began, "we're getting close to our destination. Here are just a few facts I think you should know. To start with the name of the fifty-two-old mayor is Ali Jamal.

"Why another Indian?" Doctor Doherty asked.

"Because they're so good at politics," Doctor Gruber responded.

Bobby continued: "The police captain is Paul Dhen, and our contact at St. Mary's Hospital is Doctor Vernon Lemke."

"Where're we staying?" J.R. asked.

"We're staying at the Shangri-la Hotel, which is on Chesterton Boulevard, the main drag, and located conveniently between the hospital, on one side, and city hall, on the other.

"Here's something interesting: There are many orphanages in Chesterton, one being the well-known Langalibel. This is what it says: *The Langalibel Children's Foundation is a registered non-profit organization that facilitates community based care and support for orphans and other vulnerable children.*

"*HIV/Aids in KwaZulu-Natal is now a pandemic in South Africa and the province has become the AIDS capital of the world. In a recent sample of 800 high school children more than 30% were HIV positive. We look after more than 50 HIV positive orphans . . ."*

"Where's this orphanage, Bobby?" J.R. asked. "Does it say?"

"Doesn't give an address, but it says it's next to the police station."

"Thinking about adopting a child, dad?" Elizabeth asked.

"Maybe."

"Do you think Kate would approve?"

J.R. smiled. "Only on two conditions," he said. "One, she, and I do mean *she*, would have to be pretty girl, and two, she would have to be able to dance."

CHAPTER 23

W hen they got within five miles of Chesterton, Bobby made a confession to the group; namely, that he forgot to call ahead and advise Mayor Ali Jamal that they were arriving two weeks early because they were exhausted and needed at least two weeks to recover.

"You're in big trouble, Bobby," Gruber observed with a chuckle.

Elizabeth frowned: "How could you forget, Bobby?"

"Bobby," J.R. said, getting to his feet, "why don't you call him and I'll take over the wheel?"

"Okay, dad," Bobby said, slowing the mobile and pulling off the road.

After J.R. got into the driver's seat, Bobby took his phone and retired to the first examination room.

A few minutes later, Bobby appeared. He was laughing to himself as he made his way to the front of the vehicle.

"I'm back, dad," Bobby said.

J.R. applied the brakes and brought the big vehicle to a stop by the side of the road.

"What's so funny, Bobby?" he asked as he slid off the seat.

"You won't believe this, but the Mayor actually tried to make a joke about it," he said, making himself comfortable in the driver's seat. "At first he was a little upset," he said, putting the mobile in gear, "but then he said with a chuckle: *Oh well, Bobby, I guess it's better to be early than never first in line.*

Everyone laughed as the big vehicle ambled onto the highway and slowly picked up speed.

Doctor Gruber spoke up: "You know, at first hearing it comes across like a non-sequitur, but the more you think about it, it makes sense."

"You're right, Gruber," J.R. added. "It's a paradox."

"You're both wrong," Doherty said, shaking his head. "The mayor's pithy saying is just another wordy way of saying: *First come, first served.*"

There was silence; Doherty smiled to himself. He was triumphant.

Chesterton was quiet as they pulled into town. There were no welcoming signs, and curious sightseers looked askance at the big blue and white mobile as if it were some kind of slow-crawling, beastly-looking behemoth.

Chesterton Boulevard was a wide, four lane street with a center divider carefully decorated with two rows of tall palm trees, each surrounded by foot high flowers that sprouted up from between large gray rocks. They looked similar to daisies but were known to the natives as "Treasure Flowers." The variety of colors created a dazzling rainbow display of yellow, orange, pink, red, and blue.

They passed the hospital, a modern seven-story building, and the police station, a three-story brick building that looked old but sturdy.

Next, what was supposed to be the Shangri-la Hotel, turned out to be a small shopping center with stores and a restaurant.

Bobby scratched his head and kept driving.

"That must be the hotel," Gruber said, pointing to a red brick building on the corner.

"That can't be it," Bobby said. "It's old and ugly."

"No it isn't, Bobby," J.R. interjected. "It's an example of Victorian architecture, probably built in the early twentieth century. It's magnificent."

"It's awfully small for a hotel," Elizabeth observed. "It's only got three floors."

"And there's no place to park," Bobby grumbled.

"Pull around the corner, Bobby," J.R. said. "You can park there."

As they were about to turn the corner, Doctor Gruber exclaimed: "That's no hotel, you guys; it's the city hall."

"How can you tell?" Doctor Doherty asked.

"What does it say over the door, nitwit?"

"Oh," Doherty said, "City Hall."

"Give that man a cigar."

Mayor Ali Jamal, a short and soft-spoken man with dark brown eyes and black hair, greeted his guests in his large office on the second floor. Dressed in a tailored gray suit and wearing a white shirt and a black tie, he offered each one an exquisitely upholstered high-back arm chair.

When they were all settled in, and he had been introduced to each one, he sat in his swivel leather chair, and, folding his hands, looked at his guests, smiled and said:

"I welcome all of you to Chesterton. We are happy to have you here. As you might know, HIV/AIDS is a serious problem in this part of the country. The government has largely ignored the problem; they have even denied that it exists, so we must move ahead without them. I have united with Doctor Vernon Lemke, and we are prepared to assist your efforts in any way we can. I will not get into the specifics now, but be assured that all arrangement have been made, and, in one week, we will be ready to work alongside you to fight this serious pandemic."

"In one week?" Bobby asked.

"We did not expect you for two weeks," Mayor Jamal answered. "We thought it realistic to give our people a one week of vacation because when they start working they will put in many hours, perhaps twelve or more a day. Do you not think a vacation is fair, Mr. Bobby?"

"Oh, yes, Mayor, I do," he responded.

"Now," the Mayor said, standing. "it is getting late and I know you must all be hungry. I wish I could join you, but I have a previous engagement. Do you all like good Chinese food?"

There was a unanimous response.

"Good," he said. "May I recommend The Big Wall. The food is delicious and it is within walking distance—right next door in the business mall."

He walked around the desk and took Bobby's arm. "Mr. Bobby," he said, "where are you staying?"

"We have reservations at the Shangri-la, but we can't find it."

The mayor chuckled. "You've lost Shangri-la? Dear me. What a predicament."

"We're sure it's around here someplace."

"Don't fret, Mr. Bobby," the Mayor said, walking him to the door. "You've found your Shangri-la. It's just a block up the hill. And, I just happen to know the proprietor. He's a good friend of mine. I will call him and let him know that you've arrived."

At the open door, Mayor Jamal shook Bobby's hand. "It's a pleasure meeting you, Mr. Bobby, and all your team. You are all heroes in our eyes. Thank you again for coming."

"Thank *you* Mayor Jamal," Bobby said. "You're most kind."

"Before you go, tell me, what are your plans for dinner?"

"We'll probably eat at the hotel," Bobby answered.

"Good. I will call my friend Shuka at the hotel and tell him to prepare the most sumptuous meal for our famous of friends. Does that sound good to you?"

"It sounds perfect," Bobby responded.

"And dinner is on me."

"Thank you."

Jamal shook everyone's hand and thanked them again for coming.

As soon as they were gone he hurried to his desk where he picked up a phone and pushed a button on the panel box. A moment, then: "Miss Boswell, please call the Shangri-la and get Mr. Shuka on the phone for me. Thank you."

Twelve, thirty-foot statues of carved horses lined the pathway to the magnificent Shangri-la Hotel. Standing attention at the front door were six tall men, all with thick moustaches, dressed in white shirts and knee-length jackets of red and black with gold trim, black pants, and black hats trimmed in gold.

What caught the attention of the team was not so much the carved horses, or the doormen, which they found impressive, but the architecture. The high-arched entrance to the hotel was bordered by six marble Doric columns, at least twenty feet high, all painted in pastel shades of ochre yellow, with the molding and sculptural details in red, blue, green and gold.

Inside the architecture continued to astonish the team. The lobby walls were thirty feet high and six large crystal chandeliers hung from the center of the ceiling. Complementing the chandeliers were twelve huge marble Doric columns that stood sentinel on either side and reached to the ceiling. They were painted with the same pastel colors used on the exterior columns, the only difference being that these were painted with a wide band of deep blue about one foot from the top.

At the far end of the enormous room was a comfortable sitting area. The check-in-desk occupied an entire wall. Stretching out in front of it was a marble floor thirty by thirty feet. Gold, pastel red, a soft green, and blue, played together in a design consisting of oval and diamond shapes that touched at corners then fell away in a kind of graceful dance.

To complete the scene was a large, round, glass-top table that stood in the center of the design. On top of the table was a large vase with a colorful array and variety of flowers.

As the team stood mute with admiration, a young man approached and said: "Welcome . . . to Shangri-la."

CHAPTER 24

That evening Bobby, Elizabeth, J.R. and Dr. Doherty joined together and had dinner at the hotel's Golden Horse, a large, elegant round room with indirect lighting that cast cool shades of a blue/red purple onto the ceiling. On tables that were set up along the circumference of the room, a bountiful buffet was beautifully displayed on silver serving dishes.

Bobby informed the group that Dr. Gruber had telephoned him to say that he was having a light snack and a stiff glass of whiskey in his room before retiring for the night; he did not plan to arise until eight o'clock on the third day.

"I can do him one better," Doherty said. "I'd like to hibernate for the entire two weeks."

"Oh, you lazy bums," Elizabeth countered. "I'm getting up early in the morning, packing a small bag, and heading for Durban. When I get there I'm putting on the bathing suit, rubbing myself down with suntan lotion and just enjoying the sun and the sea. I might even stay the entire weekend."

"Rubbing *yourself* down, hey?" Doherty asked, tweaking his imaginary moustache. "Mind if I come along? I know I could come in handy."

"I don't mind," she said, cutting her thick steak with a sharp knife. "Just know that I'm a black belt in karate." She gave him a sidelong glance.

"OOOoooohhhh," Doherty whined. "I think I'll just curl up in my nice little bed, pull the covers over my head, and hibernate until this is all over."

Elizabeth laughed.

"Coward," Bobby said, chuckling.

"You said it, Bobby," the doctor admitted.

J.R. looked around the table before he took a sip of wine. Putting the glass down, he said: "I know what I'm doing tomorrow. I've got a list of orphanages in Chesterton and I'm going to visit them."

"You're really serious about adopting, aren't you dad?"

He looked at his daughter, and smiled. "At first I wasn't sure; then I called Kate. She thinks it's a great idea. She would love to have a daughter, she said, but not too young."

"That makes sense," Elizabeth said.

"Want me to go with you, dad?" Bobby asked.

"Have to get up early."

"I'm with you."

With his cell phone tucked tightly next to his ear, J.R. sipped orange juice and listened intently to the voice of the young woman at the local human services department telling him about Chesterton orphanages that house AIDS' kids up to the age of fifteen.

"Are they open now and can you give me the names and addresses?" he asked. "Good . . . yes I'm ready . . ." As she talked he wrote the information on a three by five note pad.

"I got it, yes," he said. "Now, one thing more. Uh, what about paper work and all the other formalities involved? . . . Lots of red tape." He chuckled. "I'm not surprised; it's the same all over . . . What? . . . If I knew someone in government I could cut the time in half? . . . If I don't know someone, how long would it be? . . . Three to four months? I don't have that much time . . . I know the mayor of your fair city . . . He doesn't have much pull?" He laughed. "No, I won't tell him you said that . . ."

"What's so funny, dad?" Bobby asked approaching and sitting across from his father.

"Just a second, Bobby . . . Thank you for your help; I appreciate it . . . What? . . . If I knew someone in the national government? . . . I don't, but my son does . . . He's here right now . . . I'll tell him what you said . . . Thanks again . . . You too . . . Have a good day."

"What's this all about, dad?" he asked, sipping coffee from a paper cup. "Who were you talking to?"

"I was talking to a nice young lady from the human resource department at City Hall. "She gave me three names of orphanages in this city and she explained it's not easy to adopt a child. It's possible, of course, but there's a lot of paperwork and red tape involved. But, if we know somebody in government, we could reduce the whole process by half, meaning it could all be resolved in just two months."

"That's all the time we've got, dad."

"I know," he said standing. "So, bring your coffee, and let's get going."

With J.R. at the wheel of the four-by-four, Bobby acted as navigator as they made their way around the city. Progress was slow at first due to heavy morning traffic that jammed city streets.

When they finally got out of the traffic, Bobby instructed his father to the first orphanage located on Carlton Road. It was a large, modern building with a friendly staff eager to help. However, all of their children, though friendly and polite, were no older than five.

The children at the second orphanage, which was larger than the first, with a very impressive, professional staff, were even younger.

As they drove to the third, and final, orphanage, the Chesterton House, J.R. expressed the fact that he was not only disappointed but despondent as well. Bobby tried to cheer him up, but to no avail.

"Bobby, this isn't all about me," he said finally. "It's about the children. I see them all so happy during the day; there they are, running, jumping, smiling, laughing, dancing, singing, doing things, all kinds of things to keep them busy and occupied. But then I think about the night, when it's time for all of them to go to sleep. What happens to all the happiness then? Does someone wish them good night and kiss them on the cheek? Does someone comfort them and tell them that all is going to be all right? Does someone, *anyone,* hold them tight and tell them they are loved?"

"Dad . . ."

"Sorry, son," he said quietly. "I find it all so sad."

They drove the rest of the way to the Chesterton Orphanage in silence.

The three-story Chesterton Orphanage was a stately, white-brick mansion with black shutters at each window.

After J.R. parked their vehicle on the street, he and Bobby walked up the long gravel path lined with tall cypress. Two tall glass entry doors with shiny brass handles were bordered by four Doric columns.

"If I didn't know any better," Bobby said, "I'd say the Greeks must've invaded South Africa centuries ago and left their mark on the country's architecture. Besides, this place doesn't look like an orphanage; it looks more like an upscale hotel."

"I was thinking the same thing," J.R. offered, as he opened the glass door. "For a non-profit organization, they must have some very wealthy supporters."

When they stepped inside, their preconceived notions of grandeur changed. The lobby area, though spacious, was decorated simply with furniture that had been donated. The carpet on the floor was not new although it was kept clean and vacuumed on a daily basis by volunteers.

At the reception counter they were made welcome by an attractive Asian woman who wished them well and asked that they please make out a visitor's information card and pass.

As soon as J.R. made it clear to her that he might be interested in adopting a child between ten and fifteen, she smiled and said that he would have to speak to Mr. Howard Chase, the director. After J.R. nodded his agreement, she picked up a phone and dialed a number.

The call was answered and she spoke to the other person in Asian. When she hung up, she smiled at J.R. and Bobby, and pushed a buzzer to her right. In seconds, a young black boy about fifteen appeared at the counter.

"This boy," she said to J.R. "will escort you and your friend to Mr. Chase's office." She said "thank you" and bowed.

J.R. thanked her and he and Bobby followed the boy to the left down a long hall. Half way down the hall, the boy ran to a door on the right, turned, and stood at attention.

When they reached the door, he opened it for them, thanked them for coming, and bowed.

They thanked him and entered a small reception area where a young Asian woman was sitting behind a desk. Seeing them, she stood up quickly, bowed and said: "Please to take chair." She pointed to two red velvet Victorian chairs in front of a large window that was covered in long, red satin drapes that touched the floor.

After they sat, Bobby whispered in his father's ear. "Now I know where the receptionist got the Asian connection."

J.R. smiled. "Are you sure that Asian connection isn't a brothel?"

Bobby looked surprised: "What?"

"Just look around."

"Oh," he said, a glimmer of recognition on his face, "I see what you mean." He leaned over and whispered to J.R.: "It's her low-cut dress, isn't it?"

"No," J.R. shot back, "it's the *décor*."

"Oh," Bobby said loudly, scaring the receptionist. "I see. I see."

"You okay, sir?" the receptionist asked, frowning.

"Sorry," he said. "I didn't mean to startle you. Sorry."

Before she could respond, the intercom on her desk buzzed and she answered. She listened and said: "Yes sir," and got to her feet. She walked around the desk to the office door. "You go in now," she said, opening the door.

Mr. Chase's office was a larger version of the reception room. There were yards of red velvet and rare and expensive antiques.

The tall, thin, forty-something director was a distinguished-looking Englishman who wore horned-rimmed glasses and who looked more like lord of the manner than director of an orphanage; he welcomed them and offered them two large leather chairs in front of his mahogany desk.

While J.R. and Bobby sat, Mr. Chase stood at his desk reading their information cards. Finally he said: "Cronyn, Cronyn . . . I know that name . . ."

J.R. spoke up: "I'm J.R. Cronyn and this is my son, Bobby Cronyn . . ."

"Bobby Cronyn," he mused. "Where do I know that name?" The light lit. "Of course," he said smiling. "I read an article about you just recently. You're the owner of Bobby Computers and you've come to Chesterton with your Mobile Clinic to fight HIV/AIDS."

"That's right, Mr. Chase," Bobby said. "We'll be here for two months."

"Oh, Mr. Bobby, this is such an honor, sir," he said, reaching out across his desk to shake Bobby's hand.

Bobby stood and shook Chase's hand.

"Mr. Chase," J.R. cut in, "I came here to see about adopting a child."

"Of course you did, sir," Chase said. "I'm sorry." Clearing his throat, he leaned back in his chair, observing J.R. "Tell me, Mr. Cronyn, I assume you are thinking about adopting an older child?"

"Exactly."

"Good," Chase said, leaning forward and folding his hands. "Are you married, Mr. Cronyn?"

"Not as yet," J.R. said. "My fiancée is expected to join me sometime later this month; we plan on getting married in Durban."

"Excellent," Chase said. "Would you like to look at photographs of the children before we go to their unit?"

"That's a good idea," J.R. said.

"Boys and girls?"

"No, just girls."

"From ten to fifteen?"

"Why don't we narrow that down to ten, eleven and twelve?"

"Good." Chase pushed a button and the lights dimmed; he pushed another button and a small movie screen slowly lowered from the ceiling. "When you see a child you like, just say 'stop.' Here we go."

Slowly the photographs of young girls passed. Their expressions were varied: some looked happy, even joyful; others looked pensive, quizzical, even indifferent; however, none looked sad or angry.

"We're nearing the end, Mr. Cronyn."

"Stop," J.R. said. "Go back one."

"That's Natasha," Chase said. "She's ten but will turn eleven in December."

"What do you think, Bobby?"

"She's beautiful."

"What can you tell us about her, Mr. Chase?" J.R. asked.

"Well, she's a colored girl; her mother, a Zulu, died from AIDS when Natasha was two. Her father, Peter Van Brunt, a wealthy Dutchman, has not seen her for almost five years. He has AIDS, and it is my understanding that he may have a drinking problem. He is not in the best of health. Having said all of that, he continues to support her financially."

"That means that Natasha also has AIDS."

"Yes."

"Is she in reasonably good health?"

"She's in very good health," Chase said.

J.R. leaned back in his chair, looked at Bobby, then at Chase. "What are her chances for a full recovery?"

"The doctors believe her chances are excellent," he responded. "They believe she will have a full recovery."

` "If this should work out . . . That is, if she takes a liking to me and I to her, and she wants to be part of my family, could I meet her father?"

"Oh, Mr. Cronyn, the adoption could not take place without the father's approval and consent. He must sign many papers to make it legal."

"That's perfect," J.R. said, leaning forward. "You said he was not in good health."

"That's correct."

"Then why couldn't Bobby and I go to see him and bring all the necessary documents for him to sign?"

"I suppose that would be possible," he said. "Of course it would be up to Mr. Van Brunt."

"Of course."

"Good. I'll look into it," Chase said, getting to his feet.

"Does she speak any English?" J.R. asked, standing.

"Zulu is her language; however, she speaks enough English to hold a simple conversation. She's one of our best students and she is liked by everyone. At this very moment, she is rehearsing for a dance recital that we have planned for Christmas."

"She dances?"

"She's our star dancer."

"I can't wait to meet her."

Chase chuckled. "Come, Mr. Cronyn, I'll introduce you to Miss Dozinja, Natasha's supervisor."

Miss Dozinja, an attractive fifty-something, black woman with large bright eyes and high cheek bones, greeted the two men with a wide grin and asked that they follow her to the dance rehearsal in the outdoor theatre.

As soon as J.R. walked through the door into the open area, he recognized Natasha at once. Miss Dozinja explained that the dance was a Zulu woman's message of love that she was sending to her loved ones.

They sat near the stage and watched as the young girls, all dressed in long red and white dresses, swirled around the stage.

J.R. couldn't take his eyes off Natasha. There was no doubt that she dominated the group of eight dancers. A couple of times, when she broke away from the others, and danced solo at the foot of the stage, J.R. caught her eye. He was sure that she responded to his smile with a sudden shaking of her head.

"What does that mean when she shakes her head?" he asked Miss Donzinja.

"It means that she's free at last to be with her loved ones and that she has shaken off the bad spirits that surround her."

Free at last from the bad spirits. Is that not a good omen or what?

When the dance was finished, Miss Donzinja called Natasha over. Taking her aside, she spoke to the young girl in Zulu. J.R. watched closely to see how Natasha reacted to Donzinja's words.

At one point she smiled and looked in his direction. When their eyes met, he smiled at her and nodded. Natasha nodded and looked at her supervisor. They spoke a few more words before Miss Donzinja brought her over.

There were introductions all around and when Natasha was introduced to J.R., she smiled and said: "How do you do?"

As they shook hands, J.R. said he was delighted to meet her, adding that he would like to have a few words with her.

Miss Donzinja picked up the suggestion and spoke to the girl in simple English explaining to her that she walk with Mr. Cronyn in the garden by the water fall and have a little talk. She smiled, took J.R.'s hand, and led him down the path toward the flower-filled gardens that spread across the rear of the orphanage.

While they walked in the garden, J.R. learned a great deal about Natasha. Not only did she love to talk, she loved to draw, sing, and above all, dance. She wanted to become a great dancer, she said.

"You will need to take dance lessons," J.R. said.

"Yes," she said, looking at him with eyes wide open. "I want to learn how to do jazz. I like jazz. I like, too, something called break dancing. Do you break dance?"

"Break dance?" he asked, chuckling. "Oh, no, I don't think so. If I did, I'm sure I would break my head."

She laughed. "No, no, no. You would be good at it."

"What about ballet?" he asked. "The woman I'm going to marry is a ballet dancer . . ."

"You marry ballet dancer?"

"I will marry her," he said. "Her name is Kate, and she used to dance for a famous English ballet company."

Natasha stopped and looked up at him. "Does she have red hair?" she asked.

He nodded.

"Did you see a movie called *The Red Shoes?*"

"I certainly did," he answered. "It's one of my favorites."

"I've seen twice," she said, her eyes flashing. "And I would love to see again. I want to be just like her."

"But she died, Natasha."

"Oh no, no, no," she said, swishing her long black hair from side to side. "Not like that. I want to live happy and dance forever. Then I die."

"Would you like to meet Kate, and learn how to dance?"

"I would love it. Yes."

"I think we can arrange that, Natasha."

"Where does she live?"

"We both live in a place called Brooklyn; it's a borough of New York City. Would you like to live there?"

"Oh," she said quietly, turning away. "I don't know if I can."

"Why not? If you want to go, you can go. It's up to you."

"It's up to me?"

"I want you to come. I want you to be a part of my family. You met my son, Bobby. But Kate, that's my lady's name, will not only be your teacher, but she would be your mother as well. We would be family."

"Oh." She started to cry. "A family. We . . . you and me, and Kate, and . . . "We would be family?"

"Yes, a family."

She buried her face in her hands and cried repeating over and over: "A family . . . a family . . . a family . . ."

"I hope those are tears of joy," he said, lifting her chin and looking into her brown eyes.

"Joy?" she said, not understanding.

"How about *Tears of happy?*"

She understood and smiled. "Yes, yes," she said, "Tears of happy."

CHAPTER 25

J.R.'s cell phone buzzed. "Damn," J.R. yelled, as he almost tripped trying to get into his pants. Dragging them behind him, he reached for the phone on the coffee table.

"Hello," he growled.

"Dad?" Bobby asked. "Is that you?"

"No," he grumbled, "it's really the house dog."

"That's what it sounded like," he chuckled. "Are you almost ready to go?"

"I'll be down soon," he answered. "By the way, I talked to Kate this morning and she's as excited as I am about Natasha. She can't wait to meet her"

"That's great, dad," he said.

"Where are you?"

"I'm in front of the hotel."

"Got all the papers?"

"I've got everything, maps and all."

"See you in five."

With Bobby at the wheel, the four-by-four pulled into Pietermaritzburg around 9:15 and proceeded down main street through light traffic. To the men, the capital city was a revelation. J.R. read a few words from a Wikipedial: *It (Pietermartzburg) was founded in 1838. Its 'purist' Zulu name is umGungundlovu . . . The city is often informally abbreviated to PMB. It is a regionally important industrial hub, producing aluminum, timber and dairy products. It is home to many schools and tertiary education institutions, including a campus of the University of KwaZulu-Natal. It has a population of between 500,000 and 600,000 . . ."*

"Dad, excuse me," Bobby said, "Look at that building over there." He pointed to a large, three-story building on the right.

"Is that a grand building or what?"

"Wait a second," J.R. said, riffling through pages of the Wikipedia encyclopedia. "Here it is. It's City Hall, constructed in 1893, destroyed by fire in 1895, and rebuilt in 1901. This magnificent example of Victorian architecture is the largest red-brick building in the Southern Hemisphere."

"Wow," Bobby exclaimed. "It makes Chesterton's City Hall look mighty puny by comparison."

"I like Chesterton City Hall."

"Dad, look . . . that statue . . ."

"It's Gandhi," J.R. said.

Bobby slowed the vehicle to get a better look. "How does he get a statue here?"

"There's always a story, Bobby." Turning a few pages until he came to a picture of Gandhi, he read: "*In May 1893, while Gandhi was on his way to Pretoria, a white man objected to Gandhi's presence in a first-class carriage, and he was ordered to move to the van compartment at the end of the train.*

"*Gandhi, who had a first-class ticket, refused, and was thrown off the train at Piertermaritzburg. Shivering through the winter night in the waiting room of the station, Gandhi made the momentous decision to stay on in South Africa and fight the racial discrimination against Indians there . . . Today, a bronze statue of Gandhi stands in Church Street, in the city centre.*"

"This is Church Street and that is the city center."

Bobby smiled. "He looks like he's waving to us."

"There's no question about it," J.R. mused. "He *is* waving at us."

After driving for almost sixty minutes, Bobby and J.R. found themselves in the city of Jamestown in the Free State. For another ten minutes they drove through a picturesque countryside where purebred horses grazed in lush green pastures. They were looking for number 451 on Stephens Way.

Millionaire mansions stood so far back off the main street that they could not be seen from the road, except for an occasional brick chimney.

As they rounded a corner they saw an iron fence on the right. They followed it until they saw two large lions' heads on top of brick columns that supported an iron gate. The number on the mail box was 451.

"This is it," Bobby announced, turning the car into the drive and stopping.

"I like the lions," J.R. commented.

"Here's hoping there are no lions inside.'

"Nothing to be afraid of Bobby."

"Well, here goes . . ." Bobby reached for a phone that rested inside a box set into the brick column. He put it to his ear and waited. "Yes . . . uh . . . hello . . . Yes, this is Bobby Cronyn; I'm here with my father, J.R. Cronyn, to see Mr. Van Brunt. We have an appointment . . . Yes . . . Thank you . . ."

There was a buzzing sound and the gates began to open slowly. When the gate had cleared, Bobby eased the vehicle ahead slowly. They looked around.

"Is this place overgrown or what?" Bobby queried.

"It's like a jungle in here."

"Couldn't Van Brunt afford to keep the gardener?"

"Maybe he fell on hard times."

"Chase said he was very generous with his donations."

"Maybe he's just very frugal."

"Oh, dad, this is so weird," Bobby said, shaking his head. "I feel like I'm in *Great Expectations*. And Van Brunt is like the old woman just standing there in the middle of the room, all withered and old and covered with cobwebs."

J.R. chuckled. "No one can say you don't have an imagination, Bobby."

"But it is weird, dad."

"I agree. It is."

They drove another hundred feet and stopped.

"Oh, my God . . ." Bobby stared straight ahead.

"Look at that," J.R. whispered, leaning forward. "Is that a castle or what?"

"It's like a castle out of an old movie."

"With turrets and all."

"I'll bet anything it's got a moat."

J.R. chuckled. "We'll soon find out."

When they pulled up in front of the building, J.R. watched as a tall, young black man, dressed in a khaki shirt and pants, with a rifle slung over his shoulder, exited a guard shack.

"Look at that, Bobby," J.R. said. "I'm expecting a knight in shining armor, and I get a doughboy in khaki."

They both watched as he walked in stiff military fashion toward them.

Before J.R. could speak, the young guard asked him and Bobby to step out of the vehicle which they did promptly. With stoic directness the guard asked: "Who is J.R. Cronyn?"

"I am, sir," J.R. replied.

"Your identity, please."

J.R. removed a plastic case from his shirt pocket and showed the guard his driver's license. He looked at it carefully and shook his head. "Okay," he said.

Bobby opened his wallet and displayed his driver's license. Again, the guard looked at it and said "Okay."

"Wait here please," he said. Doing a kind of *about face*, he returned to the guard shack where he spoke to someone on a phone. When he reappeared, he motioned to the men to follow him.

He opened one of two fifteen-foot oak doors and stepped back to let Bobby and J.R. enter. Once inside, he closed the door behind them.

J.R. glanced behind him but the young guard was gone.

Before they could react to the grandeur of the immense hall, with its high vaulted ceilings and winding staircase, a short, stout man of about sixty with red cheeks and a ready smile, and who J.R. imagined was the butler, greeted them with a hearty "Hello," and welcomed them to Petersford Castle.

J.R. stepped forward and introduced himself. "And this is my son, Bobby Cronyn."

"Oh, I'm so pleased to meet *you*, Mr. Cronyn," the butler said. "Mr. Van Brunt has a new Bobby Computer and he's having a devil of a time trying to figure it out. He was hoping that you would take some time later to help him."

Bobby smiled and said: "I'd be happy to."

"My name is Charles, and if you have any questions about the castle, don't hesitate to ask. Now, Mr. Van Brunt is waiting for you in the great room at the rear of the castle. We can take the short cut to get there or we can take the long way. Which way, gentlemen? It's up to you."

J.R. looked at Bobby and whispered: "The long way?"

Bobby smiled and nodded.

"Very well, gentlemen," Charles said, turning. "Follow me." As they walked he continued to talk: "The castle was built by Mr. Van Brunt's grandfather starting in 1945. He named the castle after his grandson, Peter Van Brunt, who was born in 1944. There are approximately ten thousand square feet in the castle and it was built on 54,000 acres of land. There is a natural lake at the rear of the building and just below in the basement are a bowling alley and a movie theatre. In the 1940s it cost ten million dollars to build Petersford Castle."

As they walked, J.R. noticed antiques, tapestries, armor, and several large paintings of what J.R. assumed were ancestors of the Van Brunt family.

"This is the family library," Charles announced as they walked into a large, rectangular room. J.R. had expected to see high ceilings, but he figured that these were no more than twenty feet. He particularly liked the stained cross beams and old-fashioned chandelier.

The stone fireplace that rose to the ceiling was a focal point and gave the room a sense of charm, stability and warmth. And the antique sofas and high-back chairs placed around the fireplace made J.R. want to find a book and make himself comfortable. *I could get used to this.*

After they had passed through a number of rooms including sitting rooms, the games room, employee quarters, and a dining room large enough to hold a banquet for two hundred guests, Charles brought them to the great room.

"Welcome to the great room, gentlemen," Charles said, opening his arms. "Isn't it splendid?"

Bobby agreed.

"The painting over the stone fireplace is the grandfather: Franz Van Brunt."

J.R. liked the size and drama of the room, but, by contrast, he preferred the library over this room simply because it was, for him, warmer, more intimate, and was full of charm that the great room did not possess.

Natural light, from a wall of glass windows and French doors that faced the patio and lake, flooded the room. In order to provide some intimacy and warmth to the large area, a number of small sitting areas had been created. These consisted of plush sofas and comfortable easy chairs, some of which were modern in style, and others which were more traditional.

There were a number of family portraits in the room and these were of special interest to J.R. He looked for a portrait of Peter Van Brunt but found none.

When he turned around he saw a man entering the room from the patio. Although he was walking with a cane, his pace was firm and brisk.

And, despite the fact that the back light made it difficult to see the man's features clearly, J.R. knew it was Van Brunt.

After introductions, Peter Van Brunt asked Charles to bring his guests a big pitcher of iced tea and homemade biscuits with jam. He then led them out to the patio where they sat at a round table under an umbrella.

While Van Brunt reminisced about the good old days when he and his wife held parties for hundreds of people at Petersford, J.R. studied him. He thought: *He resembles his handsome grandfather—the large brown eyes, the long straight nose, the square jaw. Unfortunately, that's where the likeness ends. Even at sixty he looks ten years older. The wide strong shoulders have weakened and slumped. The barrel chest has collapsed and flattened. The crop of wavy blonde hair has grayed and deep lines have burrowed into his cheeks. AIDS has taken its toll, and I surmise he's half the men he used to be.*

When the refreshments were brought to the table, Van Brunt became even more animated. He spoke about the early days (1990) when F.W. Klerk, the country's last white president, stood up in Parliament and announced the abolition of the liberation movements and the release of Mandela.

Van Brunt commented: "It was the only time I was proud to say I was a Dutchman like Klerk."

He explained that the climate was favorable for change and that the collapse of global communism had removed the Nationalists' old fear of a communist takeover.

"But Afrikaner leaders had balked at making major reforms," he said. "They contented themselves with tinkering at the edges of apartheid. The generals were confident that they were in no imminent danger of defeat."

He said that DeKlerk's history genes suggested he too would shrink from reform; after all, he was a blue-blooded Afrikaner Nationalist and a member of the strictest branch of the Dutch Reformed Church—my church, too, by the way.

"Considering that DeKlerk's own father was an apartheid cabinet minister, it is surprising that he paved the way for a new era. But sustaining an environment where, for most of the previous three decades, leaders had tended to leave office only in a coffin or by a coup, his abdication was remarkable.

"The only flicker of life on the far right was a clumsy attempt by a group called the Boeremag, or Boers' force, in 2003 to set off bombs in Soweto. One person was killed, and the conspirators were swiftly arrested and put on trial for treason.

"For the past ten years we have put up with the crazies on the far right; until recently, they have driven by the castle and have fired their rifles at us from over the wall."

"Is that why the front of the castle is so overgrown with trees and the like?" J.R. asked. "To protect you from their bullets?"

"Yes," he answered, "but so far this year there have been no incidents, and I suspect they have run out of ammunition or the will to continue a lost cause." Van Brunt took a deep breath and said he wished to tell them what life was like around the time that he was told he had HIV/AIDS. He related that those days were wonderful, and that the mine was still open and he had 3,200 men working for him. He wanted to tell them about a black man named Aaron Mahachi (ma-hot-gee), his prodigy and friend.

"He saved my life," he said. "In 1992, I got very sick and was taken to the infirmary at my gold mine sometime very early in the morning. I was 48 and I was in great pain.

"When I was brought into the infirmary the Indian doctor examined me and determined that I had AIDS. Whenever anyone was diagnosed with AIDS the warning sirens were set off to alert the workers.

"I was told afterwards that Mahachi came to see me immediately. When he heard that there were no drugs to treat my condition, Mahachi got angry and insisted that they do whatever they had to do in order to get them.

"He agreed to take a thousand dollars and go to the Woodsville Hospital where he would purchase the drugs and bring them back. They figured it would take about an hour.

"The doctor gave him the money and the driving instructions and he left about five thirty in the morning. Sometime around six o'clock when he was traveling along a secluded country road he was ambushed by six white Afrikaans. They dragged him out of the Jeep at gunpoint and beat him severely about the head and face; they stole the money and left him to die on the road.

"Somehow he managed to get himself back in the Jeep and drive the remaining twenty miles to the Woodsville Hospital's emergency room where, after telling them who he was and what he wanted, he collapsed." Van Brunt hesitated, fighting back tears. "Less than an hour later, he died."

While Bobby and Charles played a game of billiards in the game room, J.R. and Van Brunt strolled along a path by the edge of the lake.

A fine cool breeze blew, and the sun sparkled like diamonds on the surface of the water. J.R. had a feeling of anxiety despite the familiar and usually calming effect from the scent of rose that filled the air.

Van Brunt talked and talked while J.R. listened. He knew not what he was saying; he could only concentrate on one subject: Natasha. Finally they reached a stone bench tucked between two shade trees. Van Brunt sat and motioned to J.R. to sit next to him.

Taking a deep breath, Van Brunt said: "I know you're eager for me to get to the point, J.R. So I shall do just that." He leaned on his cane and looked out at the lake. "I have two regrets in my life: one, that I allowed my wife to leave me and take my two sons away from me; and two, my daughter, Natasha. I damn this illness that has taken over my mind and my body. In a very real sense I have abandoned her. I certainly have neglected her all these years. It's true I have given the orphanage millions of dollars, but that was only to assuage my guilt. It did not comfort my soul."

He turned to face J.R. "I want you to know, J.R., that I love her; I have always loved her. I know that might be hard to believe, but it's true. And I want what's best for her; and it's not money that will make her happy or make her feel good about herself. She deserves more than I can give. I look to you, and your lady, to do for her what I did not and can not do. I want you to save her . . ."

"Oh, Peter," J.R. broke in.

"No, please," he interrupted, "let me finish. "She has no life here; but she will have a life in America. I know that. And I know that if you and Kate, and your family, love and guide her along the road, she will thrive and grow into a woman of outstanding character and accomplishment."

"Thank you," J.R. said, sighing.

"No, thank *you*," Van Brunt said, looking deep into J.R.'s eyes. "I know you've come a long way, J.R., and I know the road has been long and tedious and filled with pain. And I know, because of your life experiences, that you will take Natasha to a place where she will see the light and know the spirit of the Lord. It took me forty years, J.R., but I finally got there. I have learned that living has no meaning unless you let God into your life, because, the truth is: He IS life."

CHAPTER 26

That night, in the seclusion and quiet of his hotel room, J.R. e-mailed Kate: *Dear Kate, WE'RE GOING TO BE PARENTS. Today, Peter Van Brunt gave his permission for the adoption of his daughter, Natasha Van Brunt. He is now filling out all of the necessary papers and we can expect official sanction of this adoption. The mayor of this town has assured me that it will take effect in one week!*

I think it would be great if you could make the trip here to meet Natasha. I know you will love her as much as I do. I'm so excited I can't write any more . . . except to say I LOVE YOU . . . J.R.

P.S. Peter told me that Natasha was named for his grandmother, who was part Dutch and part Russian. That accounts for the Russian name, I guess. J.R.

P.P.S. I have permission from Peter to see Natasha outside of the orphanage, so I intend to make arrangements tomorrow to take her to Zululand, outside of Durbin to see the great dance festival featuring the famous Reed Dance. I'm sure she will love it. And, besides, it will give us a chance to bond. J.R.

Driving down to Durbin was a great treat for Natasha as she had not been there since she was seven when a number of the boys and girls from the orphanage were taken to the beach where they spent an afternoon swimming and playing games. "And being entertained," she said, her large brown eyes wide with the wonder of it. "I remember there were Zulu dancers at the pier. "They did a hunting dance to show they were brave. And they used sticks instead of spears so no one get hurt.

"They also did the umBhekozo dance. It shows how the tides come in. The men dancers moved back and forth and back again to show the moving tides. I was a little afraid. But, when they came forward, it was all right." She giggled. "When they lift their aprons and showed us their buttocks, it was very funny." She laughed and hid her face.

"What do you think it represented, Natasha?"

"The buttocks?"

"Yes."

"Oh," she said, giggling, "maybe it was the big brown whale washed up on the shore."

They both enjoyed a hearty laugh, and J.R. could not have been happier.

The road out of Durbin ran north from the city, winding through the green lushness of the North Coast sugar-belt, and skirting through the kingdom's world-renowned wildlife reserves of Zululand and Matutaland.

From there it led into the gently rolling hills and valleys of Zululand, a landscape rich with the silent memories of the heroic clashes of the Anglo-Zulu War which took place more than one hundred years ago. During the entire ride to the festival grounds, Natasha kept her face pressed against the car window less she miss a single bit of enchanting scenery.

When they reached the festival grounds, they found two seats near the front and quickly perused their programs. J.R. mentioned he had read that it was considered a great honor for the young women, or virgins, as they were suppose to be, to take part in the famous Reed Dance.

Natasha looked up at J.R., and, with a very serious look on her face, said: "If they are not a virgin, the sacred reed will know and it will die."

The sudden sound of drums called everyone to attention. Natasha sat straight up in her seat and gave her full attention to the proceedings. "Look," she said, pointing off. "Look at all the beautiful young women."

There must have been at least one thousand young women, all dressed in long white dresses and carrying a single reed that had been cut from the riverbed, and that symbolized the power that is vested in nature. It is not widely known that the reed is the building material for the typical domed or beehive hut that dots the landscape in many rural areas.

As they moved forward, the young women began to sing a jubilant melody. And, as the stately procession began to wind its way up a hill to the palace, the dancing began. Natasha was on the edge of her seat, enthralled by the graceful movements of the women as they all moved together as if as one.

The King, dressed in royal garb and flanked by his royal regiment, awaited at the gates. He put his hand out as the leader of the group, the chief Princess, knelt down before the King and presented to him a reed to mark the occasion.

As the rhythm of the drums increased, the women performed a joyful dance as a tribute to the King. To begin, many of the young women moved gracefully from side to side using the reed in a gentle, sweeping motion. When the drumming grew louder, the women began whirling round and around holding their reeds high above their heads They danced until they could dance no longer until all the young women, except the Princess, fell to the ground at the King's feet.

Natasha held her breath, and took hold of J.R.'s hand. It was if she were spellbound. He glanced at her, and looked at her hand in his, and he smiled.

To demonstrate his gratitude, the King responded with a sacrifice to the royal ancestors on behalf of all the young women and their communities throughout the kingdom.

The chief Princess, who wore the *inyongo,* the gall bladder of the principle sacrificial animal, which is a symbol of purity, and an important symbol in the Zulu ritual, led the procession from the palace.

While walking to the car, Natasha told J.R. that she had never seen a more exciting dance program. "It was amazing," she said. "I don't know how they all danced together without bumping into each other and falling down. They deserve a prize for that."

"We applauded very long and hard," J.R. said. "Is that not enough?"

She looked at him and smiled. "That is reward enough. I think."

"Where would you like to go from here?" he asked, when they got to the car.

She thought for moment. Then she said: "I think I am hungry, and I think I would like to go to *McDonald's.*"

"Oh?"

"I know where it is, and I think I can find it."

"I hope so," he said, opening the door, "because I don't have a clue."

"Very well," she said, settling into the front seat. "We shall drive to the main boulevard."

After driving around Durbin for twenty minutes, they found a *McDonald's*. Natasha ordered a hamburger with French fries and a large chocolate malt. J.R. ordered a chicken-burger and a cup of decaf.

When the food arrived, they took it and settled into a corner booth. At once Natasha started eating. "I'm . . . what is they say? Staving?"

"That's what they say," J.R. said, putting sugar into his coffee. "You go right ahead. Don't mind me."

He munched on his chicken sandwich as he watched her down the burger and fries in an instant. When it came to the malt, however, she sipped it slowly as if savoring every drop. She looked pensive. Turning to J.R., she asked: "Have you seen my poppa lately?"

When he said he had, she asked how he was, and J.R. told her his health was good. He said they had talked a lot about her, and that he would consent to the adoption. He thought it would be wonderful if she were to go to America and live with a family. "He also said that he loved you very much. And that if things were different, and he were well and strong, he would be your family. However, under the circumstances . . ."

"I love my poppa very much too," she said softly. "But I know . . . I understand . . . it's not possible. And I shall be strong. I shall go on . . ." Her voice trailed off.

"Are you all right?" he asked, putting his hand on hers.

She smiled at him. "I am all right. I am wonderful."

"You're more than wonderful," he said. "I think you're amazingly brave."

After a moment of silence, Natasha asked: "When are we going to . . ." She hesitated, looking at J.R. "I forgot the name. The *B* word."

"You mean Brooklyn?"

"Yes. That is it. Brooklyn. When are we going there?"

"I hope sometime before Christmas."

"Oh yes. I want to be there before Christmas." She thought for a moment. "Do I have any brothers and sisters?"

"You have a brother and a sister."

"What is my brother's name?"

"It's Bobby," J.R. answered. "And he's very famous."

"I will have a famous brother?"

"Yes. Have you heard of the Bobby Children's Computer?"

"Bobby? Children's computer? The computers that come in pink for girls and blue for boys?"

"That's right. You met him when I first came to the orphanage. The big, tall, young man? That was Bobby."

"I remember."

"And you will have a sister named Elizabeth."

"I love the name Elizzz-aaa-beth," she said, exaggerating the sounds. "She's the queen of the people. And I shall be the queen of the dance."

"You have a wild imagination, my darling."

"Is that bad?"

"No, that's good—very good."

"Are there lots of boys and girls in Brooklyn?"

"There are thousands," he said. "And many of them belong to the Boys & Girls Club.

"What do they do there?"

"Oh, they do many things. They play games of all kinds, they sing, and they dance . . ."

"They dance?"

"Yes. My lady teaches them ballet."

"Ahhh." She sighed. "Ballet. She shall teach me ballet and I shall be a great dancer. I shall dance all over the world. I shall be famous. That is my dream." She looked at J.R. "Is that too much to ask for?"

"Not at all."

"I shall be the very best I can be."

J.R. marveled at her courage, her determination, her spirit. He wanted to adopt her at that moment more than at any other time. He wanted to have the privilege of loving her and being able to call her *daughter.*

By mid-afternoon they were on the road to Chesterton. As they passed farms and pastures filled with horses and other animals, Natasha called out to the animals, giving each one a name as they passed.

After traveling for half an hour, they neared a horse farm that featured free rides to children. A big sign at the side of the road read: WELCOME, HORSE FARM AND FREE RIDES AHEAD!

Natasha was ecstatic. She begged J.R. to stop and let her ride a horse. She admitted that she had never been on a horse before, and said she would love to have the chance.

After checking his watch, he told her that they could stay for just a while because he needed to get her home before dark.

The wife of the owner of the farm, a pleasant Welsh lady, welcomed them to their farm and suggested that Natasha ride the small roan and not the stallion. She said the smaller horse was gentle and easy to handle. J.R. helped Natasha up into the saddle and instructed her to hold tight to the rein. He slapped the horse gently and she began the walk around the circular track.

"She's a lovely girl, sir," the woman said. "Is she your daughter?"

"She's an orphan," J.R. answered. "But I'm hoping to adopt her. Her name's Natasha. She wants to be a ballet dancer. We just came from the dance festival in Zululand."

"Oh, I'm sure she must've loved that, sir."

On the second turn around the circular track, something unexpected happened. The roan whinnied as if frightened by something. Without warning, she reared up on her hind legs, and bolted forward jumping over the fence.

J.R. heard Natasha scream as the horse took off galloping across the meadow towards the forest beyond. J.R. yelled to Natasha to hold on as he threw himself up on to the stallion and took off after the fleeing roan.

As his horse galloped at top speed across the meadow he knew he must reach Natasha before she entered the forest.

Fortunately, the little horse couldn't match the speed of the stallion, and his horse caught up with the roan a few hundred yards from the forest. When his horse was beside the roan, he yelled to Natasha to pull back on the reins as hard as she could. She did and the roan slowed. The big horse, sensing danger, nudged the smaller house and gradually slowed her to a stop.

J.R. slid off his horse just as Natalia, who was crying and close to hysterics, threw herself at him.

"It's all right, Natasha," he shouted. "You're all right now. I've got you."

As she clung to him, she cried: "Do not let me go! Do not ever let me go!"

He held her in his arms until she stopped shaking. Then he carried her to the car and put her on the back seat. She fell asleep almost at once and slept all the way back home.

When they arrived at the orphanage, he carried her into the lobby and told the caretaker what had happened. "I'd like to return tomorrow morning to check on her, if you don't mind."

"Not at all, sir," was the answer. "I'm sure she'll be glad to see you."

He thanked the gentleman, and left feeling relieved that Natasha was back home and safe.

CHAPTER 27

The following morning, J.R. got up at eight, showered and dressed and arrived at the orphanage just at nine.

He was escorted into the guests' waiting room where he sat and waited for Natasha to appear. At exactly nine-fifteen, the door opened and she appeared. When she saw J.R., she hollered his name and ran to his waiting arms. He caught her and swung her around. She laughed and kissed him and called him "my hero."

"I'm not a hero," he said. "I did what any poppa would have done."

"You are *my* hero," she said, sitting on his lap. "I don't care what other poppas would have done. You saved my life."

"But I'm not a real hero."

"If you are not now," she said, touching his cheek, "you will be someday."

Smiling, he said: "Maybe. Someday."

"What's that?" she asked, jumping up.

"That's my cell phone."

"It's a funny sound."

He took it out of his pocket and said: "Hello."

"Who is it?" she asked.

"It's Bobby," he replied. "Hello Bobby . . . I'm at the orphanage with Natasha . . . I will . . . What? . . . Yes, of course. I'm on my way." He turned to Natasha and told her that Bobby wanted to see him right away."

"I hope nothing is wrong," she said.

"I'll come back as soon as I can," he said. He kissed her on the cheek and left the room.

He was worried. He didn't like the sound of Bobby's voice. Gearing up the little rental car, he made a U-turn in the middle of the street and drove as fast as he could back to the hotel. He entered the lobby and looked around but he didn't his son.

"Dad."

Bobby's voice turned him around. "What's the matter, Bobby?" he asked. "What's happened?"

"There's been an accident," he said, turning. "Follow me to the café. I need some coffee."

"What's happened, Bobby?" J.R. asked, trying to keep pace with his son.

When they reached the café, Bobby sat in the nearest booth, ordered two coffees from the waitress, and waited until she left before speaking. Looking at his father, he took a deep breath, and said: "Martin's mobile went off a mountain road and smashed into a boulder about thirty feet down. Hugo was killed instantly."

"Oh, my God." J.R. cried, slumping down in the booth.

"Martin said he was all right and that he sustained only minor injuries. Doctor Landry was shaken up and only sprained an arm. Doctor Miles was less fortunate. He wasn't wearing a seat belt. He was thrown forward and hit his head hard on the metal dash. He's conscious but in a lot of pain."

"Where are they?"

"They're in a small hospital in Upton, a city just miles from Bloemfontein, a large city of approximately 600,000 people. Martin has called the airport in Bloemfontein and we can get a plane out of Pietermaritzburg in one hour. He also said that the hospital would send someone to meet the plane. Do you want to go with me?"

"Yes, of course," J.R. said, sipping his coffee. "I'm ready right now."

J.R. and Bobby took off from the Pietermaritzburg Airport around eleven and landed in Bloemfontein an hour later. They were met at the airport by a representative and driven the ten miles to the Upton Hospital where they were greeted by Martin and the hospital head surgeon, Doctor Roger Dunkirk, a gray-haired, fifty-something gentleman. Smiling broadly, he welcomed them to the hospital and shook their hands.

As they walked the hallways, he briefed them on the condition of Doctor Landry, who, he said, suffered minor injuries and could leave the hospital in a few days.

"Where is her room, doctor?" Bobby asked. "I'd like to see her."

"She's in room forty," he answered, pointing. "Just half way down the hall on the right-hand side."

Bobby thanked him, told J.R. that he'd see him later, and turned to Martin. Putting his arm around his shoulder, Bobby said that they needed to talk about Hugo.

As they walked slowly down the hall, Bobby and Martin made plans for shipping Hugo's body back to Cape Town to his wife and five children.

"In addition," Bobby said, "I want you to contact his wife—Hildy, I think her name is—and explain that I will personally come to Cape Town to supervise the burial of her husband, and, this is very important, remind her that Hugo was heavily insured. And, as soon as the papers are approved and signed, and all that formal stuff are taken care of, she'll get a check for almost two hundred thousand dollars. That should give her a sense of relief and security.

"When should I call her?" Martin wanted to know.

"Call her tomorrow," Bobby answered. "When you're ready to fly to Chesterton, let me know, and I'll make arrangements for you to spend a week's vacation in Durban. You deserve it."

When J.R. and Dunkirk reached Doctor Miles' room, the doctor stopped at the door and turned to his guest. "He's resting comfortably now," he said, "and I don't think we should disturb him right now."

"What's wrong with him, doctor?" J.R. asked.

"He is suffering from something called a basilar skull fracture," he responded.

"Is it serious?"

"Let me put it this way:" he began, "it's a fracture of the bones that form the base, or floor, of the skull, and results from severe blunt head trauma of significant force. A basilar skull fracture commonly connects to the sinus cavities, and this connection may allow fluid or air entry into the inside of the skull and may cause infection. Surgery is usually not necessary; however, other injuries might be involved."

He paused, taking a deep breath. "I've already requested that he be sent to the General Hospital in Bloemfontein for more tests. There's a well-qualified brain surgeon there who's a good friend of mine. I spoke to him early this morning and he has agreed to examine him. He'll be transferred there by ambulance early this afternoon."

"I think you did the right thing, doctor," J.R. said, smiling.

"Well, as I said," he began, "it may be nothing, but then it may be something. Better safe than sorry? No?"

"Thank you, doctor," J.R. said, shaking his hand.

"Please stop by my office before you leave."

"We will, doctor."

When Doctor Dunkirk turned and walked away, J.R. hurried down the hall in the direction of Landry's room.

Reaching Room forty, he slowly opened the door and looked in. Seeing that Sarah Landry was asleep, J.R. closed the door and continued down the hall.

Turning to the right at the end of the hall he found himself in a large waiting room area. He felt thirsty.

As he started to walk to a water fountain for a drink, he noticed that Bobby, just a few feet away, talking to a young doctor. They appeared to be having a robust conversation.

Just as J.R. was about to lean in to take a sip of water, he heard the doctor say: "My name is Van Brunt, Erik Van Brunt."

J.R. swung around. "Van Brunt? Did you say Van Brunt?"

"Yes, sir."

"Is your father Peter Van Brunt?"

The young doctor looked at Bobby, then back to J.R. "Why, yes," he acknowledged. "He's my father."

J.R. glanced at Bobby, then focused in on the young Van Brunt. "You're his son, all right." He couldn't believe the likeness: *I could be looking at the young Peter Van Brunt,* he thought. *The curly blonde hair, the large brown eyes, the long straight nose, and the strong jaw line. He's the image of his father. It's like a reincarnation of the fallen man.*

Bobby said something but J.R. didn't understand. "What?" he asked, still looking at Erik. "I said that Dr. Van Brunt, who just happens to be a pediatric physician, wants to join our team."

"What?"

"You heard me, dad."

"Sorry," J.R. said, shaking his head as if to clear it. "Are you sure?"

"I am very sure, sir," Erik said. "I love what you're doing and I want to be part of it."

"It's up to you, Bobby."

"I'm all for it," Bobby said.

"Don't you have a contract here at the hospital?" J.R. asked.

"No," Van Brunt said, "I'm a free-lancer."

"Can you leave tonight?" J.R. asked.

"I can leave any time I want."

J.R. looked at Bobby. Bobby nodded his approval.

J.R. smiled at Van Brunt, held out his hand to him, and said: "Welcome to the team, doctor."

They shook on it.

CHAPTER 28

O n the plane trip back to Pietermaritzburg, J.R. and Bobby brought Dr. Van Brunt up-to-date on the team's journey.

He was impressed by the scope of their success and voiced his eagerness to become a member of the team and promised to work hard and to dedicate himself completely to their mission.

Finally, when there was a lull in the conversation, Erik asked simply: "How is my father?"

J.R. knew that he would have to tell the young doctor everything. After saying that his father was well, he explained that that was because he was taking drugs . . . that were keeping him from dying . . . from AIDS . . .

Erik's stared wide-eyed at J.R. "AIDS? How can that be?"

When J.R. told him that his father had had a brief affair with a Zulu woman, Erik lowered his head and covered his faced with both hands. After a moment, he began to cry.

J.R. motioned to Bobby and they both got up and moved to another compartment.

When Erik rejoined them his eyes were red and swollen, but he smiled, said he was "okay now" and, sitting opposite J.R., asked him to tell him more.

J.R. told him that something wonderful and good came from that union. "A girl was born to them," J.R. said. "A beautiful colored girl with large brown eyes, like yours. Her name is Natasha Van Brunt and she is now ten years old. She is smart and she is talented. And I want to adopt her."

"You want to adopt her?" Erik asked. "Doesn't she live with my father?"

With a careful use of words, J.R. explained that his father was not physically able to take care of his daughter due to his illness; however, he said, his father has supported her financially all these years and has seen to it that all her needs were met.

Breathing deeply, Erik said: "Yes, I'm sure my father did everything he could to make her happy." He paused. "I was almost fifteen when I left the castle with my mother and brother and returned to Holland. I didn't know it then, but I know now that my father was a philanderer." Then, as an after thought, he said: "Is that the right word?"

J.R. nodded.

They talked some more about Natasha and her adoption. J.R. explained that that was why he had met with his father and that Peter Van Brunt had approved of it. He felt that she would be happy living in America with two people who would care for her and love her.

Erik said only that: "I look forward to meeting my half-sister."

After arriving back at the hotel and getting Dr. Van Brunt signed into a suite of rooms, Bobby and J.R. agreed that the three vacationing team members, who had returned from their Durban vacation, needed to be told about the crash of the mobile before they all met for dinner that evening.

Bobby called each one in turn and asked that they come to his suite immediately. Elizabeth swept in, looking happy and healthy and deeply sun-tanned. She greeted her brother and father with enthusiastic *hellos* and lots of hugs and kisses. Doctors Gruber and Doherty followed close behind jabbering and jesting and looking rested. The mood was festive.

But, after Bobby broke the sad news to the unsuspecting trio, the mood swiftly changed; they were silent. Elizabeth took a handkerchief from her shoulder bag and dabbed at her tearing eyes.

They were sorry to hear about Hugo and voiced concern about his wife and family and were comforted by the fact that Bobby would oversee the burial and that she would receive a handsome sum of money.

Dr. Gruber voiced additional concern about his friend, Dr. Miles. He agreed to go to Bloemfontein if Bobby thought it was necessary. Bobby and J.R. assured him that his friend was all right and that the injury was not serious. There were no complications and the doctors have assured them that Miles will have a full recovery.

"When will they be rejoining us?" Dr. Gruber wanted to know.

Bobby explained that both doctors requested a release from their contracts. "Both want to return to America as soon as possible," he said.

After the trio left Bobby's suite, he and J.R. came to the same conclusion; namely, that, although a team meeting was called for that evening, Bobby was concerned that the doctors would probably want to celebrate their loss rather than mourn it. And that, of course, would be completely inappropriate for the quiet and elegant hotel dining room.

Certainly they would not want to disturb anyone. So, Bobby contacted the hotel management and arranged to have dinner served in a private conference room where he and his team could enjoy their food while making as much noise as was necessary or allowed. It was a Friday in October. The following Monday the team would be back at work.

When Elizabeth, and doctors Gruber and Doherty, entered the conference room J.R. was surprised to see that their collective demeanors were upbeat and positive. Elizabeth looked stunning in a short, lime green chiffon dress that complemented her long dark hair and showed off her sun-tanned and shapely legs.

Everyone stood up and applauded—that is, everyone except Erik Van Brunt. He was busy nursing a scotch and soda.

While Bobby and J.R. left the table to greet the doctors, Elizabeth approached the table, and, with hands on hips and attitude in her voice, said: "Where I come from, a gentleman stands when a lady enters the room."

Dr. Van Brunt looked up, blinked, and quickly got to his feet. "I'm terribly sorry," he said, "I was off somewhere."

"I'm Elizabeth Stoford, J.R.'s daughter," she said sweetly, extending her hand. Without a word, he took it in his, and, leaning forward, kissed it. *Oh my, he is a gentleman—and tall too,* she thought. "Thank you," she said.

"It's my pleasure, Elizabeth," he said, smiling.

"You must be Dr. Van Brunt," she said, sitting opposite him.

"Please, call me Erik," he said.

"Erik."

"And you may call me Liz."

"I prefer to call you Elizabeth, because it's as beautiful as you are."

After dinner, Elizabeth went to the hotel's casino to spend a few dollars in the penny machines and sit at the bar and sip a dry martini, with an olive, of course, and think. She thought about her children and how much she missed them. She thought about her husband, Mark, and she frowned. She had received a call from her sister-in-law informing her that Mark had fallen off the wagon again and that the children were staying with her and her husband until he could get his act together.

She caught her reflection in the bar mirror. She looked hard at it and mused: *Well, damn you, Mark, I don't care what you think; that face I see there is not bad for an old dame who's pushing forty.*

"I think it's a beautiful face, don't you think?" Erik asked, laying his scotch and soda on the bar.

She heard his voice and saw his image in the mirror so close to hers. She swung around and patted the chair next to hers. "Park it there, mister."

"Well?" he asked, sitting down, "don't you think it's a beautiful face?"

"If you really want to know, I was just thinking that it's not bad . . . for an old dame who's pushing . . ." She hesitated. "Forty." *There I've said it,* she thought. *He might as well know the bitter truth right from the start.*

"I would never have guessed it."

"What would you have guess?" she asked, taking a sip of her martini.

"Somewhere around twenty-nine, thirty . . ."

She looked at him. *Liar,* she thought. "Oh, you are a charmer, doctor . . ."

"Erik."

"Erik," she said, "don't you know that I'm an old married woman with two children and a husband?"

"I've been told."

"And . . . ?"

"I'm happy for you."

How diplomatic he is.

"I might even be a little jealous."

"You've never been married? A handsome young man like you?"

"You think I'm handsome?" he asked staring into her eyes.

"I asked you a question."

"They're the most beautiful shade of blue."

"What?"

"Your eyes."

"You're avoiding the question."

He sighed and faced the bar. Taking a drink of his scotch, he turned to face her. "I tried it once when I was young and foolish," he replied.

"I assume it didn't work."

He shook his head. "I met her when I was about thirty just starting my practice in Amsterdam. She was a beautiful blonde with long shapely legs—much like yours. I fell for the package but chose to ignore the contents.

"After about two years of fighting and arguments about all the money she was spending, we parted and soon divorced. She married an older man who was happy to buy the package and everything that went with it."

"So now you're sour on marriage?"

He thought a moment: "No, someday I'll marry again."

"What will you do in the meantime?" she asked. "You're not getting any younger, you know."

"Oh, I have plans," he replied. "I actually returned to South Africa to spend some time with my father. He's getting up in years, and . . . J.R. told me that he looks well, but is physically very fragile. He glanced at her and, then turned his face away. "I remember a tall, healthy-looking man, proud and strong and full of life." He sipped his drink and inhaled. "I was only fifteen when my mother took me and my brother out of South Africa and back to Holland. That was unfortunate because it was at a time when my father and I were just beginning to build a bond between us.

"I had great respect for him and I missed him all those years I was gone. I'm hoping to renew our friendship. It's time now for me to step up and discharge my filial duty."

"That sounds noble, Erik," Elizabeth said, "but won't that interfere with your private life?"

"It needn't interfere," he responded, staring into his glass of scotch. Tilting his head he looked at Elizabeth and smiled. "I have a vision; would you like to hear it?"

"I would love to hear it."

He told the story of the Van Brunt family home in Durban that, to that very day, still sits on a high bluff overlooking the ocean. He and his brother were born there and it's where they lived until he was ten years old when his father moved them to Petersford Castle.

They had been happy living in the old Colonial with it columns and wrap-around front porch where he had played with his brother and where his father made them laugh while he chased them around the property.

Life changed almost from the moment they walked through the doors of the old castle. His father spent more and more time at the mine while his mother roamed the halls of the great manse crying tears of sadness and regret.

"I want father to sell the castle and live with me again in the old colonial on the bluff. I want to bring my bride there and I want my children to grow up there and to enjoy it as I once had. I want my father to find peace and happiness again. It's time, and he deserves it."

Elizabeth sighed, smiling to herself. Quietly, she said: "I think your vision is lovely, Erik, but you left out one person: your sister Natasha."

"Of course she is welcome to come," he said, looking at her. "I want her to be part of the family."

"You know my father wants to adopt her."

"I know," he said. "He told me, and I'm sure he'll be disappointed, but . . ."

"But he'll understand?" she asked. "Is that what you're saying?"

"Yes. No." he shook his head. "I don't know what I'm saying. Your father is a good man and I'm sure he'd be a good father to Natasha. But she's my sister whether I like it or not. He'll get over it."

"I'm not so sure," she said. "I think he might be deeply hurt."

Erik took a deep breath, picked up his glass and held it high and made a toast: "Well. Here's to you and me, Elizabeth, and to the entire Bobby team. I'm proud to be a part of it, and I drink to our success and to the complete elimination of one of the most vile pandemics that ever faced mankind."

They drank.

Silently, she rose from her chair, kissed him on the cheek, and said: "I'll see you in the morning at the mobile."

"At eight?" he asked.

"Exactly," she said, smiling. "Do not be late."

"I promise," he said, kissing her hand.

"You are a charmer," she said, running a hand through his blonde hair. "If I were younger . . . Well, let's just leave it at that. Good night." She turned and walked away.

He looked after her and smiled. *If you were younger,* he thought. *What? You would love me? Oh, Elizabeth, you are perfect just the way you are. If only I would dare . . .*

CHAPTER 29

As the days passed, it became clear to Elizabeth that she was becoming more and more attracted to the young doctor.

Words between them were limited to their positions as medical professionals; however, the unspoken words were compelling.

They worked together in the mobile in small quarters known as "The Examination Room" making it almost impossible not to feel or to sense the other's presence: their warmth, their scent, their touch. Every time he came near to her or touched her, by accident or not, she felt a wave of emotion, a tingling sensation that swept through her entire body.

By Friday, Elizabeth, usually tired and ready to rest from a grueling week's work, was energized and eager to tell Dr. Erik, as he came to be called by the other doctors, nurses and lay people, how she felt about him.

It was almost five o'clock when Elizabeth and Erik saw their last patient. While he left to wash his face, she quickly brushed her hair, applied a little lipstick, and sprayed her mouth with a breath freshener.

When she heard him coming, she stood poised in the doorway. As soon as he appeared, she put her arms around his neck and kissed him. He groaned and pulled her close to him.

"My darling, my darling," he whispered.

"Take me to Durban," she said in his ear.

"Tonight?" he asked.

"Yes, tonight," she answered. "Right now. I want you to make love to me in your house in Durban."

He held her at arm's length: "Are you sure?"

"I'm positive."

He smiled.

There was a sound. "Someone's coming," he said.

"Let's go," she said, taking his hand and leading him to the front of the mobile.

J.R. appeared at the door of the mobile. He looked surprised when he saw them. "I thought the mobile was empty," he said, as he stepped inside.

"Hi, dad," she said. "We're just leaving."

"See you guys at dinner?" he asked.

"Nope," she replied. "We're off to Durban. See you on Sunday. 'Bye."

J.R. watched as they ran off like two children just let out of school. He thought for a moment. Then it occurred to him, and he said aloud: "Oh, my God."

The sun was slowly slipping away as the little gray rental car descended the last hill into a darkening Durban.

Here and there lights dotted the landscape. In a state of silent awe, Liz watched as the sun lowered its orange head below the horizon and spread its vibrant colors across the silver surface of the Indian Ocean.

Immersed in the splendor of the scene, she snuggled close to Erik and leaned her head against his shoulder. At the third stop light, Erik turned the little gray car to the left onto King's Road. Two miles down the road he turned left, drove two blocks and turned right. Halfway down the street Erik turned the car left into a tree-lined driveway and pulled around a curve where a white colonial loomed large and imposing on a hill.

Without a word, Elizabeth jumped out of the car, and ran up the curved stone steps to the wooden porch. Turning, she looked out across the Indian Ocean and watched as wisps of deep reds and dense purples swept gently across the horizon.

"Oh, Erik," she cried. "Now I understand why you love this place. It's enchanting!"

"Not half as enchanting as you are at this moment."

"You're so sweet," she said, stroking his cheek.

Smiling, he turned and said: "Come on. Let's go in." Tip-toeing, he reached up with his hand and ran it along the top of the door. "There's a key here somewhere . . . here it is."

Holding the key up, he then put it in the lock and opened the door. She followed him into the large hall and looked around.

"Leave the door open," he said. "It's a bit musty in here."

Turning, she walked into the living room. "Erik, there's no furniture in here."

"Oh, yes, I forgot," he said. "They took most of it up to the castle."

"Well," she began, "where are we going to . . . you know . . ."

He cocked his head and looked at her. "It's all right, darling," he said. "I'm sure there's a big bed upstairs. And I promise you; I will not tell your mother."

"Oh, go on, you big silly," she said, slapping him on the arm. "Find some candles so we can see our way."

"I'll be right back."

He turned and disappeared down a darkened hallway.

When he was gone Elizabeth stepped out on the porch. Leaning against the door jamb, she ran a hand through her hair, and, as the sun continued to sink beneath the waves, Liz said to herself: "Oh parting sun, do you symbolize the end of an old day or the beginning of a new one? Or both?"

Late Friday night Elizabeth and Erik left the old colonial on the hill and signed in at a motel near the center of the city and within walking distance of the beach.

On Saturday, they saw little of the city and the beach until that night when they dressed and drove to a local night club where they enjoyed a delicious seafood dinner and danced till almost midnight to the soulful sounds of a popular local band.

They spent all day Sunday on the beach where they soaked up some rays, took long walks, and allowed themselves to be talked into playing volley ball with a group of young enthusiasts. Their game skills were seriously challenged and, although they said they had a good time, they thanked their disappointed team members, picked up their towels, and left after their first defeat.

Walking up the beach in the direction of the parking lot, Elizabeth saw a little wooden shack about a third of a mile up the beach. When she asked Erik about it, he explained that it was one of many shacks like it that lifeguards use to store equipment.

She looked at Erik. "Let's go," she said.

"It's just a shack, Elizabeth," he said. "Besides, it's not legal."

"Oh, come on," she urged. "It might be fun."

He didn't respond.

She looked at him. "You're up to it, aren't you?"

"Of course I'm up to it."

"Then, come on," she said. "Let's go."

They ran all the way to the shack. When they got there Erik was out of breath; he leaned against the side of the building.'

"Are you all right?" she asked, looking concerned.

"I'm okay," he said, breathing deeply. "Is it open?"

She tried the door and it opened. "Go on in," she said. "There's plenty of room in here."

Stepping inside, he let his bathing suit drop to the floor. When Elizabeth entered he took her in his arms and kissed her. Putting her arms around his neck she pressed her body against his. He reached behind her and released the clasp on her bra and gently pulled it loose until it fell to the floor. She felt the warmth of his hand on her breast, and, as his hot lips caressed her nipples they hardened, and she felt a growing feeling of pleasure spread through her body.

Gently, he maneuvered her down to the sandy floor so that she was on top of him. Feeling his hardness between her legs, she pulled herself back on her knees and was about to go down on him, when there was a loud noise at the door.

Before they could react, the door flew open and a lifeguard the size of a giant stood high above them. His eyes were afire and his voice thundered in their ears. "WHAT THE HELL? YOU CAN'T DO THAT IN HERE. IT'S AGAINST THE LAW. I'M CALLING THE POLICE." He slammed the door and was gone.

As they scrambled to get their things together they could hear the shrill sound of the lifeguard's whistle as he ran down the beach.

While Erik climbed into his bathing suit, Elizabeth grappled with her bra strap but couldn't fasten it. She started to giggle. "This reminds of the time mother caught me in my bedroom with Jerry. I was thirteen. He was trying to get my bra off."

"Here, give me that," Erik said, fastening it. "Wrap this towel around you. You were only thirteen?"

She smiled. "I was an early bloomer."

He laughed. "Come on. Let's get the hell out of here.

When they left the shack, they looked for the lifeguard; they could see him running along the southern edge of the beach.

"This way," Erik shouted. He started running up the beach in the opposite direction. "Fortunately, the car's not far from here." She followed close behind as they ran north to steps that led up to the boardwalk and the parking lot.

Running, Elizabeth glanced back over her shoulder. "I can see some men gathering at the far end."

"Any police?"

"I don't know, but it looks like they're pointing at something."

"At us?"

"I think so."

"Come on, Elizabeth, up these stairs." She followed close behind as they reached the parking lot.

When they got to the car, Elizabeth looked back. "Hurry, Erik, I think they're coming this way."

"Damn!" he yelled. "I dropped the key; it went under the car."

"They're coming!" she cried. "Hurry."

"All right," he said. "The car's open."

By the time Liz got into the car and closed the door, Erik had started the engine and was backing out.

Meanwhile, Elizabeth kept an eye on the far end of the parking lot. There was commotion, but no sign of a police car.

The car lurched forward as rubber burned the pavement. Erik braked the car at the exit, but didn't stop. Seeing that all was clear, he shoved the gear into high and sped up the highway.

In the rearview mirror he saw red lights flashing behind them. Liz turned to get a better look. "I can't tell if it's a police car or not."

"I'm not taking any chances," Erik said. "I'm turning off at the next turn, so brace yourself."

Sirens blasted in their ears as the vehicle gained on them. "Hold on," he yelled, as the car swerved left into on-coming traffic. Elizabeth screamed as a large pickup truck blasted its horn at them; seconds later it swerved left to avoid hitting them.

"You can relax, Elizabeth," Erik said, looking in the rearview mirror. "It wasn't a police car; it was an ambulance."

With a nervous laugh, she said: "For a second there I don't think it would've mattered."

At the motel, Erik dropped Elizabeth off at their cabin and parked the car at the rear of the building so it couldn't be seen from the street.

They lay on the queen size bed looking up at the ceiling, silent and listening. "I feel like a criminal," Elizabeth said, "wondering if and when the police will come and get me."

"Don't worry about it, baby," Erik said in a husky voice. "I won't let the police getcha."

She laughed.

"I'm sorry, Erik," she said.

"What for?"

"For insisting we go to the shack."

"It's okay."

"It was fun though."

"Want to continue?"

She looked over at him and smiled. "Oh, I don't think so," she said. "I'm tired, and besides, my heart is still pounding."

"We better stay until it gets dark."

She looked at her watch. "We're looking at about two hours."

"I've got to pee," he said, getting up from the bed.

"I'll be here."

He went into the small bathroom and closed the door.

A moment later, Elizabeth's cell phone rang. She got up and crossed to the dresser, picked up the phone, and pressed *talk.*

"Hello?" She listened. "Mark? Is that you? . . . Yes I'm here. Actually I'm in Durban . . . Could you hold on a moment? Thanks . . ." She went out on the porch and shut the door behind her.

When Erik came out of the bathroom, he looked around for Elizabeth. Seeing her outside on her cell phone, he wondered who she was talking to. He decided not to disturb her but he was curious just the same. Crossing to the front door, he opened it as quietly as he could. He listened and heard her mention her husband's name; she sounded upset about something. Not wanting to hear any more, he stepped away from the door. Within minutes she came into the room, and, without a word, went directly to the bathroom and closed the door. She was crying.

The little gray car headed up the road in the direction of Chesterton. The two occupants were silent, staring straight ahead at the open road.

Finally, Elizabeth said: "I suppose you were wondering why I was crying."

"I think I know."

"You think you know?" she asked, frowning. "What do you think you know?"

"Well, I saw you on the porch talking to someone on your phone and when I opened the front door I heard you mention your husband's name and then you reacted to something he said, and . . ."

"And what?"

"And a minute or two later you came in and you were crying and then you locked yourself in the bathroom. I know that things aren't good between you and your husband, and I thought that he had called to tell you that he wanted a divorce."

"You made that assumption?"

"I'm sorry."

"You should be," she said, glaring at him. "You had no right . . . How dare you listen to my conversation."

"I said I was sorry."

Liz was furious, fuming. "Stop the car," she yelled. "I want to get out."

"What's wrong with you?" he asked, looking mystified.

"There's nothing wrong with me," she snapped. "I just want out of this car."

"Okay, okay," he said, agitated. "There's a rest stop up ahead."

"Pull in there."

Erik pulled into the rest stop and parked the car. Before Elizabeth could get out of the car, he hopped out and started walking briskly toward the rest room.

She yelled after him: "Where're you going?"

"I'll be right back," he barked.

While he was gone, Elizabeth walked to a picnic table within feet of the rest rooms and paced back and forth while keeping an eye out for Erik.

When he appeared, she called him over to the table.

As Erik approached, she stood her ground and asked: "Let's assume, for the sake of argument, that you're right—that he did ask me for a divorce. How would that affect our relationship?"

"I don't know."

"You don't know?" she asked, turning in her seat to face him. She waited for him to say something, but he remained silent. "You're not ready yet, are you, Erik? You're not ready to make a commitment."

"I'm sorry, Elizabeth," he said, sitting on the edge of the table.

She looked at him for a moment, then, sitting on a bench, she said sadly: "Yes, so am I."

"What are you thinking?" he asked after a while.

Without looking at him, she said: "I was thinking that you're so like a child. In a way you're very much like my husband. Perhaps that's why I liked you so much."

"He must be very special."

"I think so," she said, looking at him. "As a matter of fact, that's one of the reasons I'm going back to him."

"You're going back to him?" he asked. "But I thought you said . . ."

"I know what I said," she responded. "But it's not true. The truth is those tears you saw me shed were tears of joy. He said he wanted me back and that he wanted a second chance. He said he missed me beyond imagining."

"You were testing me."

"Something like that," she said. "I wanted to be sure."

"Please don't hold it against me."

"I don't." She got up and sat next to him. "Well, young man" she began, "what will you do now? Live with your father in the big castle?"

"Yes, I suppose. We have a lot of catching up to do."

"And your sister, Natasha. What will happen to her? Will you take care of her?" When he didn't answer, she looked at him. "Erik?" she questioned. "Are you all right?"

Without looking at her, he said with a hint of sadness in his voice: "Oh, Elizabeth, all I know is how to be pragmatic. I thank God that my mother made me finish school and become a doctor. If she hadn't been there to spur me on I probably would've ended up being a bum or a gigolo.

"I'm not idealistic like you. And you're right; emotionally I'm still a child in many ways. You asked me if I'll take care of my sister." He paused and shook his head. "I have trouble taking care of myself. Remember that little episode before, on the beach, when I ran out of breath? That happens a lot. You see, I have asthma." Sighing, he asked: "How in the world can

I be expected to take care of a ten-year-old girl? I don't even know if I can take care of my father."

Putting her arm through his, she said: "Erik, that's not only insightful, it's very brave." His words had touched her.

"Elizabeth," he began, turning to look at her, "I want your father to adopt Natasha and take her to America. I know she'll be happy there."

Liz was ecstatic. "Oh, Erik, thank you so much. Bless you for that," she said, embracing him. "It will make my father very happy."

A moment and Erik said: "I'm going to miss you so much, Elizabeth. I do love you, you know."

"I know," she said softly.

"Are you ready to leave?" he asked, getting to his feet.

"Yes."

As they started back to the car, she put her arm in his and said: "There's a song that Cole Porter wrote years ago that describes our affair so perfectly. She began to sing: . . . *If we thought a bit about the end of it when we started painting the town, we'd have been aware that our love affair was too hot not to cool down. So, goodbye, dear, and amen, here's hoping we'll meet now and then. It was great fun, but it was just one of those things.*

Tears filled her eyes.

CHAPTER 30

The following week would prove a turning point in the lives of almost everyone concerned with the Bobby team.

J.R. was riding high on the news that he could adopt Natasha after all. He realized, however, that time was of the essence because it could take up to two months for the government to approve the application.

However, Bobby promised his father that he would contact his good friend, Jason Lord, who would use his influence to get the government's approval within just weeks.

The Bobby team played the game against its dreaded opponent, HIV-AIDS, and won big on several fronts: hundreds upon hundreds of women and babies were tested and treated for HIV; hundreds more were diagnosed and treated for opportunistic infections. Many children, who were found to be suffering from malnutrition, were sent to half-way houses where professional care givers would watch over them until they were strong enough to receive proper HIV drug treatment.

J.R., proud of the team's accomplishments, looked forward to Friday night—as did the others—when he could simply relax and enjoy a good meal, a bright conversation, and a drink. All of that would change in a moment.

J.R. looked at his face in the bathroom mirror. Wrinkle lines were beginning to form under his eyes and he noticed that the edges of his mouth were beginning to droop. *Age is definitely beginning to take its toll; I look tired and I feel tired.* He smiled at himself: *You'd better stop looking old, mister, or you're likely to lose your beautiful Lady Kate.*

He heard his cell phone. Grabbing a towel, he left the bathroom and crossed to the desk and picked up the phone.

"Hello," he said, wiping shaving cream off his face. "What? I can't hear you . . . Is that you Peter? Peter Van Brunt? . . . Yes, now I can hear you. It's this damn phone; I'm going to get a new one as soon as I get back to the states . . . A what?" All color drained from his face.

"Oh, no, no, it can't be," he said, trying to catch his breath. Putting a hand to his forehead, he swayed to the side as if he were going to stumble. He literally fell into a chair. "I can't believe it," he cried. "Poor Natasha. My darling littler girl . . . What are we doing? . . . Yes, yes, I understand, Peter . . . Captain Day is coming to see me? . . . All right . . . Yes, I will. I'll call Erik and Bobby right away . . . This is indeed tragic news; it's hard to believe . . . Thank you, Peter. We'll see you soon. Goodbye."

Taking a deep breath, he put the cell phone down and picked up the house phone and called in order Erik and Bobby and asked them both to join him in his room immediately. Both complied.

A moment later there was a knock on his door. He got up and headed to the door. "I'm coming," he said.

When he opened the door, standing there was a tall, rugged-looking black man who greeted J.R. with a serious "I'm Captain Day."

"I'm J.R.," he said, shaking the man's hand. "Come in please."

J.R. followed the man down the hall into the sitting room where he offered him the large easy chair. When he settled in, J.R. asked him if he wanted a drink. "Just water, please," he said.

When J.R. returned with a glass of water, he noticed that Day was staring at him. "Is something wrong, Captain?" he asked, handing him the glass.

"No, no," he said. "I just thought you might be black."

"Black? Oh, because I want to adopt a colored child?

"Yes."

"People nowadays are adopting children from all over the world. And I don't think they care what color or religion they are. Children are children and they all need love and nurturing."

"Well, here's to you, sir," Captain Day said, raising his glass.

There was a knock on the door. "Excuse me," J.R. said as he hurried to the door. When he opened it Erik and Bobby entered and walked into the sitting room. Both pulled up short when they saw Captain Day standing there.

"Erik, Bobby, this gentleman is Captain Day of the Chesterton Police Department."

They exchanged greetings and sat on the large sofa while J.R. took a position in the center of the room.

Looking at Day, J.R. asked if he could tell them the news. Day nodded.

Turning to Erik and Bobby, J.R. said: "There's only one way to tell you and that's straight out. Natasha was kidnapped today. And she's being held for a one million dollar ransom."

The trio, consisting of J.R., Captain Day, and Eric Van Brunt, flew to Peter's castle by police helicopter. Bobby and Martin stayed behind to bring the team up-to-date on developments.

As the trio was led from one room to the next by Peter's man, they were surprised to see large groups of police and a few men who appeared to be government troops. Some were lounging in chairs and sofas reading or just talking amongst themselves; some played cards, while others played billiards.

The next room they entered had been converted into an elaborate communications center. The voices of operators sounded to J.R. like a thousand buzzing bees.

Entering the great dining room, J.R. noticed that a large map of the entire area, including Chesterton, Pietermaritzburg, and Peter's municipality, was hanging on the wall to the left. He figured it had to be at least ten by ten feet.

The trio was met by Peter Van Brunt who introduced them to the principle cast of characters from the Chesterton Police Department who would be responsible for conducting all operations and the successful recovery of the kidnap victim, ten-year-old Natasha Van Brunt.

Peter introduced them first to a serious-looking Indian with intense brown eyes, who sat at the head of the long, rectangular table, as Commander Jabu Danani, head of operations. Danani, who appeared to be about fifty, got to his feet, and standing erect, bowed low to the trio.

Continuing counter-clock wise around the table, Peter introduced Lt. Paul Napier as Danani's assistant. An imposing-looking white man in his mid-forties, he stood about six feet tall with broad shoulders and a pleasant bass/baritone. He greeted the trio with a robust "Welcome gentlemen, to the Command Center."

Peter Van Brunt, Erik, and J.R. sat across from Lt. Napier, while Captain Day took the chair at the end of the table.

Commander Danani rose to his feet and declared his, and his team's commitment, to finding Natasha, stressing strongly, that they would shoot the kidnappers down like dogs, if necessary, in their efforts to bring this most vile crime to a successful conclusion.

Pausing, he took a deep breath, and, addressing Peter, Erik, and J.R., he recalled the tragic events that occurred earlier that day. He explained that a number of children from the orphanage were enjoying an afternoon at a day camp situated in a place called Greenville, a municipality of Chesterton. At around four o'clock when Natasha and a number of children were enjoying a game of soccer, three gunmen with stocking masks over their heads, entered the playground and grabbed Natasha.

One of the men put a gag in her mouth while the other two men carried her back down the road toward the highway while the third man kept the adults at bay with his gun.`

As soon as they were out of sight, several of the supervisors ran out to the highway but unfortunately all they saw was the rear end of what looked like a dark gray or black van making a sharp turn around the corner. They couldn't make out any plate numbers.

That was four o'clock. Around five, he said, this letter was left in the mail box here at the castle. He held up an eight by ten piece of white paper that was inside of a clear plastic sheet. There are no prints, he said, so you can handle it freely. You will notice that the letters were cut from a newspaper and pasted on paper to create the message:

NATASHA HAS BEEN KIDNAPPED. WE DEMAND A PAYMENT OF ONE MILLION US DOLLARS. IF YOU CALL THE POLICE, WE WILL KILL HER! WAIT FOR A CALL!

J.R. rose from his chair and asked: "May I make an observation here?"

"Of course, Mr. Cronyn," Danani answered, nodding.

"Please, call me J.R."

"As you wish."

"Gentlemen," J.R. began, "non-profit organizations that deal with children and children's services usually like to notify the local media whenever their children spend time at a day camp; they like the public to know what they're doing. It's stimulates contributions. But, gentlemen, I read most of the local papers yesterday and this morning, but I didn't see a single mention of today's outing for the children from the orphanage. So, I have to ask you, if I didn't know about it, and the general pubic didn't know about it, how in hell did three masked gunmen know about it?" He looked around the room waiting for an answer.

Finally, Lt. Napier spoke up: "I talked to Mr. Chase, the director, this afternoon as soon as we got the news of the kidnapping. He was surprised and shocked when I told him."

"And?" J.R. asked.

"He said he would cooperate with the police in every way he could."

"That's all?"

"Yes."

"But, sir," J.R. began, "with all due respect, we could be looking at complicity here. Chase might be an accomplice to a crime."

"Oh, I doubt that, sir," Napier said, shaking his head.

J.R. took a deep breath, and, leaning forward, he said: "If he's not, then we could be looking at a disgruntled employee who had access to Natasha's records. They'd know that her father was Peter Van Brunt and that he would have no trouble paying a ransom of one million US dollars."

Napier got to his feet and turned to his boss. "Should I call Mr. Chase now, sir?"

Before Danani could answer, J.R. spoke up: "I have his cell phone number if you need it."

Without glancing in J.R. direction, Napier snapped. "I have it."

Looking coldly at J.R., Danani said: "Make the call lieutenant."

J.R. sat back in his chair, and, putting his hand over his mouth, whispered to Erik: "Oh my God."

CHAPTER 31

Day/Time: Saturday, 7:00 a.m.

The carefully camouflaged police helicopter lifted off the castle pad and headed southeast, its destination: the Chesterton Orphanage to visit Mr. Chase.

Captain Day and his assistant, a Mr. Chang, sat up front while J.R. and Erik sat together at the rear.

J.R. was concerned that perhaps he spoke too frankly the night before, and he wondered what the young man sitting next to him thought about it. Turning to Erik, he asked: "Do you think I spoke out of turn last night, Erik, and do you think I exposed myself to retaliation?"

Erik thought about his answer for a moment. "Well, J.R.," he began, "I'll tell you what I think. I think what you exposed was incompetence."

"Incompetence?"

"Yes," he said. "Now, having said that, if it will make you feel any better, you might consider apologizing for speaking out of turn, as you suggest, as well as for cementing good public relations. After all, they are the police and we need them to stop these evil people and rescue my sister before they kill her."

J.R. caught his breath. "What?" he asked. "Before they kill her?"

Erik turned, looking straight at J.R. "Why are we going to the orphanage?"

"To see if one of the kidnappers was a disgruntled employee at the orphanage and . . ." He hesitated for a moment, realizing what Erik was suggesting. He looked away.

"It's just something we have to face," Erik said. "And the sad fact is, if she knows just one of her abductors, and whether they get the money or not, they will kill her."

Down below, J.R. could make out the outline of the Chesterton Orphanage. As the helicopter circled he saw the garden where he and Natasha strolled.

He saw her sweet round face; he saw her large brown eyes that sparkled when she smiled. He heard the warm, sweet sounds of her voice as she spoke. He wondered at the elegance of her dance movements and the natural strength she possessed as she swirled and leapt so gracefully about the stage. He saw her . . . and she was there . . . waving at him.

She will always be there. I'll make certain of that . . .

J.R., Erik, and Mr. Chang, who passed himself off as Van Brunt's attorney, waited in the orphanage's conference room while Mr. Chase completed his research regarding present and previous employees.

Meanwhile, the three men talked amongst themselves while they enjoyed coffee and donuts.

After about fifteen minutes the door opened and Chase entered followed by his secretary. They brought with them folders containing employee information and records and photographs. His secretary smiled sweetly at J.R. and sat opposite him.

Even before he spoke, Mr. Chase opened a folder, removed a single piece of paper and put it down on the table for the three men to see. It was a photograph of a white man.

"The man's name is Werner Menken," Chase said, sitting.

Mr. Chang picked it up and stared at it. "Why does he look familiar?"

Before answering, Chase opened a folder in front of him, and, referring to a piece of paper, said: "According to his application he was arrested once for an assault . . ."

"Oh, really?" J.R. asked, raising his eyebrows.

"In the mid-nineties, when he was thirty-eight, he was arrested for an assault on a black man. He served three years in prison."

Chang wanted to know if he'd ever been a member of the Afrikaans Resistance Movement?

"He claims never to have been a member of that movement," Chase said. "He was forty-three when he came to work for us as a handyman. We talked about his arrest and at that time he swore to me that the black man had attacked him first and that he had fought for his life.

"I made it clear to him that he would have to work part time for at least six months, after which, his attendance and work ethics would be reviewed by our board. They approved him for full-time employment, and he was hired. He was forty-three at the time."

"Where is he now?" Chang asked.

"We don't know."

"You don't know?"

"He called last Monday morning and said he wasn't coming in because he felt ill. We haven't seen or heard from him since. Yesterday morning, I had my secretary call his home. There was a disconnect message on the phone."

"You have no other number for him?" Erik questioned.

"No, sir," Chase replied, "we have no other number."

J.R. leaned in. "Mr. Chase, did you advertise yesterday's day trip to Greensville?"

"No, J.R., we did not."

While Captain Day, Erik, and Mr. Chang went off to find Werner Krug, J.R. did some shopping downtown Chesterton after which he had lunch with Bobby and Elizabeth and brought them up-to-date regarding operations at the castle.

J.R. joined Captain Day, Mr. Chang, and Erik at the police station and the four took off for the castle around one o'clock.

When the quartet got back to the castle they learned that one of the kidnappers had called just minutes earlier and had told Peter to stay close to the phone because he would be hearing from him again sometime within the next hour. Before Peter could speak, the caller had hung up.

While they waited for the call, Captain Day reported about their meeting at the orphanage with Chase and an absentee employee named Werner Menken.

Chase had given him a photograph of Menken and his home address. Then Day and Erik drove directly to what turned out to be a two-bedroom, furnished apartment on the outskirts of northern Pietermaritzburg.

The manager of the building told them that Mr. Menken had not lived there for two weeks. He gave his thirty-day notice and moved out without leaving a forwarding address; the manger said he had no idea where Menken went.

However, he mentioned that Menken was met by his cousin, Rolph—he didn't know his last name—but he was a man about forty-three and was often seen with Menken. They seemed very close, the manager said.

After Captain Day, Mr. Wang and Erik entered Menken's vacant apartment, they searched for anything that might shed some light on the kidnapping. They almost came up empty handed when Erik noticed a piece of paper in a trash can near the front door.

It was a flier promoting a parade to be held in June 2004 in Ventersdorp. Day decided to take it back to the castle.

When the Commander heard the words *"parade in Ventersdorp,"* he stood up and asked to see the flyer. He took it from Erik and walked a few steps away from the table, reading the printed words aloud to himself. When he had finished, he shook his head and turned around. There was a strange look on his face; his eyes shone with sinister awareness, and a little smirk settled in around the corner of his mouth. "I know these *sonsofbitches*," he snorted.

His eyes took in every man who sat at the conference table, including Peter. "How many of you know who Eugene Terre'Blanche is?"

The three police representatives raised their hands.

When he spoke he focused his attention to J.R., Erik and Peter. "For your information, gentlemen, Terre'Blanche is a man in his sixties, who has been a member of the Afrikaans Resistance Movement from the beginning. He is known for his paramilitary-style parades; he is a violent, hateful man, who cannot accept the fact that the country has moved on. And it is my opinion, on the face of it, that this Werner Menken and his cousin are not only two of the kidnappers, they are cohorts of Terre'Blanche. Think of it, gentlemen, a million dollars would go a long way in supporting this evil man in his efforts to destroy the fragile foundation of our newly formed government. I cannot even imagine how much blood might be shed if he succeeded in getting his hands on that money. We cannot, we *must* not let that happen." The phone rang.

The room went quiet. No one spoke or moved. The phone rang again.

Peter Van Brunt looked to the Commander for his cue to pick up the phone. The phone rang yet again.

Commander Danani pointed a finger at Peter and he picked it up.

He listened, then: "This is Peter Van Brunt, and yes, I have the money. One million dollars . . . What? . . . Wrap in newspaper? . . . Yes, I understand . . . I'm listening . . . When I leave the castle drive two miles north to Broad Street . . . turn left and go two more miles to the Royal Apartments and park across the street . . . What? . . . I'm repeating everything because I'm writing it down so I don't forget . . . What? . . . Hello?' Peter looked at the Commander and said: "He hung up."

Commander shouted across the room: "Did you get the number, Tony?"

"Sorry Commander," he yelled back, "he hung up too soon."

Danani shrugged and took a deep breath. "Okay, everyone, relax for a moment. He'll call back." As he got to his feet, he said: "Peter, don't bother writing anything down.

"When he calls again just listen to what he has to say. Of course, if you don't understand something, you can ask him to repeat it. That in itself is a good ruse; that is, even if you do understand what he's saying, you can stall by asking him to repeat what he was saying. However, if you ask him to repeat himself too many times, he's likely to get angry and hang up on you."

Straightening, the Commander turned and spoke to his men: "Tony, did you record that first conversation?"

"Yessir."

"Can you print it out?"

"Yessir."

"Good," he said, as he turned on his heels and walked back to his chair.

While they waited, Erik wrapped the million dollars in newspaper as requested by the caller and tied it with strong string. He placed it on the table in front of his father.

Ten minutes went by, then fifteen, twenty, twenty-five . Almost thirty minutes went by before the phone rang again. Everyone stiffened.

The Commander pointed to Peter and he picked up the phone: "Hello," he said, "this is Peter Van Brunt." As the caller spoke he continued to make notes.

After a couple of minutes had passed, Peter said: "Yes, I got it . . . What time? . . . Exactly one hour from now? . . . Yes . . . I'll be in a two-year-old black Mercedes sedan . . . I can't . . . because I'm not allowed to drive . . . I have no license, sir . . . My butler always drives me . . . He's an old English gentleman who has worked for me for years . . . Of course he's trustworthy. Have you ever known an English gentleman who wasn't . . . What? . . . I'm not trying to be funny, sir . . . Thank you . . . Hello? . . . Hello? . . . He hung up."

The Commander shouted: "Tony?"

"Sorry sir," he shouted back. "He hung up too soon."

After looking at his notes, Peter spoke up: "I can do this, Commander. He wants me to be at the drop point within the hour. We're to drive . . ."

Commander interrupted him: "It's okay that your butler drives?"

"Yes," Peter answered. "He approved him."

"Okay."

Peter continued: "We're to drive to Broad Street, turn left to the Royal Apartments, park across the street, take the wrapped money, and go down an alley between the apartments and a department store and leave the package in the third dumpster to the left and be sure to cover it with extra newspapers. That's it."

"Let me just add, Mr. Van Brunt," the Commander said, standing, "that once you do that, you'd better get the hell out of there." Looking around the room, he said: "LISTEN UP EVERYBODY. GET READY TO LEAVE IN FIVE MINUTES. YOU KNOW WHAT TO DO; TELL ME WHAT YOUR MISSION IS."

In chorus, the men and women spoke up: "OUR MISSION IS TO CAPTURE THE KIDNAPPERS AND BRING THEM IN, DEAD OR ALIVE, AND INSURE THE SAFE RETURN OF NATASHA VAN BRUNT."

J.R. smiled.

CHAPTER 32

The big Mercedes turned left onto Broad Street, a wide, two-lane avenue lined with an assortment of retail stores, commercial buildings, banks, and an occasional apartment house.

Inside the car, Peter sat in the back; his left hand rested on top of the wrapped money on the seat next to him. Now and then, he glanced at a piece of paper he held in his right hand that contained the address of the Royal Apartment House.

Finally, he leaned forward and spoke to Charles who was wearing a black suit, white shirt and black tie and chauffeur's cap. "Slow down, Charles, we're almost there."

The car pulled over to the left and stopped. Peter picked up the money package and put it into a large canvas bag, and grabbed his cane. He was about to open the door when it suddenly swung open. He looked up, startled. "What?"

When he saw Charles holding the door open for him, he growled. "Damn, Charles, what the hell do you think you're doing?"

"What I always do, sir," he said. "Opening the door for you."

"Not now, Charles," he snapped. "Get back inside the car."

"Yes, sir," he said. "Sorry, sir." He walked briskly away.

Peter got out of the car and slammed the door. Traffic wasn't with him. He waited for a bus to pass, then a large truck and several cars. When they had passed, he walked halfway into the street and waited for more vehicles to go by.

When he was finally on the other side of the street he looked up the alley and saw three green-colored dumpsters against the side of the apartment house.

Satisfied that no one was about, he walked as fast as he could down the alley to the dumpsters. He thought to himself: *The third dumpster on the left. Here it is. Put the money on the right side under some newspapers.* He lifted the lid and let it fall backwards until it hit the wall. Reaching down he took the money package out of the bag and placed it in the dumpster. When he thought he heard someone or something he stopped and looked around. Nothing. He realized that he was shaking and that his heart was pounding in his chest. *Damn it, Peter. Breath, breath!*

Retrieving loose newspaper from the bag he covered the money package until it was completely hidden.

Before he left, he looked up and down the alley; it appeared deserted. Folding the canvas bag and making it as small as he could, he took a deep breath and started walking toward the street.

Unbeknownst to Peter, J.R., Erik and Captain Day were sitting in an unmarked car directly in back of his Mercedes.

They watched as Peter crossed the street and got into the Mercedes. They heard the engine roar and waited until they were out of sight.

Twenty minutes passed and no action. Forty, fifty minutes passed and still no one showed to pick up the money.

"I don't think they're coming," Erik said.

J.R. agreed.

"Be patient, men," Day said. "Be patient."

Twenty minutes later, Day's cell phone rang; it was the Commander. "Yessir," he said, "I understand."

"What's up, Captain?" J.R. asked.

"Time to get the money," he responded.

"They're not coming?" Erik inquired.

"Why don't you go and get the money, Erik?"

"Why me?"

"Because you're your father's son, and I'm a policeman."

"Sounds like a good idea, Erik," J.R. remarked. "We don't want to upset these bastards too much."

"Okay."

When he was out of the car, J.R. asked Day why the kidnappers were doing this. "Is it a test?" he asked.

"You might say that," he answered. "It's also a way of throwing us off. Complicating the game by changing the rules."

"I don't like it," J.R. said. "I don't trust them."

"Nobody trusts them, J.R."

"I'm afraid they'll kill her."

"Why should they kill her?"

"Because it's very possible she knows who they are. She can certainly identify Menken. He worked at the orphanage."

"If my memory serves me, J.R., all three men were wearing stocking masks when they kidnapped her. They did that for a reason; they didn't want to be identified by her or anyone else. They're not going to hurt Natasha, J.R. I'm sure of it. They want that money and that's all; they don't want to spend the rest of their lives in jail for murdering a young girl."

"Are you suggesting that Menken is still wearing his stocking mask?"

"Yes."

"I hope you're right, Captain," J.R. said. "I hope to God you're right."

Tension in the Control Center was high. The time was twelve noon. Several hours earlier Peter had talked to one of the kidnappers regarding Erik. The man wanted to know who the hell he was and when Peter tried to tell him that he was his son visiting from Holland, he called him a liar and screamed in his ear that he was one of the police. When Peter contradicted him insisting that he was his son, the man hung up.

An hour later, when the man called back and asked personal questions about Erik, Peter suggested that he call the Shangri'la Hotel in Chesterton and ask the manager if there was a young man registered there, about thirty, tall and blond, by the name of Erik Van Brunt. Without answering, the caller hung up.

Thirty minutes later the man called and, in a calmer voice, advised Peter to let Erik drive the Mercedes for future drops. Before Peter could respond, the man hung up.

J.R. turned to Erik: "Looks like you're going to be around for a while."

Erik looked at J.R.: "Should I call Bobby and tell him I'm going to be a little late?"

"You want me to do it?"

"Sure, if you want to."

J.R. reached for his cell phone and called Bobby. As the phone rang, he got up and took a few steps away from the table. "Bobby? . . . Yeah this J.R. Got some news regarding Erik. The kidnappers want him to drive the car for the money drop. There's no telling when he'll be back at work . . .

What? . . . You are? . . . Hold on." J.R. turned to Erik. "Bobby's in a pinch; two doctors are out ill. Got any suggestions?"

"I have one," Peter said. "Have Bobby call Doctor Reynolds at General in Pietermaritzburg and explain the situation. Mention my name and he'll give you at least two staff doctors well qualified for the job. And be sure to add that Van Brunt will reward their humanitarianism with a generous stipend."

J.R. smiled at him. "You're a saint. You know that?"

"Yeah, I know."

Three days passed with no word from the kidnappers. Commander Danani paced the floor mumbling to himself. His men and women were already beyond restlessness. Some slept while others passed the time by playing cards or billiards.

Erik took the sun while his father rested and J.R. made himself comfortable on one of the plush sofas in the great room and read.

On the fourth day, exactly ten minutes after five in the evening, the phone rang.

Danani, who was enjoying a juicy steak, dropped everything. Throwing his napkin to the floor, he got on the intercom and yelled to his staff to come to attention. Within seconds everyone was in combat mode.

J.R. ran in from the great room to help Van Brunt walk from the chaise, where he was resting, to his chair at the table. Erik appeared directly after and took his place at the table.

The phone rang again.

Commander Danani, now wearing an ear plug that allowed him to listen in on conversations, motioned Peter to pick up.

Clearing his throat, Peter picked up the phone and said "Hello." What he heard was a woman's voice:

"Hello," she said. "Is this Mr. Van Brunt?"

"Yes," he replied, looking at the Commander who signaled him to continue.

"Is this *Peter* Van Brunt?"

"Yes, it is."

There was silence for a moment, then: "My name is Marie Schneider. I'm a friend, or should I say ex-girl friend, of Werner Menken."

"How can I help you, Miss Schneider?" He glanced over at the Commander who gave him the thumbs up signal.

"I have information that might be of interest to you," she said in a voice close to a whisper."

"I can barely hear you, Miss Schneider," he said. "Can you speak up a little?"

"I'm sorry," she said. "Can you hear me now?"

"That's better," he said.

"Months ago I gave birth to Werner Menken's baby. At first, he promised to marry me. But, as time passed, he lost interest and was gone from the house for days on end. He'd come home drunk and angry and when I confronted him he'd curse and beat me until I lost consciousness. When I threatened to call the police, he packed up and left. I have not seen him since."

"That's a terrible story, Miss Schneider, but how can I help you?"

"It's not how you can help me, Mr. Van Brunt. I'm calling because I might have information that could help you."

The Commander nodded vigorously, waving his finger in the air.

"I'm listening, Miss Schneider."

Peter could hear her sigh. "Before he left," she began, "he told me how he was going to kidnap your daughter and that he was going to hold her for ransom."

"And that he has done, Miss Schneider."

"I'm so sorry," she said. "Have you called the police?"

He looked at the Commander who was scowling and shaking his head.

"Miss Schneider," he began, taking a deep breath: "The kidnap note warned that if the police were called, they would kill her." He paused. The Commander waved him on. "You said that you have information that might help me?"

There was a pause. "Yes," she said. "I know where they've been hiding out. It's a ramshackle old place on the corner of Wright's Road just off the old highway."

"I know where that is," he said, writing it on his pad. "Are they there now?"

"I don't know," she said. "They might still be there. There are at least three men, maybe more, and they are armed and very dangerous. Please be careful."

"I will," Miss Schneider," he said. "I assure you. I'll be very careful. Thank you so much for calling."

"I have to go now, Mr. Van Brunt, because my baby's crying. God bless you." She hung up.

The room erupted in hoots and hollers and laughter and applause and whistles. Captain Day did a dance; Wang went to strike the gong in the great room while Erik hugged his father and J.R. hugged Erik, and everyone just went wild with joy and celebration.

Everyone that is, except the Commander. He sat still, staring into space, thinking and wondering if that woman on the phone was for real. Was she who she said she was? Was she still working for Werner? Was it a cleverly planned ruse to persuade old Van Brunt to admit that he had called the police? He didn't know for sure, but he was sure he didn't trust her—despite an award-winning performance.

Sure, he thought, they would go to that nasty little shanty on Wright's Road, but he was certain they wouldn't find anything that would lead them to the kidnappers and Natasha.

CHAPTER 33

Captain Day ordered Chang to push the unmarked police car up to eighty when they pulled onto the old highway that would take them to Wright Road.

J.R., who was sitting in the back, checked his watch; it was five-thirty. He figured that it would be dark by six.

J.R. leaned forward to address Day: "What's the backup plan, Captain?"

Day turned to look at him. "Basically two unmarked cars with approximately eight police," he said. "They'll reach the destination point before we do and position themselves in strategic areas around the house. You won't even know they're there."

"It's turning dark," J.R. remarked.

"If the house is empty, we may have to use flashlights."

A few minutes later, Day advised Wang to slow down because the light up ahead was Wright Road.

As they neared the cross-road, the light turned green and Wang made a left-hand turn into a residential neighborhood that consisted mostly of small one and two-bedroom cottages with neat front yards and a car in almost every driveway. Wang reduced the speed to thirty.

Lights shone in every home, but when they got to five-eleven Wright Road, they found the corner house dark.

"Drive by slowly, Chang," Day said, "I want to see if there's any activity there."

"It looks deserted," J.R. said.

"Go down a block or two and turn around."

Chang drove a block, made a U-turn, and, coming back, slowed the car to twenty miles an hour. As they approached the house, Day told him to pull over and stop.

"I think you're right, J.R.," Day said. "It does look deserted. I don't see any lights or signs of human activity. We'll leave the car here and walk across the lawn to the front door.

"What about flashlights, Captain?"

"You should find them in a box back there."

"Yeah, they're here," J.R. said as he removed two and handed them to Day. "Okay," Day said. "Let's go."

J.R. grabbed one for himself and climbed out of the car. He fell in behind the two policemen as they walked slowly across the brown-weed lawn to the front door. Even through the darkness, J.R. could see that the little house was in dire need of repair. Window glass was cracked and paint was peeling off the siding. When Day tried to force the rusty old screen door open it came off it hinges and fell with a loud crash on the cement flooring.

J.R. froze and Chang instinctively reached for his gun. Day smiled and advised the men to relax. But when he tried to get the front door open, it wouldn't budge. "What's the matter, Captain?" Chang whispered. "Having trouble?"

Snorting, Day stood back, and, taking a deep breath, lowered his right shoulder and attacked the door like a crazed bulldog. It flew open taking Day with it. He ended up on the floor of the living room in a pile of filthy, ant-ridden garbage.

"My God," he cried, getting to his feet, "what the hell is that disgusting odor?"

With a straight face, Chang said: "Shit."

"Put your bandanna on," Day said to Chang. Looking at J.R., he asked: "Do you have a handkerchief?" He nodded. "Put it on."

While Day and Chang searched the living room and bedroom, J.R. flashed the light around the kitchen searching for anything that might lead him to the kidnappers and what they had done with Natasha.

All he found were dirty dishes in the sink, garbage strewn on the floor, and what had been an oak dining room set left broken, cracked and useless. As he flashed the light around, J.R. saw that someone had punched big round holes in the walls and they looked like large black eyes, like someone had died in them.

He flashed back to the feelings of fear and hopelessness as he lay on that basement floor fighting for his life. The dense, odorous darkness of the tiny kitchen brought on a sense of claustrophobia. He felt ill, weak, like he might faint. He fought against it as best he could. *I've got to hold on,* he told himself.,

Before long, he heard Captain Day call his name; they were ready to go. Turning, he flashed his light one last time against the opposite wall and saw an old white refrigerator. It was covered with magnets of all sizes and shapes. Most of them held magazine photos of pretty young women in various stages of undress.

"J.R., we're leaving," Day said.

"Coming, Captain," he answered.

He was about to turn away when his light picked up something that . . . he walked closer to get a better look. He removed a piece of paper from the refrigerator and turned away. "Captain," he called.

"What?"

"Come here," he responded, "I think I've got something."

A second light flashed across the kitchen wall; it was Day. "What's up?" he asked.

"Look at this," J.R. answered, handing the paper to Day.

Day examined it closely and said: "I think we've got something here. Look at this Chang. What do you make of it?"

"Looks like a map to me."

"It is. You see what's written at the top? *VB Gold Mine.* That can only mean one thing: Van Brunt Gold Mine. I was there once or twice. This box here near the entrance is the office, and this box, just in back of it, represents the infirmary. This box back here must be the mess hall."

"If you ask me, boss," Chang said, "this is where the boys are holding Natasha Van Brunt: VB's old gold mine."

"Exactly," Day said. "Let's get out of this hell hole. I've got to call the Commander right away."

Before they left, Day slapped J.R. on the back and said: "Good job old man."

As they walked across the dried up lawn to the car, Captain Day contacted the Commander on his cell phone. He explained to him how J.R. had found a hand-drawn map of Van Brunt's gold mine on the refrigerator and that they were in agreement that the kidnappers must be using it as their hideout.

When they reached the car and J.R. was about to get in, Day said: "Yes, Commander, it's a great break." He listened. Then, shaking his head, said: "Yeah, we'll head back to the castle."

"NO," J.R. blurted out.

"What?"

"I'm not going back to the castle. I can't . . ."

"What are you talking about, man?"

"We've got to go to her," J.R. exclaimed. "My daughter needs me."

"She's not your daughter."

"She's not my daughter *yet*," J.R. shot back. "But I'm adopting her."

Captain Day looked confused. "Is this true, Chang?"

"Yes, sir," he said. "It's just not official yet."

"Please, Captain, please take me there," he said.

"This is crazy," Day remarked.

"Please, Captain."

"I'm probably going to regret this, but . . . All right. You've got to promise to stay close."

"Yessir," J.R. said, sighing deeply. "You won't have to worry about me, sir. I know how to take care of myself."

"All right," Day, said, opening the car door, "get in."

Once inside, Day took the hand-drawn map from Chang and shone a flash light on it. "Look here, guys," he said. "Let me explain a few things to you."

In as few words as possible, he described the location of the mine as one mile off the old highway and that the office and infirmary were located in a park setting. "Van Brunt's aesthetic dictated that he provide beautiful surroundings for his men for whom he had a high regard. For him, the park with its annuals, bushes, trees, benches, fountains, and boulders, some at least seven feet high, was a way to show his men that he cared for them."

"I have a question," J.R. said.

"Yes J.R.?"

"What do the abductors do for light?" he asked. "Do they have electricity there?"

"Uh, some years ago Van Brunt equipped the main buildings with emergency generators. If they don't work, well, I guess the bad guys are burning a whole lot of candles—at both ends."

Chang and J.R. laughed.

"All right you guys," Day said, starting the car, "fasten your seat belts. We're going to push this baby to the limit."

CHAPTER 34

J.R. sat close to the window staring out into the darkness wondering if he'd made the right decision. He took a deep breath and chided himself for even *thinking* he shouldn't go to the mine.

Are you a coward? Your daughter is there and God knows what they're doing to her. She needs you and she needs you now! You can't turn your back on her and leave her fate in the hands of strangers, trained policemen or not.

If she were hurt, or worse, you would never forgive yourself.

Now firm in the knowledge that he was doing the right thing, he steeled himself for the outcome.

The car turned right off the old highway onto a narrow, two-lane unpaved road and slowed for the remaining mile to the mine entrance. During the ride, J.R. could make out the outline of a high metal fence that ran along the perimeter of the mine. The car pulled to the curb and stopped.

Captain Day turned and peered over the top of the seat at J.R. "Mind you stay close to us, young man."

"Yessir," he said, saluting.

They got out of the car. All around it was pitch black.

Chang and J.R. stayed close to Captain Day who flipped his flash light on and led them along the fence to what he called the pedestrian entrance where he stopped and looked around. Turning, he whispered to J.R.: "You may not know it, but this place is surrounded by our men. As we proceed, stay close to the man in front of you."

After the men had walked about two hundred feet along an old gravel path, passed stone benches and overgrown foliage, J.R. could see the front part of the mine office building from light that filtered through the surrounding bushes and trees.

Instead of going left with Day and Chang, J.R. held back, and quickly slipped away taking a path to the right.

At first, the going was uncertain. There was little light and he was forced to grope his way along. Then, about ten feet ahead, J.R. saw an illuminated path that appeared to fall away slightly to the left. When he reached it, he hid behind a huge boulder and slowly shifted the upper portion of his body. He surmised that the lighted building in front of him must be the infirmary.

Leaning hard against the boulder he slid his body along its rough surface until he could make out a row of beds against the far wall. Unfortunately, there was no sign of Natasha.

He was about to turn back when there was an outburst of loud, angry voices. He recognized Captain Day's voice shouting: "GET YOUR HANDS UP OR WE'LL SHOOT."

A man appeared at the infirmary window. J.R. couldn't make out his face, but he was sure it was Werner Menken. The man stood tall and dark against the pane as he shielded his eyes and peered out into the night. J.R. froze.

There was more commotion and Menken disappeared. J.R. took a deep breath and moved as fast as he could along the dirt path another twenty feet or more until he reached a tall metal fence and a dead end.

A narrow passageway about three feet wide to his left gave way to a wide expanse of dirt road. Moving sideways along the narrow divide he managed to reach yet another large boulder; it was at least seven feet high by seven feet wide.

When he looked out he saw that the southern end of the infirmary was approximately thirty or more feet away. Light from the building spilled out on the ground, and J.R. could see that large bushes and trees opposite the structure blocked his view from the rest of the pathway. Still, there was no sign of Natasha.

As he reached behind him for the gun that he had stashed in his belt, he heard screams and men shouting for someone to stop. The silence of the night erupted in ear-splitting gun shots that echoed through the deep canyons of the mine.

Standing close to the boulder, he pulled the gun out, and released the safety.

He heard someone coming down the path toward him. A man's voice rang out: "COME AND GET ME YOU BASTARDS."

J.R. stood poised and ready.

Out of the darkness Werner Menken and Natasha appeared in the opening. She preceded him as he pushed her forward; she was gagged and her hands were tied behind her back.

J.R. pulled back so she wouldn't see him.

A loud voice rang out: "STOP MENKEN, OR WE'LL SHOOT."

He stopped, and as he whirled around, he maneuvered her so she was shielding him.

Now, Menken's back was to J.R. He realized he had to act. As the shouting continued, JR. reached for a hefty rock at his foot. Taking aim, he threw the rock as hard as he could at Menken. It hit his leg and he reacted.

Letting go of Natasha, he spun around and was about to get a shot off, when J.R. fired. The bullet hit Menken in the left shoulder. He screamed in pain and stumbled. At that moment, Natasha ran back down the path toward the infirmary.

J.R. was about to get another shot off when Menken fired. J.R. ducked as the bullet hit the boulder above his head. When J.R. looked back for Menken he was gone.

There were more shouts and warnings and then a shot rang through the canyons. A moment later JR. saw Menken staggering down the path toward him. He was holding his side, and his white shirt was soaked in blood.

Without hesitating, JR. stepped out in the path directly in front of Menken and called him by name.

Menken looked up, and when he saw J.R. he raised his gun. Before Menken could get a shot off, J.R. fired at him.

Like in old Westerns, the action happened in slow motion. The villain dropped his gun as his head fell to his chest and his knees began to buckle. At the same time, his upper body, collapsing, fell face down into the dirty dust. He was dead.

While J.R. just stood there staring at the dead man at his feet, Captain Day and Chang appeared on the scene. They couldn't believe their eyes.

Without a word, J.R. approached Day and offered him the gun. Day looked at it and said: "You shot him with this?"

"Yes."

"Where'd you get it?" he asked.

"In Chesterton after our visit with Chase at the orphanage."

"How much did you pay for it?"

"About fifty US dollars."

"This is a piece of crap," he said, frowning.

Chang, who was examining the deceased, spoke up: "That piece of crap shot this guy right between the eyes."

"I'll be damned."

"How's Natasha?" J.R. asked. "Is she all right?"

"She's fine," Day assured him. "A police doctor is examining her in the infirmary now."

J.R. looked at Day. "Thank you for everything you did today, Captain. I'll never forget it."

"I don't think I'll ever forget what you did here tonight."

J.R. smiled. "I did what I had to do."

Shaking his head, Day said: "I know."

J.R. patted the Captain on the back and hurried off to find Natasha.

He entered the infirmary to find Lt. Napier surrounded by his men who were laughing and joking about their two captors.

When Napier saw J.R. he frowned. "Mr. Cronyn," he said, getting up from the table, "what are you doing here?"

Before he could answer, Captain Day stepped between them and said to Napier: "Meet the gentleman who killed Menken . . ." Opening his hand to reveal J.R.'s gun, he continued: . . . "with this."

Just one glance at it and Napier began to laugh. "That's not possible," he blurted out. "That's just a piece of crap."

Day smiled: "That's what I said."

J.R. added: "I got him right between the eyes, Lieutenant."

Napier looked at him for a long moment, then asked: "Do you believe in God, J.R.?"

"Yes sir," he responded. "I do."

"Do you believe he had anything to do with this—miracle?"

"You think God's hand was on the gun?"

Without expression, Napier looked at J.R. and said: "If I took that gun and went outside and shot at a target, not too far away, I would miss it by many, many, many inches. Difficult for me to do, because, you see, I am an expert shot. And I have medals to prove it."

"I feel blessed, Lieutenant."

Napier smiled, and putting his hand on J.R.'s shoulder, said: "Congratulations. You're a hero."

"Thank you."

"J.R." she cried out. "J.R."

He turned and saw Natasha on the far side of the room reaching out to him. She looked so small, so frail in a long white wrap-around. "Natasha darling," he said approaching her with out-stretched arms.

She ran to him and wrapped her arms around his waist, pressing her face against his body. "You see? I told you once. You are a hero! But you must promise me you will never leave me again."

Putting one arm around her, he gently stroked her hair with the other and said: "Dear, sweet, Natasha. My child. I promise; I will never leave you again."

CHAPTER 35

Several days after the shooting, J.R. wrote in his journal: *I've thought many times over these past few days about what Napier said to me that night at the mine. He made me realize that I could not have killed Werner Menken with that "piece of crap," without the Lord's help. I believe He was with me that night. I believe that His hand was on the gun. If that were not true, I wouldn't be sitting here now writing in my journal. I would be dead.*

What followed were a series of tedious events including personal interviews for both newspapers and television. The public became fascinated by J.R.'s story especially when they found out that he was the father of the famous Bobby Cronyn.

However, J.R. wanted nothing more than to get his hands on the adoption papers as soon as possible and return with Natasha to America and to his beloved Kate.

Regrettably, the government of South Africa would keep him waiting.

In the meantime, however, Bobby lost no time in planning a party for his dream team to celebrate their huge contribution to the fight against HIV/AIDS. Impressed with Bobby and his success, Peter Van Brunt insisted on hosting the great occasion at the Castle. Bobby was only too willing to accept the generous offer.

One Week Later

J.R.'s Room

From his journal: *I was happy for my son, but, quite frankly, I wanted to skip the whole affair, travel to Pretoria and press the government to sign my adoption papers. I would've been content to miss the party and return home.*

As J.R. was getting dressed for the day at the Castle, he told his son what he had written in his journal the night before. Bobby became apoplectic. His large body swayed from side to side and he groaned; holding his head, he said: "I feel dizzy, dad." J.R. reached out to grab him, but he eluded his father's grip and collapsed into an overstuffed easy chair.

He mumbled, "Don't do this, dad." He took a deep breath. "You don't have to go to Pretoria because Jason Lord is already there. I should have told you, but, well . . ." He hesitated, looking a little sheepish, "It's about Kate."

"What about Kate?" he asked. "What should you have told me about Kate?"

"Before I say anything," Bobby began, "you've got to promise me you won't get mad."

"Why should I get mad?"

"Promise me?"

"Okay, I promise."

"Kate's coming here for the celebration, dad," he said, getting to his feet and placing the chair in front of him. "The plans are that you two are, uh, getting married this afternoon—at the castle. "

"What? " J.R. exploded.

"You promised, dad."

"Why didn't you tell me?"

"We wanted it to be a surprise. Was it?"

"Oh, you bet it was."

"Would you've been angry if we'd told you earlier?"

"Probably."

"Are you angry now?

"Probably." J.R. lost his composure and started to giggle.

"Is that an angry giggle, dad?" Bobby started to giggle.

"Probably."

Both laughing, they embraced each other with a big bear hug.

"Now I know why you made we wear this monkey suit."

"It looks great on you."

"I can't wait to see Kate."

"She looks great.'

"You've seen her?"

"Of course."

As J.R. fumbled with his bow tie, he said: "You know, Bobby, I wanted nothing more than a civil ceremony with a few friends in attendance. Nothing fancy. Nothing the least bit pretentious. Just simple, simple, simple."

"Well, dad," Bobby said, trying to help him with his tie, "she was delighted to come. She said she agreed to your plan of a civil ceremony to please you. But when I asked her if she wanted to come to South Africa and get married in a castle like a princess. She is a princess, isn't she dad?"

"She's a queen."

The Great Room. Standing in front of a large mirror that hung on the wall over an antique Queen Ann sofa, Peter Van Brunt examined his image with a critical eye. Not liking the look of a slanting bow tie, his large, knurled fingers fumbled with it in an effort to make it straight.

Frustrated in his attempt, he turned to find Natasha standing at his side. She smiled at him and took his hand. "Let me fix it for you, father," she said quietly.

While she worked on his tie, he noticed that she was not yet dressed for the wedding and that her large brown eyes, usually bright and clear, were red from crying. "Are you all right, Natasha?"

Not answering, she straightened his tie, patted it, and turned away.

Puzzled by her behavior, he sat on the sofa and asked her to join him.

She sat on the edge, looking at her hands.

After a moment, he asked: "Why are you so sad, Natasha?"

Finally, she looked up at him, the flicker of a smile on his face. "Father, may I ask you something? It's been on my mind for a long time."

"You can ask me anything, Natasha."

Taking a deep breath she said: "I know why you put me in the orphanage all those years ago. I was sick and so were you. I knew you could not take care of me. But . . ." She looked away.

"But what, Natasha?"

She looked up him, her eyes filling with tears. "Father, I must know. If you were well—I mean, if you did not have AIDS, would you have put me in an orphanage? Would you have let me live here with you in the castle. Just the two of us, like father and daughter?"

Van Brunt sighed and smiled broadly. "Oh, my darling girl, my Natasha, I would never, ever have put you in an orphanage if I didn't have AIDS. We would've lived like father and daughter right here. And I would've been the king and you the princess of all the land, including, I might add, all the gold." She laughed. "And there certainly was a lot of gold."

She laughed again and put her arms around his neck. "I love you, my father, with all my heart. And I will never forget you."

"And I love you, my daughter, with all my heart."

The Castle
Two Hours Later

There must have been at least two hundred and fifty guests at the castle. All the men were dressed in tuxedos and most of the women wore floor length gowns.

After Bobby thanked his team for their dedication that went beyond the call of duty and that culminated in the saving of thousands of young mothers, women and babies from the scourge known as HIV/AIDS, he announced his father's wedding to Kate Winfield in the east garden, and invited everyone to attend.

The garden was a large grassy area set between two rows of high flowering hedges that were perfectly groomed. A hundred urns filled with beautiful displays of red, yellow, and white roses, decorated the area.

The guests sat on white wooden chairs with cushions. The sun hid behind clouds and the temperature stayed at a mild and steady sixty-seven.

The tall, lanky, English Episcopalian minister stepped up on a platform that substituted as an altar, smiled at JR., and wished him a good day. J.R. wondered: Doesn't he know that I'm the groom?

When the wedding march began, everyone turned in their chair to see the bride. Natasha appeared, looking very pretty in a long pink dress, and carrying a large basket; she moved gracefully like a wood nymph, dropping rose petals in the path of Kate and Bobby as they walked down the aisle.

As the service continued, Erik took his place beside J.R. and Elizabeth and the Mayor's wife acted as bridesmaids. When Bobby stepped up next to his father, he whispered in his ear that he had the rings.

Kate was a vision in an emerald green gown with puff sleeves and a V neckline. She smiled at J.R. and mouthed the words: I love you. Hypnotized by her beauty, J.R. got through most of the ceremony not hearing a single word the minister said. Bobby had to nudge him and whisper: Say 'I do.'

"I do," J.R. blurted out.

Kate scolded him with her eyes.

Fortunately, J.R. regained consciousness before the ring exchange and was eager to kiss Kate when the minister said: "You may kiss your bride."

Afterwards, J.R. and Kate strolled arm-in-arm along a garden path that led through rows of tall cypress trees and rose bushes to an Italian-like stone fountain carved with four grotesque faces where narrow streams of water trickled forth.

They were about to sit on a stone bench when J.R. heard Natasha's voice calling "Poppa, Poppa."

When he turned around, a vision in pink flew into his arms, almost knocking him over. Kate stepped to the side and laughed heartily as she covered her face.

"Poppa, Poppa," she cried, wrapping her arms around his neck. "You're my hero."

J.R. laughed.

Turning to Kate, she asked: "Don't you think he's a hero?"

"I certainly do, Natasha," she answered. "He is a hero."

"Hear that, Poppa? We both think you're a hero."

"Well," he said, smiling, "I guess that makes it unanimous." They laughed. "I just have one question: where did this 'Poppa' come from?"

"Oh, all the girls at the orphanage who have fathers, call them *Poppa.* That's why I like to call you *Poppa.*" Turning to Kate, she added: "And I like to call you *Momma*. It that okay? Is it American? I want to call you something American."

"Yes, darling," Kate began, putting her arms around Natasha, "It's very American. You can call me *Mom* or *Momma,* whichever you like."

Kate and Natasha looked at J.R. for his approval. "Yes, yes," he stammered, "Poppa's just fine." He put his arm around her. "It's been a long time, but I'll get used to it." Kate, amused by his obvious discomfort, smiled.

"Now, one thing more," she began, "I want you to call me Tasha. All the girls at the orphanage call me Tasha, and I like it, because it's more . . . African." She looked at Kate. "Do you like it, Momma?"

She thought about it for a moment, then said: "Tasha. Yes, I like it; I like it very much."

"Poppa? Do you like it?"

He smiled. "I like Tasha . . . Tasha."

She laughed.

Bobby's big voice filled the air and everyone turned to greet him as he lumbered down the path toward them.

Without saying a word, he swooped Natasha up in his arms and started carrying her away, saying that they were off to the ballroom for cake and ice cream. She squealed her delight. At the end of the path, Bobby called to his father: "Hey, dad, you and Kate had better get a move on; the Krug is flowing, but you never know how long it'll last. Just warning you."

J.R. waved back and sat on the bench.

Kate paced slowly up and down as she brought him up-to-date on the "family" back in Brooklyn. She told him that Jack Johnson would spend the holidays with his family in Missouri and that he would not be coming back. Old Carl had finished the book and that an agent was interested in it; however, significant changes needed to be made and Carl wanted to know if J.R. would help him. He said yes.

The second bit of surprise news concerned Puddles. In early May, he left the house and didn't return for almost a month. Kate told J.R. that she was terribly upset because she knew that he would be angry if she lost his dog. So, she had many copies of a LOST flyer made and posted them on telephone poles all over town.

They did no good, she said. Finally, after about three weeks, on a sunny Sunday afternoon, while she was sitting on her porch reading, she heard his bark; she looked up and saw him walking up the path toward her followed by a pretty little brown and white shaggy female followed by a sweet little puppy that looks exactly like Puddles. Now we have three dogs, she said.

J.R.'s groan was followed by a chuckle.

Hundreds of guests filled the castle ballroom on the second floor. J.R.'s first dance with Kate was a waltz. He, along with many guests, were enthralled with Kate's grace and beauty as they glided around the floor. When the dance was over, the guests showed their appreciation with thunderous applause. Kate smiled, and curtsied.

After an exquisite buffet and the best cake J.R. had tasted in years, they were joined at their table by Bobby, Elizabeth and Erik. When the band started playing a two-step, Elizabeth coaxed Erik out onto the dance floor. With Kate leading, she and Tasha quickly found the rhythm and performed an energetic and entertaining dance that the crowd applauded enthusiastically.

When the band took a short break, doctors Gruber and Doherty approached Kate.

Before Doherty could speak, Gruber took Kate by the hand and asked: "Isn't this our dance, my dear Kate?"

Looking a little bemused, she said: "I don't know."

"I'm sure I'm on your dance card."

"What dance card?" Doherty wanted to know.

"You wouldn't understand," Gruber said, staring into Kate's eyes.

"How do I get on this dance card?" Doherty asked, looking perturbed.

"You don't," Gruber answered.

"That's not fair."

"Life's not fair."

A smile flickered across Kate's face as she looked from one to the other. "Are you on the card?" she asked Gruber.

"Of course I'm on the card."

"If you're on the card, then *I* can get on the card," Doherty shot back.

"It's a very special card," Gruber said, turning his back on Doherty.

"What is this card anyway?" Doherty demanded to know.

"I told you. It's a dance card."

"I know but, but *where* is it?"

"Oh, you're so annoying."

"I want to know where it is!" Doherty whined loudly.

"It's up your nose, you idiot."

Kate broke out laughing and pushed the boys away.

"Did you think it was funny, Kate?" Gruber asked.

"Yes, I thought it was funny, but . . . Was this all a joke?"

"Yeah," Doherty said. "We were trying new material out on you. I hope you don't mind."

"I don't mind, but why? Why do you do it?"

"It's a comedy routine," Gruber said. "In our spare time back home we perform in a local comedy club. It's fun and it relieves tension. It's a break from our usual work."

"Are you coming back next year?"

"I'm coming," Gruber responded, "but I want to find a place for my wife in Durban so she can spend part of the year with me."

"I know just the place," Liz said, appearing as if from out of nowhere, and taking Gruber by the arm. "There's this beautiful, four-bedroom colonial on a high hill overlooking the ocean that's just sitting there waiting for people to occupy it and bring it back to life. It belongs to Peter Van Brunt but I'm sure you could make a deal." She and Gruber walked off together with Doherty tagging behind like an obedient puppy dog.

Kate shook her head and smiled to herself. Hearing a voice behind her she turned to find Erik standing there. "Erik? Are you all right? You look terrible."

"I'm okay."

"What is it?"

"It's my father. He looks so vulnerable."

"Appearances can be deceiving, you know. He may not be the robust man he once was, but, in the way, he may be even stronger. I'm talking about his heart and his spirit. It shines through his eyes. And I've seen him when he looks at you. He's so proud of what you've accomplished. He loves you very much. And I think he's grateful that you're here at last."

"I love him, too, Kate," he said softly, tears moistening his eyes. "And I'll be here for him for as long as he needs me."

Smiling up at him, she asked: "Would you like to dance?"

"Yes," he said, his eyes glistening with hope. "Please."

Alone with Bobby, J.R. pressed him on the subject of Jason Lord and his efforts in obtaining the government's approval of the adoption. Bobby said that he'd spoken to Jason that very morning and that he had assured him that he'd be at the castle by five o'clock with the signed papers.

"Then why do you look so concerned, Bobby?" J.R. asked.

"I look concerned because, based on Jason's information, we took the liberty of booking you, Kate, and Natasha on a nine o'clock flight tonight back to New York."

J.R. looked at his watch. "That's not too bad, Bobby. It's five now; that gives us four hours."

"All right, dad," Bobby said. "I'll take a breather and call Jason now on his cell phone. I'll get back to you." He walked away.

The music ended and when the band started to play another waltz, Kate came to the table and literally pulled J.R. out of his chair and started dancing with him.

Not wanting to be left out, Tasha approached Kate and took her hand and, before J.R. knew it, the three of them were doing a kind of circular waltz. They whirled around the floor, laughing and enjoying their silliness. When the music ended, J.R. heard his name.

Turning, he saw Peter Van Brunt in his wheel chair and Charles standing behind him. Peter beckoned to them. As they approached, Peter said: "I'd like to have a few words with you and your new family, J.R., before I retire for a nap. Too much Krug you know."

J.R. smiled. "Of course, Peter," he said.

Van Brunt pulled an envelope out of his coat pocket and said: "On this beautiful occasion, J.R., I thought it appropriate that I present you and your lovely family with a gift, a token of my love and appreciation for everything that you've done." He handed J.R. the envelope.

He opened it and withdrew a check. When he looked at the amount, he gasped. "Peter, this is a check for one hundred thousand dollars. This is so extravagant."

"Not at all," Peter said. "If you consider that there were two hundred and fifty guests here today, and if each one had given you a gift worth say, four hundred dollars, it would come to that amount."

Smiling, Kate stepped forward and, leaning over, kissed Peter on the cheek. "Thank you so much Mr. Van Brunt. We'll be sure to put some of this away for Tasha's college education."

Taking her hand, he kissed it and said: "Don't be too concerned about that, dear Kate. Before that time comes, she'll be a very wealthy young woman." He wished them a safe journey, gave Tasha a hug, and motioned to Charles that it was time to leave.

When Van Brunt was gone, J.R. opened his arms: "Group hug?"

Without a word, Kate and Natasha moved to his open arms.

The band played a fox trot.

When the dance was over, J.R. looked at his watch. It was 6:50. *How time flies,* he thought. He looked around for Bobby but he was nowhere in sight.

Kate tugged on his arm. "Why so pensive?" she asked.

"It's almost seven," he answered. "And our plane leaves at nine."

"Any word from Jason Lord?"

"I don't know. That's why I'm looking for Bobby."

"I saw him over by the . . . Oh, here he comes. I don't like it."

"What?"

"He doesn't look happy."

Joining J.R. and Kate in the middle of the dance floor, he told them that Jason's assistant had called and that he was still in Pretoria and that he did not think he would get here until eight-thirty, too late to make the plane to New York.

J.R. shook his head. "Bobby," he began, taking a breath, "that's not what this is about. This is all about Tasha and whether the government approves our adoption papers. I don't give a damn if we get on that plane tonight."

"I'm sorry, dad."

"It's not your fault, son."

"I know why your father is so upset," Kate interjected. "If this adoption is not approved, we . . ." Kate took a moment to breath. "Your father and I will be devastated. Our hearts are set on this adoption. And we've made such plans . . ." Not being able to finish, Kate walked off the dance floor.

"Excuse me, Bobby."

Bobby watched as his father joined Kate and embraced her. She was crying. Taking a few steps away, Bobby reached for his cell phone and dialed a number. When a voice answered he said: "Let me talk to Jason Lord." He waited. Another voice: "Hello, is this Jason? . . . Oh . . . What did you say? . . . He's still in Pretoria? . . . I see . . . No, I understand.

Thank you." Ending the call, he put the phone in his pocket, turned, and walked away. It was 7:10.

At 7:30, Kate and J.R. were on the dance floor with their arms around each other swaying back and forth to the rhythm of a slow fox-trot. While she choked back tears, he held her tightly in his arms.

The music played and the minutes ticked away. J.R. checked his watch; it was 7:45.

At exactly 7:46, their quietude was interrupted by a loud Bobby who, standing at the double doors of the ballroom, urged them to get a move on because Jason Lord was waiting for them in the great room.

Instead of taking the elevator down, J.R. and Kate ran down the stairs. J.R. was so excited that he could feel his heart throbbing in his chest. When they got to the great room, J.R. saw Bobby, Erik, Elizabeth, and finally, Tasha, grouped together at the far end of the room.

Jason Lord stood alone by the French doors that led to the patio. Dressed in a dark suit, white shirt and black tie, he looked stiff and as stoic as usual. Judging by his demeanor, J.R. was sure that the news was not good.

Letting go of Kate's hand, he approached the single figure and said "Hello, Jason. How are you?"

"I'm not sure yet," he answered.

"I understand, J.R.," Jason said. "It's been a long and hard struggle. They didn't want to do this, you know. The government didn't want to approve of this adoption; they didn't want to lose one of their daughters, as they put it. And, in the end, I didn't think they would approve the adoption even after Peter Van Brunt so eloquently wrote about you and your character and how much this experience would help shape and develop his daughter and that it was what he wanted. Even then, after all of that, they were skeptical. But skepticism doesn't always shape outcomes, you know. In the end, I am happy to say, that it didn't in this case." A small smile crossed Jason's face, and J.R. began to feel a sense of relief, of victory.

"Are you saying what I think you're saying?" J.R. asked excitedly. "That we got the approval for the adoption?"

"Yes, J.R., that's what I'm saying."

Ecstatic, he threw up his arms and shouted: "Kate! Kate! Tasha! Tasha! We've won! We've won! We've won!"

Kate and Tasha ran to him. They hugged each other and kisses were plentiful. Kate cried and thanked Jason for his help in making the adoption happen. "I'll never forget you for this, Jason," she said through her tears. "Never."

They shared a group hug with Jason and he presented a signed document to them and said: "This is your wedding gift from the government of South Africa. Treasure it always as you would treasure your adopted daughter."

Bobby interjected that they had better hurry if they were to catch that plane to New York. He added that the limousine was waiting for them at the main door and that their suitcases had already been put into its spacious trunk. They were ready to go.

After Bobby thanked his old friend, Jason, for his help, Jason informed him that the government of South Africa had found a place to build his factory. Cheered by the good news Bobby assured Jason that he would make himself available to negotiate with the government any time they wished.

Jason asked Kate if she'd mind if he walked out with her husband. "I'd like to have a few words with him," he said. She gave her consent but urged them to hurry along.

Turning to Bobby, she asked: "May I take your arm . . . son?" Surprised, he looked at his father, then at Kate. "You certainly may . . . mom." Looking at Tasha, he inquired: "Want an arm . . . sis?"

Tasha giggled, took his arm and said: "Thank you, brother."

J.R. beamed as he watched them walk away. He was a happy man.

As they walked through the labyrinth of castle rooms, J.R. and Jason talked of many things. Finally, Jason asked J.R. what he planned to do when he got home.

Smiling, he replied: "Kate and I will probably take Tasha to Macy's and spend a lot of money on new clothes for her.

"And after that?"

He glanced at Jason. "Oh, write a book, I guess."

"About?"

"Oh, about AIDS and South Africa, inequality, the spirit, God. There's so much I want to write about."

"Than write about it all."

"I may have to."

They chuckled.

"And you, Jason?" J.R. began, "Where do you go from here?"

"In a few days I'll be flying back to New York. I have to write a holiday speech I'm giving in December at the United Nations."

"That's a big order."

"Do you mind if I use you for a sounding board?"

"Not at all."

"With America at war in Iraq, with men dying for a cause that so many feel is wrong, and with Secretary General of the United Nations, Kofi Annan, declaring the war as not in conformity with the UN Charter and therefore illegal, I'm inclined to go with the people and rally against it. What do you think?"

J.R. thought for a moment. "This is a time of joy and peace and love. I would use the war only as an introduction to show the vast disparity between war and peace. Use your theme of one world where the evils of destruction and war are conquered by the brotherhood of man, peace, and love. I think that's the kind of message people want to hear this time of year."

"One people under God?"

"Yes."

"In line with that," Jason added, "I like what Jesus said: 'Love thy neighbor as thyself.' He could've been speaking about a world concept of brotherhood."

Nodding, J.R' said: "We're all united in a single humanity, as Tolstoy believed. It's God's wish that we all come together in peace and harmony, because, in the end, we are all one with God."

Jason stopped, looking at J.R. with renewed respect. "May I quote you, J.R."

"Of course," he responded, adding with a bit of whimsy: "Just so long as you give me credit."

They laughed together and hurried through the last room to the grand entrance hall. The two men embraced and shook hands. Before he sent J.R. on his way, Jason gave him his card and asked him to please call him in one week. J.R. promised to do so.

"Just one more thing before you go," Jason said. "How long has your journey been?"

J.R. smiled and shook his head. "The journey has been a life time, my friend," he said, taking Jason's hand. "I thank you for everything. And

Kate. And Bobby. And God." He paused, adding: "But not necessarily in that order."

Jason slapped J.R. on the arm and sent him hurrying out the front door to the waiting limousine. "I'll call you when I get back to New York," J.R. yelled as he ran.

Standing in the doorway, Jason watched and waved as the long car pulled slowly out of the driveway. While he stared at its red lights fading into the moonlit night, Jason thought: *Oh, I think the hand of the Lord must be upon you. You're very special. And I expect great things from you, James Russell Cronyn.*

THE END